THE ACADEMY

*To Steve and Lesley —
Enjoy your visit to
The Academy!
Scarlett Dean*

THE ACADEMY

...Inside the manhole, Grant kicked at the probing muscle inches below his feet.

"Pull me up!" he screamed.

"What is it?" Joe called.

"Just do it!"

Grant's body jerked upward as the chalk-colored mound lurched, missing his left shoe. He slammed against the tunnel's murky walls, cursing when his hands sunk into its soft tissue-like warmth. Joe seemed hundreds of feet above, feverishly pulling the rope.

After several more tugs, Grant reached the hole's opening. Sweat burned his eyes as he fought to pull himself to safety.

Joe could barely contain his excitement. "What is it? What did you see?"

Grant tore the rope from his waist and dropped, pressing his forehead against the damp, but solid, ground. He tried to shake the image and catch his breath. Finally, he looked up at his roommate's expectant gaze and said, "It's alive."

PRAISE FOR THE ACADEMY

"With spine-tingling chills and unrelenting suspense, Dean takes good versus evil to new heights. This one's a keeper…"

—Lee Driver
Author of the *Chase Dagger Series*
Winner of the 2005 IPPY Award for Best Horror

"Scarlett Dean crafts a fast-moving tale with believable characters caught in a deadly struggle of good versus evil. The creepy, claustrophobic atmosphere of *The Academy* provides lots of visceral scares that build to a hair-raising climax…"

—E. F. Watkins
Author of *Dance With The Dragon*
Winner of the 2004 EPPIE for Best Horror

Also By Scarlett Dean

Destiny's Call
Unfinished Business

THE ACADEMY

BY

SCARLETT DEAN

AMBER QUILL PRESS, LLC
http://www.amberquill.com

THE ACADEMY
AN AMBER QUILL PRESS BOOK

This book is a work of fiction. All names, characters, locations, and incidents are products of the author's imagination, or have been used fictitiously. Any resemblance to actual persons living or dead, locales, or events is entirely coincidental.

Amber Quill Press, LLC
http://www.amberquill.com

All rights reserved.
No portion of this book may be transmitted or reproduced in any form, or by any means, without permission in writing from the publisher, with the exception of brief excerpts used for the purposes of review.

Copyright © 2005 by Scarlett Dean
ISBN 1-59279-769-5
Cover Art © 2005 Trace Edward Zaber

Layout and Formatting provided by: ElementalAlchemy.com

PUBLISHED IN THE UNITED STATES OF AMERICA

For James

Once again, thank you to Darden Hood of Beta Analytic Labs for DNA and carbon dating knowledge and expertise.

Much appreciation to Elliot Lounsburg of R&S Locksmiths for allowing me to pick his brain.

A special thank you to Chrissy for remaining adamant that this is her favorite book.

Much appreciation to David Morrell for his sound advice and encouragement.

As always, thank you to my children and husband for putting up with me.

*And he said: "I tell you the truth, unless
you hange and become like little children, you will
never enter the kingdom of heaven. Therefore, whoever
humbles himself like this child is greatest
in he kingdom of heaven."*

Matthew 18: 3-4 (NIV)

And he replied, "I give you my truth unless their souls are freely relinquished unto me, their physical presence will endure and the final battle will be lost. Therefore, whoever offers himself will be the greatest servant in the kingdom to come."

Buell 18: 3-4 (Satan's Bible)

CHAPTER 1

Jordan, 1600 B.C.

The boy poked the snake with a stick. One ebony eye gleamed in the sun while the other side of the serpent's horned head lay buried in the steaming sand. It was different from any snake he'd ever seen, with two rows of callused spikes running helmet fashion along the back of the head. Its mud colored body was as thick as his fist with scales so parched they curled into translucent scabs.

The snake did not move.

The child squatted, closer this time, watching the creature for any sudden movement. He poked it again. Satisfied it was dead, he ran a tentative finger along its hardened body, letting the brittle texture scrape his fingertips.

A sudden wind gust forced the boy to bury his face inside his cloak as blowing sand bit the back of his hand. The fierce wind ended as abruptly as it started, but he stayed within the protective covering. He knew from experience that sandstorms could be tricky, raging just when it seemed safe.

He regretted straying too far from home as an angry wind scraped sand across his cheek. But the dark mound in the sand had captured his imagination. His heart soared at the idea of bravely killing a snake and showing the other boys. Now he looked at the harmless find and frowned. There would be no adventurous tale to share over a dead snake.

A severe underground tremor caused him to lose his balance and land hard on his bottom beside the rigid serpent. Its hook-like fangs lay inches from his foot. Images of the snake jerking to life and sinking them into his leg made him scramble out of reach.

The bright cerulean sky dimmed as if God had stepped in front of the sun. When the ground shuddered again, the child toppled face first onto the dead creature. He pushed away screaming, aware no one would hear him.

Desperate to get away, he crawled against the blinding sandstorm. Which way home? His heart pounded in his ears over the screeching winds.

Sand and dust flared, surrounding the boy's face in a dirty cloud. He coughed and sputtered as he struggled to get up. He cowered when a threatening presence towered overhead, its shadow as wide as the road. Heavy darkness surrounded him and he dropped to his knees fighting for air. A deafening whir consumed his mind and he prayed he would die quickly.

Fire seared his back and he called out for God's mercy. His stomach lurched to his throat when his body grew suddenly weightless. His feet dangled like a doll as he soared upward; a vice grip clenched his waist. *Surely, this is death, for an angel holds me fast.* Then he looked up to behold his abductor and screamed.

*   *   *

The demon, Malik, soared higher, screeching in victory as he clutched the boy. He knew Michael, the Archangel, wouldn't be far behind. Michael, guardian of man, would learn too late that he'd been purposely lured from his heavenly home.

Malik sped higher with the squirming child, and savored the moment. This victory had been a long time coming.

The sharp sound of a drawn sword turned Malik's attention behind him, and he saw Michael's great wings pounding the skies in challenge. The angel's crystalline eyes blazed with the light of God and his breastplate encapsulated the brawn of his luminous form. His shining black hair fanned over his shoulders like a royal cape as he stared hard at his nemesis.

Malik spied the purple sash, known as the belt of truth girding his waist. He chose his next move carefully.

Michael's silent glare made clear his warning, but Malik felt no fear. Victory loomed inches away.

Malik released the squirming child and watched him twist and writhe as he fell helplessly toward Earth.

Michael sheathed his sword and raced downward. Anticipating the move, Malik quickly darted beneath him, and thrust his lance through the Archangel's belt, severing it. Michael arched violently and fell with great speed, powerless without God's truth. Lightning lit the skies against the roar of deafening thunder signaling Michael's legions were on their way. Malik knew they would be too late.

He sneered at Michael's last attempt to do good as the angel enfolded the boy with his body to cushion him. As Michael exploded into the ground below, the heavens shook, throwing Malik off balance in the air. Pride filled him as he viewed the large crater in the sand below, and he relished the glory in accomplishing what Satan himself could not.

As the blackened heavens opened to pour forth Michael's angelic army, Malik fled their wrath knowing he'd forever be known as the one who'd slain the Archangel Michael.

* * *

Malik drew a rancid breath and moved across his lair in an agitated, sinuous motion. His large scales scratched the craggy rocks as his swollen belly slithered over steaming piles of vomit. He'd escaped Michael's army to hide in a cave like a rodent. It disgusted him that he had yet to receive his deserved recognition. Perhaps Satan believed he alone was worthy of all glory.

His guttural jeer grew deep and full as he peered out of the lair's opening at the Earth's vastness. He found great pleasure at the plan forming in his mind—one in which the master would become the servant.

"Malik!" the archaic rumble filled the lair. He knew Satan had arrived.

"You are greatest in my legions, and I will see you are rewarded for your victory. For now, you must remain hidden from God's angelic army. Therefore, I will set you in a place of high authority on the Earth."

Malik turned violently. "That is a punishment! Why send your mightiest warrior to dwell among the lowly creatures of Earth?"

"You will do as I say!" Satan's voice shook the cave's walls. "There is need for a new ruler in the stone city of Petra. This task I give you as a reward for the Archangel's death. You will be safe disguised as a human king, and better able to protect my written word—my bible.

"One day you will lead my army in the battle of Armageddon for you have found favor in my sight, Malik the Great."

The demon swallowed the title like venom. It did not please him to serve this master as a humble human. Satan departed, leaving Malik to consider the *reward*. He moved to the lair's opening, his large jaws unhitching to spew forth the vomit that had built up inside. One bitter defeat after another.

He raised his head in defiance. "I alone had the power to defeat Michael and yes, I will lead the army of Armageddon, but they will be *my* soldiers! After Armageddon is won, I will lead them to erase the name of Satan forever!"

* * *

Malik watched blood run over the altar as the crowd chanted. As king of the Jordanian city of Petra, he observed all formal activities from his stone balcony. How he hated the sound of human voices praising nonexistent gods. The fools need only worship one deity—Malik the Great!

He raised his fist to Jehovah's heaven shouting, "What is man that You are mindful of him!"

Demons Rajan and Tau stood beside him in human form watching the ceremony reach its crescendo. They were but two of the hundreds of demons sent by Satan to serve and protect Malik during his reign as king.

Malik savored the irony. The demons had already pledged their loyalty to him, vowing to fight in the war against Satan. Combining the human soldiers of Armageddon and his demon hoard, Malik knew he would not fail.

Rajan spoke first. "What is mankind indeed? Yet God cherishes them greatly."

"Man is nothing but putrefied bones with a selfish will of his own! But, he has been placed high above all creation and given command of the earth. He views himself as a god, but he is unworthy!" Malik's eyes glowed white in the darkness.

Tau offered a respectful bow. "Do you require anything, my king?"

"Only your allegiance when the time comes. You and the others have vowed to follow me as you did Lucifer during the rebellion. I rely on your word."

"Of course." Tau nodded. "And you have given *your* word to us, your promise of great reward after the final battle. "

Rajan stepped forward. "I ask only for the privilege of destroying the demon Buell. He has become too powerful. His meat will bleed sweet in my mouth."

"You have served me well, Rajan. Take whomever you wish. I have only one desire—to remove Satan from his dark throne. When we reign victorious after Armageddon, Satan will sit on God's throne as it is written in his word. We will have but one enemy yet to smite. Satan will feel my wrath and cower in my presence when his own army sets out to destroy him.

"But first, we must build the army that will defeat God and his angels."

"We stand ready for your command," Tau said.

Malik gazed over the human crowd below as they retreated for the night. He pointed at a young woman leading a child by the hand as the multitude pressed through the city gates. The little girl stumbled, and the mother quickly gathered her into her arms.

Rajan and Tau listened as Malik explained his plan.

"The human soldiers of Armageddon will have power over God."

"How is this possible?" Rajan asked.

"God has one weakness. It will mean His destruction."

"God is perfection," Tau reminded him.

"Jehovah is the creator! *That* is his weakness." Malik trained his gaze over the crowd once more.

"Therefore, I seek the children. Mankind will realize too late that the purity and innocence of a child remains their only defense. It is for their pride that humankind will fall. Just as in Eden!"

CHAPTER 2

Present day

The seaweed colored Chevy sped along the parched stretch of road toward Knollwood Academy. A brief spot of sun glinted off the car's patchy chrome, then ducked behind clouds as thick as sour cream, turning the sky into dirty paste. A sense of foreboding filled the car after turning off the main road.

Fourteen-year-old Grant Taylor watched the barren trees zip past in a rapid blur. He glanced at his mother, noting her sunglasses didn't hide her furrowed brow, a look that had come to mean trouble for Grant. The tired old car forged ahead while radio static and a pine-drenched deodorizer suffocated the air.

"Can't we wait a few days?" he asked her profile.

Amanda Taylor bit her lip. "Sorry, Grant. I think this is for the best."

Grant's breakfast curdled in his stomach. He had expected to be nervous. Who wouldn't be? By this afternoon he'd been in prison, for Christ's sake. Not really prison, he reminded himself. Knollwood Academy housed boys—bad boys.

He'd overestimated his luck this time and it was going to cost him dearly. Although his black curly hair and freckles made him look younger, his stocky build and smart mouth had gained him access into the wrong sort of company at Fontaine High School. He'd quickly fallen in with an older group of troublemakers who liked a bit of action in their humdrum high school careers, where detentions and suspensions were weekly events. Still, they remained his friends.

He defended them, asking himself, *who* helped take up the time when his mom worked double shifts at the hospital, leaving him to channel surf and eat cold pizza? *Who'd* gotten him out of a tough jam the day he'd tried shoplifting?

It had been his friends.

Thinking back, he realized he hadn't even wanted the stupid magazine from the Quick Pick Grocer. It proved more of a personal dare. Boredom and loneliness shadowed him since his dad died, and occasionally Grant needed to show he had some balls. So he picked up a cheesy magazine—*no big deal.*

The grocer owner hadn't seen it that way. If not for Paul Tyler saying he'd gone ahead in line and Grant must have thought he'd paid for him, he would have seen the inside of a squad car first hand. He'd never told his mom about that one.

This time he'd received a year's expulsion for having a pocketknife at school. After Columbine, a lot of shit had changed on academic turfs across the country and he supposed his small hometown in Fontaine, Indiana had to keep in step.

Grant recalled how Principal Beck's faded brown eyes gleamed at the find. He held up the dull knife like a rare specimen—something never seen before by human eyes. The man's pencil thin top lip lifted into a sneer as he snapped the weapon closed, tossing then catching it with his left hand.

"You just bought yourself expulsion, Taylor. Go clean out your locker while I call your mom."

The principle's eyes strayed to Ms. Baron, the school secretary, passing them in the hallway.

"Hello," she said on her way to the office.

Beck nodded then turned his attention back to the knife.

"It's not mine," Grant snapped.

"Doesn't matter. You have possession."

Grant's hand suddenly shot to his forehead as a voice echoed in his mind.

He stared at the principle in shock. He tried to shut them out, but the man's thoughts grew louder before they stopped.

"What did you say?" he asked Mr. Beck.

"I said, 'you have possession.'"

"No, after that. You said something about Ms. Baron."

The principle paled. His beady eyes narrowed. "You're mistaken."

"I heard you say you wish she'd use more tongue."

Beck's jawed dropped. "How..." He stopped. "What kind of game are you playing, Taylor? You couldn't possibly hope to get out of this by any means, especially false accusations."

"But I didn't..." Grant suddenly understood. "You're gettin' it on with her, aren't you? Boy, wait till the superintendent hears this one."

Beck straightened with a patronizing smile. "Mr. Taylor, a moment ago I might have been persuaded to let this go with a week's detention. I like your mom and don't want to force any undo hardship on a single parent. But now I must say, that you are expelled."

Now he'd done it.

He quickly changed tactics. "Mr. Beck, I swear I was only holding the knife for someone. Can't you let it go this time?" Grant hated himself for begging.

The man's slim smile lingered. "Zero tolerance. You know the rules. Go get your stuff."

The back of Beck's white dress shirt puffed out over his too tight, too short, and too eighties slacks. Grant watched the billowing white sail retreat to the office and offered it a double finger salute.

That afternoon, the hardest part had been the silence in the car on the way home. His mother kept her eyes on the road. She didn't even seem to notice he was in the car. In the principal's office, she'd surprised Grant by offering no argument or rebuttal to the sentence. Perhaps she understood zero tolerance better than he did. She'd accepted the sentence with no show of emotion. He never told her he could have avoided the expulsion if not for his mind reading experience.

Grant couldn't recall a time in his life when he hadn't had the ability to occasionally hear what people were thinking. He wished he could put it to good use, like picking the teacher's brain for test answers, but it came when he least expected it, often during some sort of trouble or when a person became excited. He'd certainly blown it with the principle, thinking he could blackmail him into letting him off.

Two days later, his mother finally broached the ordeal with him and dropped the bomb. She'd leaned in the doorway of his bedroom, her expression tired and too pale against her floral print blouse.

"You've left me with no choice. You'll be going to the Knollwood Academy for boys."

He let the football he'd been absently pitching up and down drop to the floor. "Knollwood is for fags!" he argued. "Send me there and in a few weeks my ass will whistle."

She tried to joke him out of his mood. "Good. It won't be a waste of time if they'll develop your talents. We leave at eight."

He'd spent a sleepless night fighting the demons of fear and remorse while trying not to cry. The last time he'd shed tears had been two years before at his father's funeral. That had been a different kind of sadness, though, like sinking by inches into quicksand and suffocating in helplessness and despair. He slammed his fist into his closet door for disappointing his mother—again.

Grant knew his mom worked hard to give him the best. Her job as ICU nurse at Fontaine General Hospital provided a steady income, but it took her away from him. She was sole provider now and pulled additional shifts many times to pay for extras like his football uniform and movie money. The guilt burned him like acid.

Now he fidgeted in the passenger seat, tinkering with his favorite keepsake deep inside his coat pocket. He'd brought it along to feel less alone in his strange new home. Although his dad had proven more of a hurtful jerk than a loving husband, Grant couldn't bring himself to hate him. Right now memories were all he had.

As the car slowed, his father's key chain felt solid against his fingers, a tangible connection with home.

"I don't know how you can afford this place," Grant said.

"Since when are you concerned with money?" His mom kept her eyes on the road.

"Isn't this place private?"

"Yes. I was able to get some financial assistance through the school, and the rest will have to come out of the insurance money from your dad." She pointed. "Look, it's up ahead."

Grant glanced out the window and frowned. The road resembled a winding black tentacle leading to a body of redbrick buildings clustered like open sores on a patch of dry skin. The brochure his mom tossed at him earlier boasted housing for over two hundred boys and *spacious grounds,* which Grant figured, meant far enough from anything or anyone that might lure the boys into trouble. A prison without the bars.

As they went, his eyes fixed on something strange. Black trees lined the roadside, their trunks and most of the branches slick ebony. Every tree looked the same, like polished clones. When the car slowed around a tight bend, his mouth went horribly dry. He squinted hard at a nearby tree. It looked glossy for a good reason. A thick coating of black beetles covered the trunk.

"Mom! Look at that!" He palmed the window.

"Not now. You want me to end up in a ditch?"

"Jesus, there's bugs all over it. Turn this pile of junk around. I'm not stayin' here."

"Stop swearing. And you *are* staying here, even if there *are* bugs."

"I'm tellin' you that tree was covered with beetles. Huge black ones as big as my fist! What kind of hole is this place?"

"This *hole* is the only facility I could get you into on such short notice. You should be grateful you won't miss a whole year of school. If everything works out, you'll be back at Fontaine High next year."

She sped up as the road straightened.

Grant shook his head. "Why can't I just have a tutor? I could sleep in my own bed and help out around the house."

Her incredulous look withered his ploy.

"Grant, let's be honest. You don't help out around the house. All I get is attitude and lip service when I ask. You've been in trouble for truancy, loitering, and now carrying a weapon—"

"Pocket knife," he corrected.

"A knife just the same, and you know better. Ever since Dad died I've been working to support us and trying to be both mother and father, but it's not enough. Somewhere along the way, I've failed." She stopped abruptly, choking out the last word.

He let the silence hang a moment. "I'm sorry, Mom. It was just a stupid mistake and now you're sending me away." A lump tightened his throat.

"I'm sorry, too. But I'm afraid because I don't want to lose you. Let's get through this so we can get back on track. That's all I'm asking. Just give it some time."

They pulled up the semicircle drive in front of a redbrick Tudor with white shuttered windows. Gold knobs embellished the matching double doors. No beetles.

His mother touched his arm. "Promise me you'll watch yourself."

"Don't worry. I won't drop the shower soap."

"That's not what I mean. Keep your *thoughts* to yourself."

"I will if everyone else does," he frowned.

"I mean it, Grant. This is your last stop before military school. Keep your mouth shut."

She reserved this tone of voice for serious matters. Her eyebrows looked pinched enough to hurt and her lips were framed in harsh lines.

She always warned him that using his *gift* was impolite—like eavesdropping, and told him he should try to shut out the thoughts.

That could be tricky. He had little control over what he heard in people's heads. It just happened.

"Yeah. I'll try," he said.

Grant got out of the car and followed his mother up the steps to the doors. He glanced warily at the large placard bolted to the face brick that read:

KNOLLWOOD ACADEMY
Training boys to serve a just cause.

Before he could comment, the door opened and a short balding man with pudgy cheeks, and lips the color of plain Chap Stick stared at them.

His mother broke the silence, extending a hand. "Hello. I'm Amanda Taylor and this is my son, Grant."

The fifty-something man accepted her greeting with little expression except for the tight smile pasted under his pug nose. His sausage-like fingers swallowed her delicate hand.

"Welcome, Mrs. Taylor and Grant." He half turned to acknowledge the boy.

Grant didn't like the way he looked at him and decided to stay clear of the guy.

The man continued, adjusting his black suit coat over a slight paunch. "My name is Elias Mumsford, headmaster of Knollwood. I'll be overseeing your paperwork and tour of the grounds today. Afterward I'll see Grant to his room so he can begin the transition," he said the last word with emphasis and directed a thin smile at Grant.

Grant shifted uneasily under the sudden scrutiny and asked, "Hey, what are all those beetles on the trees down the road?"

"Ah. An inquisitive mind!" Mumsford led the way inside. "You'll do well at Knollwood. We find curiosity a fine tool of education. As for the beetles, I can't say I've ever seen any. Those trees have been standing sentry to the academy since its creation one hundred years ago. Trust me when I tell you they are not diseased in any way."

"But I saw—"

"Grant," his mother cut in. "Let it go. The sun was in your eyes. There aren't any bugs."

Inside Mumsford's office, Grant remained standing while his

mother began the paperwork.

He turned the tree image over in his mind. The sun couldn't have been in his eyes. It hadn't been shining since they'd turned off the main road. Grant knew what he'd seen.

He gasped when something clambered over his right foot.

Mumsford looked up in question.

A mewing sound came softly from under the desk and the headmaster bent down to expose the culprit. "I am sorry, Grant. It seems my cat, Frederick, has poor manners. I usually keep him in my room, but he occasionally sneaks out. I assure you he's the only non-human here at Knollwood."

Grant wasn't convinced.

CHAPTER 3

Mitch Blair turned his Harley onto Cutter Road feeling the rumble between his legs. He'd stripped off his greasy mechanic jumpsuit, glad to be out of the shop and back in jeans and a T-shirt. Quitting time at Bill's Auto signaled his favorite part of day. Time to shit, shower, and shave as his old man used to say, and raise a few brews down at Smalley's Pit Stop.

As he glanced west, his balls crawled toward his stomach when he glimpsed the rear side of Knollwood Academy. Taking the back road never quite quelled his feeling of dread. The school had become a tick in the armpit; except, it proved more than a simple annoyance. It had grown, unbeknownst to the town's people, into a festering sore infecting everyone in some diseased way. It drained goodness and hope, replacing them with the poison of evil and defeat.

The Academy creed ran through his mind and he wondered just who or *what* the boys really trained to serve? In Mitch's opinion, if things happen for a reason, fate had some bizarre reasoning. His parents had been justified in sending him there, but the real punishment came unexpectedly. From the moment he entered the school, he knew something evil lurked inside and considered himself one of the lucky ones, when he had the chance to leave.

He recalled meeting the headmaster the first day, Elias Mumsford, whose clammy handshake matched his sweaty bald spot. It amazed Mitch that parents and teachers never saw through the shady little man. Even at the age of seventeen, Mitch had already reached his full height of six-foot-two and towered over the fat little shit like a tall oak. He liked that, Mumsford didn't. The headmaster's watchful gaze never seemed far and Mitch had landed in detention hall three times the first week.

But it hadn't been Mumsford, the strict regimen, or even the crappy food that made Mitch realize he had to get out. A cold penetrating presence tried to suffocate his soul. He remembered his first night.

As his roommate, Cliff Travis, lay snoring in his bed across the small bedroom, Mitch leaned against the wooden headboard feeling the coolness against his back. Over the cricket's chirrup, heavy, check patterned curtains tossed up and down in the breeze of the open window. Sleep wouldn't come because his frayed nerves bristled at something he couldn't explain. Not exactly a noise and nothing tangible.

He stared at the walls, then the window, then back at the walls, expecting them to vibrate or begin pulsating in the moon's pale glow. The eerie silence screamed something was terribly wrong.

Nothing happened. Finally, when he couldn't hold his eyes open any longer, he slipped beneath the sheets and waited for sleep or whatever lay close, to take him.

Suddenly, his body pressed hard against the mattress and he tried to kick his legs, but they were dead weight. He couldn't catch his breath against the increasing pressure on his chest.

I'm paralyzed!

Mitch fought hard for release. He forced breath into his burning lungs and found the room smelled of fresh blood. Starting to wretch, he feared he might choke to death on his own vomit.

He watched a fetid cloud hover over his bed, then slowly dissipate. The pressure eased on his chest allowing fuller breaths. Finally, the presence lifted and Mitch's limbs return to normal.

He threw back the sodden sheet, rubbing thumb against index finger. Cold slime. What the hell had just happened?

He slipped a T-shirt over his shivering skin and went to his roommate.

"Hey man, wake up," he shook Cliff's shoulder.

No response.

Mitch stared at the kid in the dark. He shoved him a little harder.

Cliff's arm shot up in defense nearly connecting with Mitch's jaw.

"What the hell?" Cliff bolted up.

Mitch flipped on the small bedside lamp. "Did you hear anything?"

"What are you talkin' about? I was asleep for Christ sake!" Cliff tore back the bed covers and swung his legs over the side. He rested his forehead into his palms.

Mitch tried again. "You didn't hear anything?"

Cliff slowly raised his head and squinted. A putty colored facial scar along his left cheekbone glistened like a chubby night crawler in the light of the dilapidated lamp. Mitch could hear the annoyance in his voice.

"No! What did you *hear*?"

"I don't know. It wasn't a sound. Something was in here and all over me."

"Fucking baby. It's first night freak out, that's all. Go call your mommy so *I* can get some sleep."

Mitch grabbed his bed linen and shoved it in front of Cliff's face.

"Here. Look. Am I imagining *this*?"

Cliff pushed his arm away without looking. "So you had a wet dream. Congratulations. Get used to 'em because there aren't any girls around here. The closest thing we got to a female is Mumsford, and he's only interested in his damn cat."

Mitch sat back down on his bed. The crickets continued their serenade, filling the dead silence. Finally, Cliff lit a cigarette and leaned back against his headboard.

"A piece of advice," he said to Mitch. "If you're gonna survive here, you've got to fit in. Mind your own business and do what they tell you. That's it."

"Is that what you do?"

"Yup," he blew out a thin smoke stream.

Mitch shook his head. "Something's not right about this place. I can feel it."

Cliff coughed out a laugh and shook his head. "No shit, sweetheart. That's the whole idea—to make us miserable enough to be good." Snubbing his cigarette into the bedrail, he said, "But I'll tell you what, it'll never happen. Most of us will end up in jail or an early coffin after we leave here. A bad seed is a bad seed. Sometimes I think that's what this place thrives on." He got up and headed into the bathroom.

* * *

Mitch swung the Harley into the graveled parking lot of Smalley's Pit Stop and cut the engine. A heavy bass beat thrummed the building, as a red disk of sun slipped behind the forest wall to the west. Rows of beat up cars told him there was a full house tonight. As he headed for the faded, brick building, Cliff's words still rang in his memory, and most likely always would—*I think that's what this place thrives on.*

Mitch's boots scraped along, spraying rocks ahead of him. He passed a group of Harley's with their chrome gleaming deadly under the lot's lights. The smell of beer and cigarettes reached him before he pulled on the rusted metal bar that served as a door handle.

In all the nights he'd spent at Smalley's he'd never met anyone he'd known from his academy days. They'd all just disappeared. Even Cliff's whereabouts remained a mystery. Mitch had tried to keep in touch after he'd left, but learned Cliff couldn't be found; whatever that meant. Finally, he'd quit trying and assumed his old roomy either didn't want to make contact or had moved on.

Mitch stepped inside the small bar allowing the darkness to enfold him like a cocoon.

A bad seed is a bad seed.

His mouth watered for a shot and a beer.

Sometimes I think that's what this place thrives on.

Mitch took a seat at the bar and ordered. He knew the stream of alcohol would drown the voices of the past.

CHAPTER 4

Dreeson Cooper better known to his students at Trace High School as "Coop," kicked at the rubber puddle that used to be his Jeep tire. It had been slashed into black coleslaw. He ran a hand through his lanky brown hair. "Shit."

A group of teen boys ambled by on the sidewalk playfully shoving each other and talking loudly. One called out, "Hey man, looks like you gotta problem." More laughter followed as the boys moved on.

Coop removed the spare from the back of the Jeep. "Yup. Looks that way, Devon." He pinned one of the boys with a stare.

He remembered the kid from earlier in the school year. Devon had been in his first period class, but had dropped out of high school before the second semester, apparently pursuing other interests.

The boy turned away as if he hadn't heard, but his brief backward glance told Coop otherwise. Devon looked almost apologetic. Coop's arm hairs rose when he realized that Devon, or one of his friends, had slashed his tire. He held his temper as the boys disappeared around the building, reminding himself that there were five of them and one carried a knife. At six-foot with a lean but muscular build, he knew he could stand his ground, but his street-smart youth had taught him to choose his battles wisely.

He changed the tire fighting down the urge to pull the boy out of the group and kick his ass. He didn't know what angered him more, the realization that Devon would purposely hurt him, or that the street kid was bound for bigger things—like prison. In five years of teaching at the inner city high school, Coop had seen both menace and miracles walk through the school's security doors and out into the world. He hoped Devon turned out to be the latter.

Coop felt proud to be an art teacher, knowing he could bring a change of perspective into his student's lives; a sense of beauty in an environment so often hideous. In short, he tried to make a difference. Devon proved the plan didn't always turn out. There were other forces, seemingly stronger ones, working against it.

A familiar saying crept into his mind as he changed the tire. *Young men think old men fools and old men know young men to be so.* That's what his Uncle Eb had always told him when he'd bailed Coop out of trouble during his teens. If not for his uncle, Coop believed he would have been like Devon, or worse.

After Coop lost his father at the age of fourteen, he'd gone on a rampage, setting the tone for his delinquent teenage years and giving his mother more than her deserved share of grief. He'd started hanging out after school with the wrong crowd, drinking, and smoking pot. Eventually, he stopped going to classes and ended up close to expulsion when his father's brother, Eb, stepped in.

One steamy July day, his uncle's old Buick crawled past the back alley where Coop stood smoking a joint with his friends. When the car rolled to a stop, the boys took off over a nearby fence, leaving Coop to take the rap. Eb got out of the car and approached him, his crisp button-down shirt wilting against the scorching temperatures.

Coop stomped out the cigarette and blew a defiant smoke stream in Eb's direction.

Eb's voice echoed between the faded gray, brick walls on either side. "You missed another day of summer school."

Coop shrugged. "Mom sent you?"

"Nope." The man unbuttoned his left shirtsleeve, folding it into a neat roll just above his elbow.

Coop watched in silence as the man stopped only a foot away and began working his other sleeve upward. Eb's dark brow had become one serious line. His usual pleasant expression twisted into pursed lips intent on making a point.

"What are you gonna do?" Coop asked taking a step back.

"Something I should have done months ago."

"What do you mean?"

"I mean...if you're going to run the streets like a hoodlum, you need training. You'll need to know how to defend yourself, because one day somebody's going to try and take you down."

Before Coop could come up with a rebuttal, his Uncle's fist slammed into his eye. Coop stumbled backwards and fell over a garbage can, spilling soda cans, gooey wrappers, and the contents of someone's kitty litter box.

"What the hell did you do that for?" he asked his uncle, trying not to cry. His eye throbbed and felt twice its normal size.

Eb's hand reached out and lifted him up by his collar. He twisted a handful of Coop's unruly brown hair, forcing the boy to his knees among the cat turds and soggy paper towels.

"You fucked up, boy!" Eb's eyes burned a hole through him.

It was the first and only time he'd ever heard the college professor swear.

"What did I do?"

"For starters, you left yourself open for that hit. Not smart. If you're going to play tough, you first have to *be* tough. Second, you're breaking your poor mother's heart and she's already lost one man in her life. That really bothers me."

Coop blinked hard. He hadn't cried since his father's funeral and he feared if he started now, he'd never stop. The grip on his scalp eased and he edged clear of the sour smelling garbage around him. Eb's blackened shadow loomed overhead. Coop waited for the rest of the beating he knew he deserved.

Then his uncle did something Coop knew he'd never forget. He sat down beside him and started to cry. Coop didn't know what to say, where to look, or what to do. Eb's tears mingled with the sweat stains of his dress shirt as his body shook in silent sobs for several minutes.

Finally, Coop laid a tentative hand on the man's shoulder. "I'm sorry, Uncle Eb. How can I fix it?"

He gazed at Coop with an unreadable expression. He didn't say anything for quite a while and Coop decided to wait it out. When he did speak, he became the self-assured professor, choosing his words carefully, in order to drive the point home.

"It's quite simple, Coop. Don't be afraid to be a man—the man your father was."

The incident had only been sixteen years ago, but he'd changed a lot in that time. He'd gone on to finish high school and graduate college with a teaching degree. His uncle had saved him from himself, and he would always be indebted him.

He hoisted the tire remains into the back end of the Jeep and locked up. He pushed back a strand of hair from his eyes watching the sun droop below the western rim of sky. The evening shadows grew tall against the brownstone building known as Trace High and he stared hard at its stoic frame. He had one more item to take care of before he could call it a day. His last day.

A man appeared outside the double glass doors of the school. Lamppost thin in baggy tan trousers and a rumpled white shirt with rolled up sleeves, he waved at Coop. "Dreeson. I'm glad I caught you. Can you come up a minute?"

Coop brushed the dirt from his hands and started up the cement steps toward Arthur Friend, the school's principal. He popped a piece of gum into his mouth to fight the sour taste. His stomach churned.

The man held a door open for him, explaining, "We need to talk."

"Is there a problem, Art?"

"Yes. I'm afraid so."

Inside the principal's office, Coop took a seat.

The cramped quarters were stuffy against the stacks of paperwork and old education volumes the principal had accumulated over the years. The smell of burned coffee wafted past his nose, forcing him to open a new pack of gum. Somewhere down the hall a floor polisher hummed, providing a comforting background noise, and then his boss broke the lull.

"Bad news, Coop. They're cutting the art program next semester. Lack of funds and the arts go first."

Of all the possibilities Coop had anticipated, he'd missed this one. He stifled a smile at the irony of the situation. Earlier in the day, he'd tried several times to gain a private audience with Art. Due to conflicting schedules, and a bathroom brawl on the second floor, he'd been unable to do so.

"God, I'm sorry to hear that, Art."

"That's it? No fireworks? I've had a knot in my stomach all day—couldn't even eat lunch in anticipation of your reaction, and all you can say is 'God, I'm sorry?' Would you at least throw something and make me feel better?" The man's forehead wrinkles eased in relief.

"You're in good company, Art. I had a similar knot in my stomach when I thought about what I had to tell *you*."

Art's eyes widened.

Coop sighed. "I'm giving notice, effective immediately."

After a moment, the principal's stunned expression formed into a slight grin. "That's right, I remember now. You always have to be one up on me. Never play poker with Dreeson Cooper. I've learned that lesson the hard way."

"Art, I'm serious. I'm leaving. I have no choice. My Uncle Eb died over in Knollwood yesterday, and I promised him a long time ago that I would keep the house. I owe the man, and want to honor his wishes, but that means moving to Knollwood. I have to leave today to make funeral arrangements, and I won't be back."

"I'm sorry to hear about your uncle, but I can't believe you're serious about leaving the city. You're really moving?"

"Yes. But what's the difference? I'll be out of job by January anyway."

"What will you do? You love teaching. It's your life."

The truth stung. He did love to teach; his students meant everything to him. But he'd given his word.

Coop shrugged. "Maybe this is a good time for me to get back to the business of serious artwork. I haven't painted in so long I doubt if I even remember how to hold a brush. Who knows? The country life might inspire me and I'll have an art show by summer's end. Shall I invite you?"

"You know I'd be there. But I don't believe you'll give up teaching. It's not your way. I give you six months and you'll be back behind a desk. Starving artist, you know."

"We'll see." Coop didn't mention the fact that thanks to Uncle Eb's smart investing over the years, he'd received a handsome inheritance along with the estate. It provided a solid way for Coop to enjoy an early retirement. *Who would believe an art teacher could retire at thirty?*

He couldn't deny it would be difficult to leave his career, and he wondered how long it would be before the lure of spitball warfare would call him back to the teaching trenches.

CHAPTER 5

Mumsford led the way into Grant's new living quarters. Grant watched his mom's reaction. It matched his. She turned to hide her frown, but Grant couldn't keep quiet.

"Yuck."

"You'll get used to it." Mumsford offered a plastic smile.

"Don't bet on it." Grant tossed his suitcase onto the bed.

"Grant, that's enough," his mother warned.

Mumsford clasped his hands in front of him. "Well, I'll leave you to unpack and get settled. Mrs. Taylor? You may stay as long as you like, but the boys are to have lights out at ten o'clock."

"Thank you," his mother said as the man left the room, closing the door behind him.

Grant spread his arms out. "Mom, look at this place. It's not much bigger than my bedroom!"

"So?"

"*So*? I have a roommate! How can two people share this room?"

"Like Mr. Mumsford said, you'll get used to it."

"And like I told him, don't bet on it."

His mother zipped her coat. "I suggest you start unpacking. It's almost time for dinner and you don't want to be late."

Grant watched in disbelief. How could she leave? He'd thought she'd at least stay long enough to help him get settled and maybe even go with him to the cafeteria. Disappointment filled him. What about her teary, regretful good-bye? She acted liked she couldn't wait to get away and be rid of him.

"Fine," he said, and opened his suitcase. He felt her staring at his back.

"Grant." He heard her say softly. He opened a dresser drawer expecting a swarm of beetles to spew out, but found it empty, not even a mouse turd.

She rested her hand on his shoulder. "Grant look at me."

He turned to find her smiling. How could she look happy?

She used her mom-knows-best tone. "Honey, this will all work out. You'll see. I don't know what else to do. I don't want to lose you."

Grant didn't want to hear excuses. He felt deserted, like when his father died.

"You're not losing me, you're giving me away."

* * *

After his mom left, Grant finished putting his belongings away, and heard a commotion of muffled voices in the hallway. The door burst open and a tall kid with dark hair wearing jeans and a Metallica T-shirt filled the open doorway. His eyes narrowed.

"Who the hell are you?" the kid asked.

Grant watched him strut across the room to the closet, take down a shoebox, and toss it onto his bed. He quickly stripped his shirt exposing a trim, muscular torso and a generous crop of chest hair. The kid moved to the window and opened it a couple of inches.

"You work out?" he asked Grant.

"No." Grant grabbed the football he'd brought from home.

"Well, you better start. A guy like you will end up as someone's girlfriend if you don't toughen up."

Grant turned back to his bed. He had drawn a real jerk for a roommate. He jumped when a large hand clapped him on the back.

"Don't take it personal, man. Just tryin' to help. I'm Joe Blockman. You got a name?"

Grant relaxed a little when Joe grinned. "I'm Grant Taylor," he said.

"That's cool. We'll get along okay as long as you mind your own business." Joe sat on his bed and opened the shoebox.

He pulled out a small bulging baggie and some rolling papers, making quick work of the job at hand.

Grant watched the joint tip glow bright orange and die as Joe took the first hit, and then offered it to him.

"I thought you said I should mind my own business," Grant said.

Joe shrugged. "Your loss, man. I'm just tryin' to break the ice." He took another drag.

"Aren't you afraid you'll get caught? I mean, a shoebox in the closet isn't the best place to hide your stuff."

Joe laughed. "You think they check? This isn't prison. Besides, I'm the star center for their basketball team. As long as we bring home the championship trophy every year, they leave me alone. You play ball?"

"Football."

"I never liked it. But Knollwood has a pretty good team, if you don't mind putting up with the coach. He's ex-army and thinks he's running a boot camp instead of a football team."

"I'm not going to be here that long."

Joe snorted. "That's what we all say. I'm here two years already. Just like you, I turned out to be a major disappointment to my parents."

"What did you do?"

"The usual. Drugs, truancy, petty theft, and just an all around bad attitude."

"Yeah. Me, too," Grant admitted. "What's the point of this place? I mean, putting us all together only fuels the fire. Don't they know we'll learn more from each other than we could ever learn on our own?"

"You think they care?" Joe asked. "Do you think they're here for us?"

Grant didn't follow. "Aren't they?"

"Wrong. *We're* here because our parents or guardians or whatever, don't know what else to do with us and the big shots here are only in it for the bucks."

Joe got up suddenly and went into the bathroom to flush the joint down the toilet. He closed the window and returned the shoebox to the closet.

"Better get ready," he told Grant as he pulled his T-shirt back on.

"For what?"

"Time to eat."

Grant put on his shoes, glad he didn't have to go to the dining room alone. He looked up to see Joe staring at him as if he had bad news. The kid leaned close enough for Grant to smell the rancid stench of smoked weed on his breath.

"Let me tell you somethin'. Knollwood isn't what it seems. Just remember I said that."

"What do you mean?"

"Things happen that shouldn't. You'll see. All I can tell you is to watch yourself."

Grant straightened. "I'm not afraid of a bunch of delinquent punks."

"I'm not talking about the students."

* * *

Amanda Taylor yelped and drew back a bloody finger. She pressed her lips over the wound and tasted the sanguine flavor while the sewing machine whined at her. Luckily, the needle had only caught the side of her finger when she'd tried to pry the wadded material loose from the hungry contraption.

"Damnit. Another item for my growing fix-it list." She checked the wound and noted that the bleeding had stopped.

She appreciated her nursing skills, especially raising a son alone. Grant had experienced the usual childhood incidents like sprained ankles and chicken pox, but she'd saved herself a fortune in medical bills and stress by knowing when to race off to the doctor, or treat at home. Her work in an ICU unit had taught her to handle almost any situation requiring medical attention, except the one area she couldn't seem to heal—her own heart. She doubted those scars would ever heal.

Ancient history, she reminded herself. No one ever quite recovered from something like that, did they? Her main focus now should be Grant. She'd thought of nothing else for weeks, fighting over the decision to place him at Knollwood Academy. It would be on his permanent record, but it couldn't be helped. Besides, there were worse things he'd never be able to hide from his background—things like school expulsion for holding a weapon, and petty theft. The hard truth of his childhood would follow him forever, and as much as she'd hated to enroll him in the academy, she realized she'd needed to take drastic measures before something truly catastrophic happened. Amanda couldn't bear to lose another person in her life.

The doorbell rang; and she welcomed the distraction. Her neighbor, Jill, had phoned earlier to say she'd be bringing coffee. Jill's devil-may-care attitude never failed to perk her spirits. After leaving Grant at Knollwood yesterday, she needed all the perking she could get.

"Come in," she called on her way downstairs.

The front door bounded open. "Hey, what's up?" Jill precariously balanced two plastic cups from a neighborhood coffee bar, while trying to close the door behind her.

Amanda led the way into the kitchen. "I'm getting ready to take a buzz saw to my sewing machine. Care to watch?"

"Sure. I'll go get my toaster. It burned its last bagel this morning."

Amanda accepted a cup of steaming coffee and sat. Jill's short-cropped blond hair stood at attention in tiny spikes as her vivid green eyes narrowed.

"I thought we were dieting," she scanned the contents of a donut box on the table.

"We are." Amanda wafted it under Jill's nose. "We can only have one apiece."

"Now *that's* a diet!" Jill grabbed a chocolate long john and sat down yoga style on a kitchen chair. She munched thoughtfully for a moment and then asked, "So? How did it go yesterday?"

Amanda stopped mid-bite into a powdered sugar donut. "Fine," she lied.

Jill's left eyebrow shot up. "Really?"

"The grounds at Knollwood Academy are beautiful. The staff members are professional and seem nice. The whole place is too good to be true, but…"

"But what?" Jill wiped her chin.

"Grant thinks I've abandoned him. He wants to stay home."

"Of course he does. He's got it made here. He knows you're running scared. Stick to your guns and all that." Jill popped the last bite into her mouth.

"I feel guilty. If Mick were here…"

"Mick would take care of business! But he's not. So move on, girlfriend. Since you only have to answer to yourself, do what you feel is best."

Amanda knew Jill wanted to help, but she and her husband Tony had moved next-door only a few months before Mick died, and for most of that time he'd been on the road. They never really got to know him. But then, apparently neither had she. No one had been more shocked to learn of Mick's extramarital affair than she. The love of her life turned out to be a two-timing jerk. His one redeeming quality had been his love and devotion to Grant.

Jill was right about Mick's reaction if he were still around. Grant probably wouldn't be able to sit down for quite a while.

She'd never been able to play the tough guy role and that's what her son needed. She hoped the academy could provide it.

Amanda licked the powder from her fingers. "I've never been in this position before. I got married at twenty, had Grant before our first anniversary and then went to nursing school. Guess I did it all backwards. Now I have to find a way to be the hard-nosed disciplinarian. It's not my thing. I'm never sure if I'm making the right choices with Grant."

Jill nodded. "It's the same with little Brad. He's a handful, and Tony isn't much help. Sometimes I feel alone when it comes to raising our child."

"Brad is two. He's supposed to be a handful. Besides, at least you have another adult around, someone to talk things out with."

"Look, I know things have been tough on you and Grant for the last couple of years. But frankly you seem less stressed now that Mick is gone." Jill picked at the pink icing on the box lid.

Amanda avoided her friend's eyes.

"What is it? I know when something's on your mind," Jill warned.

"Sometimes I feel like Mick is still around. Like he's watching me. Does that sound strange?"

"Nope. He probably is. I don't believe all that die and go to heaven stuff. I think our spirits hang around for a long while."

Amanda drained her cup and headed for the television. "C'mon, it's time for our work out show." And a subject change, she decided. Now that she'd be alone in the house, she didn't want to dwell on Mick's spirit on the loose. The idea terrified her.

CHAPTER 6

The next morning, Grant followed close behind Joe as he elbowed his way through the Saturday breakfast line.

"C'mon, move it." Joe nudged the boy in front of him. The kid turned, frowning. Suddenly his full lips spread into an even smile.

"Screw you, Block*head.*" He let Joe cut in front of him.

"That's Block*man*, as in the *man* you'll never be." Joe laughed.

Grant got in front of Joe and took a tray. He looked around the large cafeteria trying to remember the names of the boys Joe had introduced him to the night before at dinner. A few memorable faces and names had stuck with him. The tall black kid behind Joe named Terrence Treybelle, shared a room with his twin, Thomas. Joe had explained they were both on the basketball team and nicknamed, Double-trouble, or the Terrible Two.

They'd been placed with an aunt when both parents died, but they'd found their share of trouble, and she'd enrolled them in the academy to prevent a catastrophe.

"All they ever talk about is goin' home to Aunt Betty. It's kind of sickening," Joe had scoffed.

Grant knew how the twins felt, but kept it to himself.

This morning, in a sea of faces, he picked out a nerdy kid named Billy Parker who didn't seem delinquent enough for Knollwood Academy. The night before, Billy had made the mistake of bumping Joe's tray causing a near miss with the floor. Joe quickly recovered his grip and warned the kid to watch it. Billy's eyes had gone large in fear behind thick glasses. He'd stuttered something about it never happening again, and hurried off to sit alone at the far end of the table.

Joe had laughed when Grant asked, "What's his story? He doesn't look like he belongs here."

"Billy-boy doesn't fit anywhere. I'm surprised he's lasted this long."

"What'd he do?"

"Social service pushed his enrollment because he was abused. He's done his share of truancy and drugs, but I'd say putting him here is overkill."

"Why?"

"He's got too much potential."

This morning Grant noticed Billy sat alone again.

"Move it, Taylor." Joe bumped his tray into Grant's.

Grant slid the blue plastic tray along the polished metal rungs, and reached for a cup of chocolate pudding. Before he could claim it, a large hand grabbed it up.

"Put it back," Grant ordered, regretting it immediately. The hand belonged to a kid twice his size in both height and width.

Grant looked up to see a thick black uni-brow across a canvas of severe acne. The boy's penetrating stare caused Grant to step back. Before the bully made a move, Joe stepped between them, placing his palms on the guy's shoulders.

"Leave it alone, Artie."

Grant hid a grin. *This Goliath's name is Artie?* No wonder the kid bullied people.

The kid leaned toward Joe. "What's it to you? Is he your girlfriend?"

Joe grabbed him by the collar and the dessert cup dropped to the floor splattering pudding all over Artie's shoes.

The boy's cheeks burned crimson as he seethed, "You'll pay!" He hauled back a fist, but Terrence caught it.

"Is there a problem, *Arthur?*" he said, towering over the kid.

Artie lowered his arm slowly and shook his head as he pushed Joe aside on his way to the napkin dispenser.

Joe slapped Terrence a high five, while offering Grant a bit of advice.

"Stay away from him. He *thinks* he's tough and that's the worst kind."

Grant nodded. "No problem."

At the table, Terrence's brother, Thomas, joined them and proved that the twins shared only physical qualities. Thomas ate his breakfast in silence, offering an occasional laugh, while his brother led the conversation in a loud, boisterous tone. When introduced to Grant, Thomas merely nodded then turned back to his food.

As Joe and his friends talked about the upcoming basketball season, Grant's attention drifted to Billy Parker at the end of the long table.

Joe nudged Grant. "Hey, wait here. I'll be right back."

Grant watched him leave with Terrence, then shot a glance over at Billy. Dread washed over him when Billy slid over beside him with his tray.

"You're Grant, right?" He stuffed a spoonful of oatmeal into his mouth.

"Yeah," Grant said looking around for Joe.

"He'll be back. He's probably lookin' to make a dope deal." Billy gulped his milk.

When Grant didn't answer, the kid eagerly filled the silence.

"Knollwood isn't a bad place. Kind of strange sometimes with all the rules and weird noises, but you'll get used to it."

"That's what they say," Grant said absently. He wished the kid would go away before Joe came back. He sensed the kid had become a regular target with the other boys, especially Joe's crowd.

As Billy rambled on, Grant noticed the kid scratched at his hands and wrists the whole time, as if he had fleas or something. He noticed Billy had started to bleed from the claw marks he'd created. He watched in horrified silence as Billy talked and scratched. His fingernails were coated with fresh blood and his skin looked as though it had been smeared with pink watercolor.

Grant moved over a few inches.

Billy didn't seem to realize he was scratching.

Grant saw Joe and Terrence heading his way and seized his dirty tray. "I have to go. See ya."

When Billy didn't answer, he turned to see the boy tearing at fresh territory on his forearm.

As they left the dining room, Joe turned his attention to Grant. "Get your coat. I want to show you something."

Grant followed orders, still thinking about Billy. Should he mention it to Joe? What if the kid had a disease? He found his jacket and hurried to meet Joe outside. As curiosity took hold about what his roommate wanted to show him, his concerns over Billy faded. He hoped Joe wasn't including him in a drug deal as Billy had warned. He didn't need any new trouble.

The sun hid behind threatening gray skies. Grant zipped his coat as a gust of brisk autumn air seeped through.

"C'mon," Joe called taking off down a sidewalk from the main house to the school building about a hundred feet away.

"Where are we going?" Grant asked.

"You'll see." Joe veered onto the grass between the two buildings.

Grant followed him behind the school to a row of mature trees, marking the beginning of a dense forest. He watched Joe brush dead leaves from a place on the ground. Grant tucked his hands inside his coat pockets to keep warm. He fought off an ominous feeling of impending danger. *Why is this place so creepy?*

The twisted tree trunks looked as if they'd been exposed to radiation and the shed leaves on the ground were an iridescent maroon color. The sour smelling air made him breathe through his mouth. Grant thought the Knollwood grounds were diseased and rotting.

"C'mon, Joe. Let's go." Grant turned around.

"Wait. See this?" Joe called, tossing his book bag aside.

He bent to look at a metal disc planted into the ground.

"It's a manhole cover." Grant pushed aside more leaves. He judged the copper colored plate to be about two and a half feet in diameter and at least three inches thick. The ornate border carved onto its surface surrounded by unusual markings reminded him of ancient writing.

"What the hell is it?" he asked Joe.

"I don't know, but I don't think it has anything to do with the sewage system."

"Does anyone else know about it?" Grant asked.

"Not a soul. It's my secret."

"Maybe it's some kind of Knollwood emblem," Grant suggested.

"Don't think so. Our symbol is a knight in armor. The Knollwood Knights."

Grant traced the lettering with his finger and found the metal unusually warm.

"And check this out." Joe placed the heels of his hands against the edge and pushed. The cover slid with a loud grating sound against the cement rim. Grant jumped back when several large black beetles skittered from beneath and disappeared into the grass.

"God! What *are* those things?"

Joe didn't flinch as he continued to push. The hole now looked like a giant half open eyelid over an empty socket.

The boys peered into the black abyss and winced at a sudden gust of musty air.

Joe's eyes gleamed. "It's a tunnel."

It looked bottomless to Grant. He picked up a nearby rock, and pitched it in to determine how deep it went. He never heard it hit bottom.

Joe shrugged. "I think we should take a look."

"We are," Grant stated.

"No. I mean a *real* look."

Grant spread his arms. "Go for it."

"Listen. You're better built for this than I am." He unzipped his book bag and took out a thick rope and a flashlight. "You wouldn't be able to hold my weight."

Grant knew he'd been duped. "You brought me out here to drop me down this hole? Fuck you." He turned to go.

"I promise I'll only lower you a little ways down, not all the way. I just want to see what this thing is." He picked up the rope. "Look. All you have to do is tie this around your waist and I'll haul you up at the first sign of trouble."

An idea dawned in Grant's mind and he grinned at his roommate. "This is some kind of initiation, huh?"

Joe wore an incredulous expression. "No way. I just want to know what's down there and I can't do it by myself. Will you help me?"

Grant thought a moment about how Joe had taken him around to introduce him and then the way he'd stopped Artie this morning. He didn't need an enemy at the school, especially with Joe's popularity.

He grabbed the rope. "All right man, but you *owe* me."

"You got it," Joe said.

As Grant descended, he tried to avoid touching the tunnel's shiny sides, jerking his hand back when it brushed the cold, rubbery interior. He couldn't stop thinking about something grabbing his feet as he dangled from the rope. He forced several deep breaths and made himself think of something else. Suddenly, he stopped moving and heard Joe call.

"See anything yet?"

"No," he yelled back. "Why don't you bring me up? There's nothing down here."

"Just a little more," Joe hollered over the edge.

Grant realized he'd stupidly put his fate into the hands of a delinquent teen that he hardly knew. "What a dumb—" Something bumped his shoe.

"Whoa!" he called out. Grant tried to rationalize the situation. It's a rock sticking out of the wall, he told himself, fumbling with the flashlight.

The tunnel turned out to be a narrowed mass of reddish folds that formed into a puckered hole. He knew why he hadn't heard the rock hit the soft, shiny, muscle inside.

Suddenly, he yanked the rope hard. His throat felt desert dry and his heart roared in his chest.

The puckered center opened and a bulbous mass shot up at him.

Grant kicked the probing muscle inches from his feet.

"Pull me up!" he screamed.

"What is it?" Joe called.

"Just do it!"

Grant's body jerked upward as the chalk-colored mound lurched, missing his left shoe. He slammed against the tunnel's murky walls, cursing when his hands sunk into its soft tissue-like warmth. Joe seemed hundreds of feet above, feverishly pulling the rope.

After several more tugs, Grant reached the hole's opening. Sweat burned his eyes as he fought to pull himself to safety.

Joe could barely contain his excitement. "What is it? What did you see?"

Grant tore the rope from his waist and dropped, pressing his forehead against the damp, but solid, ground. He tried to shake the image and catch his breath. Finally, he looked up at his roommate's expectant gaze and said, "It's alive."

* * *

Inside the Knollwood Academy chapel, Billy Parker shredded his history test over the linen draped altar. He watched in satisfaction as the red-inked bits of paper lay in a mound before him like a bloody sacrifice. No one would know he'd failed again—especially his dad.

The chapel had become a safe haven for Billy, where he could hide from his classmates' glaring eyes, and pray for his deliverance. Each Sunday, Pastor Jack gave a non-denominational religious service for those who felt the need. Billy attended regularly, finding comfort within the dark paneled walls and golden candlelight.

The classroom-turned-chapel remained vacant between services, serving as Billy's quiet place for meditation. He confessed and conversed to the statue of Christ above the altar for almost two years now with promises to do better and become the son his father would finally be proud of. Maybe then he could go home.

Looking down at the paper pile before him, he knew it would be a major set back in his father's eyes. Failure was not an option in the Parker household. Everything had changed after his mother disappeared, never heard from since. The last five years had taken its toll on Billy and his father, turning the man into a control fanatic.

He remembered all the abuse his old man had dealt out from his high and mighty couch throne. At times, it overwhelmed Billy and he wished for siblings to share the deluge of punishments.

Tears rolled down Billy's cheeks, recalling his father's favorite phrase—the one he drilled into his head every time Billy screwed up.

"What's eatin' ya boy!"

"Nothing, Dad." Billy backed away from the couch.

"Don't give me that. I see those lazy, useless, bums you hang with."

"They don't hurt anyone."

"Come 'ere!" he commanded.

Billy inched forward. The man grabbed his wrist. He felt his skin burn as his father twisted it. "Who robbed that drugstore on forty-fifth street?"

"How would I know?" Billy struggled to get away.

"I think ya do." His old man's breath reeked of whiskey.

"Dad, I told you, I don't know anything about that!"

The man's hand met his cheek with incredible force, sending Billy to the floor. His glasses smacked the wall behind him.

Anger surged as Billy picked them up, and saw the bent frames. "You broke them!"

His father guzzled from a nearby bottle on the coffee table, and let his bloodshot gaze travel over the boy. "Oh? And what are you gonna do about it?"

Billy lowered his eyes.

"Uh-huh. That's what I thought. You're weak, just like you're mother. Weak! Don't you look at me like that!" He jumped from the couch and stood overhead with clenched fists.

Billy pressed against the wall, raising his arms in defense. He knew what was coming, and regretted his lame attempt to stand up for himself.

"What's eatin' ya boy!" The man's chuckle poured into his ears like acid as he felt the first blows.

Billy shook himself from the images and focused on his shredded test paper. He picked up a few bits and shoved them into his mouth.

Christ's image watched as he stuffed in the rest. He chewed while he wandered behind the altar to gaze up at his savior. He knew Jesus would probably have quite a bit to say about his deception, but it was the only way to get rid of the test. His father could never know about it. Billy silently promised the statue to do better in history, if He would let this incident slide.

Suddenly, the replica's face looked down and smiled. Billy couldn't believe his eyes; surely it was some sort of miracle. He smiled back. Maybe this time he would be forgiven. Then he saw the plaster split, sending chunks raining down on Billy's upturned face. He backed away seeing his father's image scream, "What's eatin' ya boy!"

CHAPTER 7

Uncle Eb grinned up at Coop from the mortician's table. Even death couldn't erase the man's trademark, impish grin. He looked downright happy.

Beside Coop, stood a tall man in a drab black suit, that matched his stoic expression. The owner of Marshall's Funeral Home, explained, "Your uncle had made most of the arrangements beforehand. He seemed to know just what he wanted."

Coop nodded. Uncle Eb had made his wishes clear, long before his death. He'd wanted no wake or services, and was to be cremated as soon as possible. Under the circumstances, however, things were moving a bit too fast for Coop.

It never occurred to him that Uncle Eb would die alone with no witnesses. When he'd received the call from the Knollwood Police, he'd been numb. How could a man as cautious as Uncle Eb, accidentally die in his own home? The man could have written a safety manual.

That night on the phone, the police chief delivered the final verdict, telling Coop, Ebenezer Cooper, had apparently fallen down his staircase, receiving a fatal blow to the head. The chief's tone failed to reflect any sympathy as he gave him the funeral home's address and phone number. He hadn't even allowed time for questions.

Coop turned to the funeral director. "Mr. Marshall, I was under the impression that accident victims were automatically autopsied. May I ask why they didn't do one?"

"They're done in unusual circumstances, but a home accident involving an elderly person isn't considered suspicious. We see a lot of that." When Coop frowned, he added, "You may request one if you'd like."

"No. That's fine. He looks content. Just wondering."

The man nodded and said, "I'll be in my office when you're ready."

Coop waited until the man left before lifting the sheet.

Eb wore nothing but a red-green hue. Coop cursed his nosey nature, then drew the cover all the way back. The neck and jaw hung slack, with the arms locked close to the body like a soldier at attention. Coop didn't know what to look for exactly, but he felt compelled to examine the body thoroughly. The sketchy information revealed only that Eb had hit his head on the way down the stairs.

Coop leaned closer. The small cut above the brow didn't look treacherous enough to kill, and he didn't see any other unusual marks, not even a bruise.

He moved to the feet and stopped. The bottom of Eb's left foot shone, like it had been painted with egg whites and left to dry. Coop scraped it with his fingernail and watched crusty flakes fall to the floor. Between several toes, he found a yellow, curd-like substance, and wondered if this had been the cause of his uncle's slip down the stairs. He knew Eb would have avoided a mess like that. The story didn't make sense.

He covered the body, said a silent good-bye, and headed to Mr. Marshall's office.

Coop declined the funeral director's offer of coffee and got straight to the point. "I'd like to know what's on my uncle's foot. It looks like eggs."

The man's eyes widened.

"What is it?" Coop pressed.

"Well, we believe your uncle was fighting a bout of flu because…his foot appears to be covered in dried vomit. The police suggested he'd slipped on his way down the steps. I'm sorry you had to see that."

Coop heard a touch of annoyance in the man's tone, and figured he'd overstepped his bounds in peeking at his uncle. He suddenly felt foolish. Maybe things had happened like they'd said. No mystery, after all.

He realized he was plagued with guilt that Uncle Eb died alone, like his father had. But Dad had died in a hospital, he reminded himself, with a morphine drip to ease his pain and anxiety.

When he visualized Eb's last moments, he shut his thoughts down. Guilt could eat a man alive, and he knew Eb wouldn't want that. Accidents happen. Time to move on.

He grabbed a pen and signed the cremation papers.

* * *

Coop jiggled the doorknob again and wondered if he had the wrong key. The lock finally gave, and he entered his new home. Dust motes and stale air accosted him on his tour throughout Uncle Eb's two-story farmhouse.

The carpet lay threadbare and the rooms needed a fresh coat of paint, but he decided it proved a decent place to live alone. Well, not alone, he amended when he noticed mouse turds on the kitchen counter. His hopes rose when he found the spacious parlor provided great light exposure from tall windows and more than enough room to set up his art studio.

He stopped at the foot of the steep staircase and looked up toward the second floor. This had been where Eb died. He pictured Eb's fall and how he might have hit his head hard enough to kill him. Again, doubts surfaced when he tested the railing and found it secure. As he started up the steps, he couldn't find any signs of vomit, or blood, not even a stain. Had the police cleaned up the mess? The further up he went, the farther the story stretched.

He startled when his cell phone rang. He recognized Arthur Friend's number. "Miss me already?" Coop answered.

"Don't you wish? I'm just calling to apologize again. I feel like I left you hanging."

"You didn't let me go. *I* did."

"I thought by now you'd be job hunting." Art chuckled.

"Looks like I already have a job."

"Oh? Doing what?"

"Fixing up my new home."

"That bad, huh?"

"I suppose I could cover the walls with my art."

"There are more interesting ways to spend time," Art hinted.

"Like what?"

"Getting out and meeting people. Dating?"

Coop knew where this was heading and smiled at Art's concern. "Okay, Cupid. I'll take that into consideration."

"Right. Well, call if you need anything. I know relocating can be rough, not knowing anyone and all. If you get lonely, give a holler."

Coop thanked him and disconnected. He headed back into the living room taking a good look at his new digs. Although age had had its way with the house, his artistic eye caught and held its beauty. Decorative plaster cornice painted eggshell white, enriched the living room and parlor with tasteful elegance. The archways offered a unique welcome to each of the rooms, and he appreciated the generous sunlight spilling through the first floor windows. It gave the old farmhouse surprising elegance amidst mice and creaking stairs. No wonder Eb loved this house so much.

Coop sighed, considering all the work ahead, from change of address forms to the much-needed repairs, but realized he'd have plenty of time now. *Retired*. He didn't like the word. It had become an age definer instead of an employment status. It conjured images of wrinkles and white hair, and usually followed other adjectives like, elderly or senior citizen. At the age of thirty, he shared none of the old age traits, except one—loneliness.

He thought about his conversation with Art and realized his friend had never understood the lack of romance in his life. Coop had little regret in choosing not to marry. His decision to remain single had come after a routine medical exam in his twenties. He could recall the doctor's words vividly. "According to my findings, I feel I can safely tell you to toss your rubbers. I'm sorry Mr. Cooper, but you'll never father children."

Consequently, he'd decided it wouldn't be fair to ask a young woman to remain childless because of his inadequacy and so although he dated occasionally, he'd never let anything get serious. Instead, he'd fallen in love with teaching and let the students become his *children*.

His art filled the void for a while as he submerged himself in the goal of making a name in the great galleries of the world. Eventually, he'd put that dream on hold to teach full time. It became his true love. But now retirement had ended that relationship, and he wondered if he'd made the right choice.

He paced in the dust-riddled parlor trying to recapture the enthusiasm of his younger days at the prospect of painting full-time, but found the emotion lacking. Instead, his mind traveled to images of teenagers in tattered jeans and T-shirts rolling their eyes at the prospect of having to draw a vase. The familiar image felt comfortable, like reminiscing about family members.

Later that afternoon, Coop rearranged the living room furniture to his liking. He'd opted to leave his worn apartment furniture behind since he'd also inherited all of his uncle's furnishings. Although Uncle Eb's decorating tastes differed from his own, he hadn't had the time or enthusiasm to go shopping for new furniture.

He relaxed now that all of his personal items had been put away. But a survey of the kitchen cabinets reminded him that he'd neglected to stock up on groceries. He slipped on his jacket with the idea of heading into town for some basic bachelor nutrition.

On his way to his Jeep, he glanced over the property and noted the three acres were full of mature trees and hilly areas. The spacious farmhouse held a special charm surrounded by Uncle Eb's meticulous landscaping. The neatly trimmed hedge had lost its bush-like quality to the autumn season, but it framed the front yard nicely. Decorative stone wove its way around the house, with redbrick edging where mums and other flowers still held their vibrant colors.

Across the front yard, he saw the large garden area where Eb's talents really came to life. The man had a creative spark that fueled his love for beauty. When Coop had asked him why he'd taken the tough job of landscaper after retiring, the man had chuckled and replied, "It's not for the income, but the diversion. I'm bored, my boy. Beside, I love to see nature come to life."

A faded pole barn stood in place of a garage several yards from the house, met by a gravel driveway. Situated outside of town, the home was extremely secluded.

A chill gripped him as he buckled his seatbelt. The skies over Knollwood looked as though they might dump a generous portion of snow before the day ended, but it wasn't the temperature that had him shivering. A heavy foreboding feeling had sunk into his bones.

He shook off the dark mood and turned the key. The Jeep's engine whined and choked. Once again, his busy schedule had caused him to neglect a badly needed tune-up. It looked like his car had made a change in *his* priorities, shooting to the top of the to-do list. After several tries, the engine finally turned over with a rattling cough.

The ride into town proved a lesson in patience when he crawled at twenty miles an hour behind a tractor. After several failed attempts to pass it, he decided to kick back and enjoy the rural scenery with livestock in the fields and the smell of manure in the air. Several miles down the road, he craned to see a group of redbrick buildings on a rolling stretch of hills. He caught a glimpse of the sign. The Knollwood

Academy intrigued him as a new resident and a teacher. What *kind* of academy? The grounds were as large as a small town. Experience told him it must be privately owned.

Coop grinned when he entered downtown Knollwood. He'd been a city boy so long he'd forgotten such a quaint town could exist. Eventually the shop owners would probably call him by name and he'd become a person instead of a number. He figured there were probably many things he'd have to get used to in Knollwood.

He slowed when he came to Bill's Auto. A beat up Harley sat parked on the side of a building that housed three empty car stalls. He pulled up to one of the garage doors.

Inside the shop's office, a John Stamos look-alike glanced up from his *Playboy* magazine. The greasy jumpsuit said *mechanic*, but the name patch read, Mitch. Coop nodded and waited for the man to get up from the roller chair and meet him at the counter.

"What can I do for you?" the man remained seated.

"I've been having trouble starting my Jeep."

The mechanic nodded. "Okay. Pull it in and I'll have a look."

"Now?" Coop asked.

"Yeah."

"No wait?"

Mitch looked around with a shrug. "Well, the customers aren't exactly waitin' in line."

"Right," Coop turned to go and reminded himself he wasn't in the city anymore.

The mechanic made small talk while he worked on the Jeep. "You don't look familiar. Just passin' through?"

Coop popped open a can of Pepsi from the vending machine and leaned against the wall. "I just moved in."

"Where?" Mitch wiped a palm on the front of his coverall.

"The Cooper house off of Route 41."

"Oh, yeah. I heard the old man died."

"That was my uncle," Coop informed him.

"Sorry." The mechanic wiped the dipstick and continued. "So where are you from?"

"Up north, in the city. I'm a teacher."

"That's cool. Are you going to work at the academy?"

Coop caught the man's dark expression and wondered if he'd discovered a terminal problem with the engine.

"I'm retired," he said realizing how strange the phrase sounded.

Mitch glanced up. "Kind of young, aren't you?"

"Inheritance." Coop changed the topic. "Have you been in Knollwood long?"

The man snorted a chuckle and said, "All my life and then some."

"What do you mean?"

"No one ever leaves Knollwood."

Before Coop could comment, the mechanic slammed the Jeep's hood. "Simple adjustment, but I suggest a full tune-up and oil change soon. I'd do it now, but it's closin' time."

"I see. Can I stop by on Monday?"

"Sure. We open at nine." Mitch cleaned his hands on a greasy rag.

"You know anything about the Knollwood Academy?" Coop asked.

Mitch threw the rag into a large corner bin. "Yeah. Why?"

"What kind of place is it?"

"Good question."

"Pardon?"

"It's a boys school. For delinquents. I used to go there." Mitch's lips tightened.

"I see," Coop said.

"Look, if you're thinkin' about teaching there, you might want to reconsider."

"Why is that?"

"Because the place isn't right. It has a way of getting to a person. It's like I said before, no one ever leaves Knollwood—the town or the school."

* * *

Billy couldn't believe it. Joe Blockman had told him to go to the main house backyard tonight at seven. At first, he'd feared it was a ploy to get him outside so Joe and his friends could beat him up. His nerves calmed when he saw only one cigarette tip glowed in the dark. Joe stood alone.

He met Joe halfway across the yard standing beside a dark lump in the grass. Suddenly a bright beam cut his eyes as Joe turned his flashlight on him.

"You didn't wuss out. That's a good sign," Joe said.

Billy tried to sound brave. He didn't trust Joe. "Course not. What do you want?"

The flashlight poured over the grass and onto the mound beside him. It was a book bag.

"What's that for?" Billy asked.

"It's for our little expedition." Joe opened the bag and took out a thick rope.

Billy wanted to run. What the hell had he gotten himself into now? "Look, I need to get back—"

"Not so fast. I want to show you something. C'mere."

The wind had picked up, blowing leaves across his cheek, as black clouds buried the moon's light.

"Billy," Joe called. "Get over here."

The boy obeyed, wishing he could turn away, but he knew that would be a mistake. Something in Joe's tone told him things would go much better for him if he did what he was told. *Just like home.*

Joe got down on his knees and shoved a manhole cover from its place in the ground. "I know you've been having some trouble with the guys. They give you a hard time because they don't know what you're made of."

He stood, brushing his hands clean. "So, I told them we need to get to know you better. This is your chance." He handed Billy the rope.

"What do you mean? Chance for what?"

"To prove yourself. If you do this, I promise the guys will never bother you again. You'll be one of us, man. Just like a brother."

Billy took the rope, not sure what to do.

"Now listen, I've done this a hundred times. No one ever gets hurt. It's more of a formality than anything. Kind of like a college fraternity stunt. Tie that rope around your waist, and I'm going to lower you into the hole."

"No way!" Billy started to give back the rope.

Joe stepped forward. "No more teasing, Billy. You'll have a place in our group. Think about it man."

Billy looked into the black mouth waiting to swallow him. He feared dark close places more than anything after spending countless nights locked in the hall closet at home. His father's idea of tough love.

He pictured himself walking into the cafeteria with Joe and his group to the shocked stares of other students, no longer a nerd, finally accepted and respected. They'd call him Bill, not Billy. The idea appealed to him more than his fears.

He secured the rope around his waist and sat on the hole's edge.

"You won't regret this. You're doin' the right thing," Joe promised Billy.

CHAPTER 8

Monday morning Grant poked his oatmeal with a spoon looking for his appetite. The inside of his eyelids felt like they were coated with sandpaper. Sleep had abandoned him since his Saturday night tunnel experience. Joe still didn't believe his story about the mouth-like hole behind the school and the fact that it had tried to eat him.

"It's all in your head, man. You just got freaked." Joe had laughed at him.

"I'm telling you there was something down there that grabbed for my foot. Like a long, gray tongue."

Joe brushed him aside and moved on. "Forget it, kid."

Back in their room, Joe had rolled on his bed with a hideous cackle. He threw his pillow hard enough to hit Grant in the head. "Grow up, Taylor."

Grant ignored his taunts as he searched his dresser for his dad's key chain. He hadn't seen it in a couple of days and wondered where he'd put it. He hoped Joe hadn't taken it as a joke.

"I don't really give a shit if you don't believe me." Grant slammed the top drawer of his nightstand.

Joe reached into his closet for some weed. "You pussy. Grow up. It was all in your head. In a few days it'll be ancient history."

When Grant called home and relayed the experience, his mother had taken a casual attitude and warned him to stop playing around. He cringed when he realized everyone thought he'd overreacted.

By Sunday evening, he started doubting the experience himself. His mind rationalized the blurred images into something more palatable. The muscle-like lining of the hole became wet clay; the great writhing tongue, a loose section of pipe or plastic tubing. With his fears vanquished, he expected a peaceful night's sleep before his first day of classes at Knollwood.

Instead, he'd tossed and turned, wrestling with the truth in his heart—the tunnel was dangerous. Sleep came after he had made the conscious decision to stay clear of the manhole. He'd managed two hours of sleep before the alarm sounded.

Now as he fought to remain alert, he heard Joe's voice calling him from across the cafeteria.

"Hey, Taylor! Let's move it!"

Grant emptied his tray and took off after his roommate, lugging his book bag.

Outside, thick clouds broke apart, exposing a blue backdrop. Grant caught up to Joe as he flicked his cigarette butt across the dried grass. As they passed the open area between the main house and the school, Grant avoided looking in the direction of the manhole. Never again, he promised.

Above the trees, he saw a great flock of black birds circling overhead.

"Jesus, look at those birds. There must be a hundred of them!" Grant said.

Joe glanced up with a knowing frown. "Those aren't birds. They're bats."

"Bats?" Grant squinted skyward. "In the daytime?"

"I know. It's weird."

Grant ducked when a heavy plop hit his shoulder. He knew what had happened without looking.

"Shit!" He moved ahead of Joe.

"Yup." Joe grinned and hurried toward the school.

Another tap on Grant's coat signaled a second strike and he seized up a handful of leaves to wipe it off. They came away covered in a slimy, red substance.

"What is this stuff?" He showed Joe.

"Looks like blood, man. Time to go."

Grant's breakfast rose to his throat as he ran for cover from the blood-dripping bats.

* * *

THE ACADEMY

The fluorescent classroom lights did little to brighten the dreary paint of Grant's first classroom. The instructor, Mr. Peterson, however, turned out to be a sufficient diversion with his enthusiasm and funny anecdotes. Grant found World Geography more interesting than he thought it would be. Still, bats beat South America in the "what's interesting" department and he found it difficult to concentrate.

Looking around the classroom, he saw one or two familiar faces, one of them, Billy Parker, who sat in the next row. Billy offered a brief wave as he took his seat and proceeded to claw at his bruised left forearm.

Halfway through the class, Mr. Peterson assigned a short project and asked everyone to pair up with a partner. Billy quickly made his way to sit beside Grant.

"Since you don't know anyone," he explained.

Grant nodded glumly and edged his desk a few inches away.

The boy's longish hair drooped over his left eye like a black veil. He had to keep pushing it back in order to see.

"What happened to your arm?" Grant nodded toward the bruises.

"I got in Joe's way again. You know how it is." Billy shrugged.

He did know. For the past several days, Joe had dished out extra helpings of verbal insults to the kid. He wondered what triggered Joe's wrath.

As they worked in class, Grant thought the clock must have stopped. He couldn't wait to get out of here. Billy's scratching made him itch, and hideous open places were bleeding.

He watched in disgust as Billy absently brushed a small scab from his paper and continued working.

"Let me have that brown marker, will ya?" he asked Grant.

Grant handed it over; making sure their fingers didn't touch.

Billy swiped his neck and went back to work on his map of South America.

A tiny black bug lay dead on the desk. Grant stared hard at Billy's skin as the boy colored his paper. The kid's skin swarmed with gnat-like insects. No wonder he itched.

When Billy reached in front of Grant to return the marker, he noticed the boy's hand was riddled with tiny red bite marks. Billy was being eaten alive!

Grant jumped when a hand rested heavily on his shoulder.

"Everything all right here, guys?" Mr. Peterson asked.

Grant knew he had to act. If he didn't speak up now, he never would. One of Billy's little black bugs headed his way. He moved his chair over, and wondered how he could be discreet in front of Billy.

Suddenly, Mr. Peterson leaned close and took a long look at the student's hands. Grant caught his horrified expression.

"Billy?" the teacher said. "Would you please come with me for a minute?"

Grant watched them leave the room, relieved that he hadn't been the one to tell. He knew from experience that tattling usually ended in disaster.

Grant leaned back in his seat and sighed, feeling the need to shower. When the bell rang, he collected his supplies, all but the brown marker, and headed off toward his second class of the day in hopes that Knollwood had no further surprises for him.

* * *

Arthur Sikes stroked his pet hamster, Einstein. The butterscotch fur reminded him of the hard candy he'd favored growing up. That had been ages ago. At seventeen, he considered himself an adult, after surviving on his own since twelve when his father went to prison and his mom went to the bar. A street gang became his surrogate family, providing the human bonding he never received at home. His new family taught him the meaning of loyalty and sacrifice, a foreign concept to his parents.

He'd run the streets for a while, until someone called family services on his mother. It hadn't been long before his court appointed guardian shipped him off to the academy. It should have been a new beginning. Now he was alone again and his only friend was a rodent. Better than most of the trash he'd met at Knollwood, he decided.

He'd learned to keep his distance from the other students on the first day when several older boys attacked him in the back yard of the main house. Joe Blockman had put an end to the beating, but had had an agenda of his own. Artie still smelled the musty odor of the slimy tunnel that day. His heart had pounded so hard he thought it would burst through his chest. Since then, he'd been plagued with nightmares and a sense that something watched him while he slept. Artie had few regrets so far, but that was at the top of his list. He never should have gone down that hole.

Einstein climbed up his arm toward his favorite spot on Artie's shoulder. Animals fascinated him and he hoped to become a veterinarian someday. If he survived the academy.

Artie thought about the new guy, Grant Taylor. The kid didn't know what he was in for, and Artie decided he wasn't going to be the one to tell him.

"What good would it do?" he asked his pet. "It's too late for Grant now that he's friends with Joe."

Artie jerked around to an empty room when the floor creaked behind him. His nerves were live wires, snapping and twitching inside his brain. *Something was after him.*

He held the hamster close to his face. "You understand, don't you? I know you've heard the weird sounds late at night, too."

Artie looked over at his clothes hamper, his stomach churning.

This morning he'd awakened, naked, his legs and feet covered in dried mud. His soaked pajama bottoms lay in a heap beside the bed. Artie knew he'd been outside—again.

They're after me, Einstein, if only I knew *who*."

The rodent's whiskers twitched in delight as Artie placed him onto his exercise wheel.

"I'm going to buy you a new wheel. I have to oil this one to keep it from squeaking. If anyone found out, Mumsford would make me get rid of you."

Einstein did laps while Artie pulled down a book from a nearby shelf and started reading about common canine diseases. Deep in concentration, he soon forgot about the night terrors.

CHAPTER 9

Mitch groaned when the euphoric release rushed to his head like an illegal drug. If this feeling could be bottled, no one would be able to afford it. He rode the last few waves of pleasure and rolled over onto his back.

Sandy, a waitress from Smalley's Pit Stop, lay softly panting beside him with her sweaty blond bangs plastered to her forehead. She pulled the cotton sheet over her naked rump and turned onto her side. Mitch got up to grab a couple of beers, but Sandy lay asleep with her full lips slightly parted against the pillow.

In the kitchen, he glanced at the clock on his way to the refrigerator, and noted he had less than five hours before he had to get up. His boss, Bill Deeken, had turned over the fine job of opening the shop to his number one, and only, mechanic. *Lucky me.*

The beer can's pop-top echoed in the small kitchen and he enjoyed a long guzzle.

"Ah, nectar of the gods," he said and belched loudly.

His bare feet made a sticky sound as he walked across the faded linoleum and he reminded himself it could probably use a good scrubbing. He hated housework. An idea ignited and quickly died like flash paper when he considered asking good ol' Sandy to do it. She worked two jobs, and from what he'd seen of her place, she'd never get the happy homemaker award.

"She'd probably tell me to go to hell." He chuckled to the four walls.

After another long draw of beer, he pulled back the dingy living room curtain to look out. The dark silhouettes in the yard were familiar. An overturned Johnny boat and a car engine covered with a tarp sat abandoned beside the garage. The building itself stood nearly filled to capacity with boxes, tools, and an engineless 1969 GTO that he'd been *restoring* for years.

Beyond his gravel driveway, heading west, he gazed onto Route 41 that stretched into a dark ribbon of solitude as it wound its way into town past farm fields and small bungalows. He knew his world; his kingdom would never change. Grand ol' Knollwood.

He'd inherited the house and the small patch of land when his parents died, and it had provided every reason to stay and make a life in the town where he'd grown up. He knew the real reasons for staying ran deeper than that. It had little to do with his inheritance. His short stint at the academy had been long enough to inject its poison. Once it got into you, escape was impossible.

Part of it boiled down to raw fear; the kind that sinks deep into the bones and stays. The other part of the twisted puzzle was the guilt he'd lived with after leaving the school. Guilt for burying his head over the serious issues involved there. It had worn somewhat dull over the years, but instead of fading away, it had spread into his subconscious like cancer. Its roots grounded him in Knollwood forever and made it a part of him.

Mitch crushed the can in his hand and tossed it aside on his way back to the bedroom, where Sandy, the girl of his dreams, lay snoring. He climbed in beside her and wished he could count on pleasant dreams of the waitress and what her full lips could do to him, but he knew what he'd be in for once he slipped through the doors of sleep.

He reached for the exhausted blonde and she knocked his hand away half drunk with sleep. "Go to hell," she mumbled.

Been there, thought Mitch.

Mitch at seventeen again, jogged effortlessly toward the redbrick face of the Knollwood field house that hosted basketball games, graduations, and housed an Olympic size swimming pool.

He knew his friend, Jake Connally, would be doing practice laps for the upcoming swim meet, and Mitch needed the science quiz answers before Jake got started. Once "Red", named for a head of carrot orange hair, got into the pool, there'd be no talking to him. He had less than an hour before the quiz.

Mitch smelled chlorine before he reached the pool as he hurried down the long gray-tiled corridor. When he pulled open the locker room door, he heard the echo of shouts from the swimming area. Coach Betz's whistle pierced the wet air signaling the end of class as Mitch pushed through the door.

Jake sat on a bench in his Knollwood swim trunks looking impatient as the freshman class took their time getting out of the water. After last minute dunks and towel slaps, the boys finally cleared the area.

Mitch gave a sharp finger-whistle, and headed onto the wet floor.

Jake tossed his towel on the bench and waved. "What's up?"

"Before you start your water ballet, I need those science answers. Did you forget?"

Jake's freckled face broke into a grin and he nodded. "Sorry. They're in the locker room. Go get 'em." He tossed Mitch the key from under his towel. "Locker forty-two."

In Jake's locker, Mitch found the folded paper with the answers tucked inside a copy of The Catcher In The Rye. He'd heard of the book and wondered who the hell would read a story like that? Now he knew.

Mitch couldn't help looking through the locker and book bag even though he'd already found what he'd come for. He noted that Jake was taking a few honors classes, not to mention Latin as his language choice. Mitch stuffed everything back inside and realized that if anyone had the potential to make it out of the academy, really make it out, it was Jake.

Mitch knew the kid didn't belong here. He'd been a victim of abusive parents, as well as a foster family system gone wrong. His brief career of truancy and small crimes had unjustly landed him at Knollwood.

Mitch stuffed the paper in his back pocket and returned to the pool. Jake did his laps at a smooth, effortless pace. He made it look easy. The tips of Mitch's boots stuck out over the pool's edge as he peered down into the deep blue water. A dizzying sensation caused him to step back. He'd always feared the water since he'd nearly drown as a little kid at a public pool. He could still feel the pressure of the water on his chest and the helplessness as he sank. Now his vivid imagination played tricks as he caught a glimpse of a long white stick lying on the bottom. When he looked closer, it wasn't there. A reflection, he told himself, and he turned to go.

Suddenly Jake dipped under the water. Halfway across the pool, Mitch watched as he vanished like the chick in Jaws. Jake resurfaced a second later, and Mitch called out, "Very funny."

Jake coughed up water like Mitch had done after his near drowning incident, and thrashed violently in the churning water.

"Jake!" Mitch started around the side of the pool. "What's wrong?" He looked for the coach.

The boy didn't have time to answer before he went under again. Mitch stood frozen when the water turned murky red. Fear seized him when he could no longer see Jake. He reached a hand into the water in disbelief and stumbled back when he pulled out a handful of stringy, crimson clots.

More white sticks bobbed up and down on the surface, and he gagged when his hand gripped a human skull. Its empty sockets cried bloody rivulets when he pulled it from the pool.

Mitch yelled and tried to get up to run, but his boots slipped on the surrounding pink puddles. His screams rose above the bloody water.

He jerked awake to see his bedroom, Sandy beside him, with her mouth gaping open like a large-mouth bass. Drenched in sweat, he got up and once again headed into the kitchen. He opened another beer and drank deep in the dead silence of his home and hopes.

* * *

Grant's second day of classes proved uneventful and he headed to his room. He didn't have much homework and planned to drop off his books and get over to the field house to find the football coach. He hoped he could still try out for the team.

Before he reached his door, he heard a deafening howl down the hall and saw Artie Sikes, tearing out of his room in a rage.

"All right! Who did it? Who fuckin' did it?" He ran down the corridor beating on all the doors.

Joe stuck his head out of the bedroom at Grant. "What's *his* problem?"

Grant shrugged and started toward Artie's room with Joe following in his briefs and crew socks.

Artie's face had turned dangerously red, twisted into a painful grimace. His boulder-like frame rumbled awkwardly down the hall.

"I'll kill you all!" He rammed a wall with his beefy shoulder.

Grant stopped to listen when he heard Artie's voice suddenly pound inside his brain. *I know it wants me dead. This is just a warning of what's coming. I'm going to die!*

Grant looked after him as he raced down the hall.

When Grant and Joe reached Artie's room, they saw football

posters, trophies, and stacks of videos of his favorite NFL team. The clutter made the room seem much smaller.

"Where's his roommate?" Grant asked Joe.

"He doesn't have one. The kid left last month."

Grant's eyes scanned the small desk by the window and stopped.

"Oh-oh," Joe said, coming up beside Grant. "Looks like ol' Artie had a pet. That's a big deal with Mumsford. No animals at Knollwood, except for his."

Grant wondered what a guy like Artie would want with a pet. He didn't seem like the type to own anything but a rattlesnake. He glanced at the empty hamster cage.

They moved to the desk and Grant saw what had sent the six-foot bully screaming like a lunatic.

The hamster had been skinned, gutted and pinned to a square of corkboard like a science project. The animal lay positioned like Christ on the cross with its front legs stretch out and its back legs crossed with feet fastened together. Blood splattered the desk in large congealing drops. Chunks of tan and white fur lay strewn everywhere.

Grant turned from the mangled body when he heard heavy footsteps coming down the hall. He followed Joe toward the door and on his way out, he caught site of several books pertaining to Veterinary medicine and the care of animals. Artie, a vet? He shook his head. Somehow, the big guy didn't fit that picture, but why else would he have the books?

"What's that?" Joe asked.

"Check this out. Maybe Artie isn't such a hard guy after all." Grant shoved a book at him.

A fresh round of wails broke out down the hall and Joe pushed Grant ahead of him. "C'mon. Let's go."

They leaned outside the doorway and watched several teachers take hold of the hysterical boy. Mr. Mumsford pushed past Joe and Grant, entering the scene of the crime.

"Good God!" he cried and made a hasty retreat. "Who did this?" he demanded, eyeing the bystanders. "I *said*, who did this?"

Artie screeched. "You did, you bastard! It was your mangy cat!"

Grant doubted that a cat could have performed the neat pinning job he'd seen on the corkboard, but Artie had lost all common sense in his anger.

Mumsford's face went from pale to burgundy. "What did you say, Mr. Sikes?"

The boy showed no fear. "You heard me!" He struggled to break free, shouting, "Let me go! Let me at him!"

Grant watched Mumsford's eyes narrow.

"Arthur Sikes, you now have *two* detentions. One for housing a pet and a second for threatening a staff member." His thin lips formed a vicious smile. "I don't have to tell you that a third detention will be your ticket to sit out the first football game."

"You can't *do* that!" Artie roared and dropped to his knees.

Mumsford turned his back on the scene and started away, barking orders to a nearby teacher. "Get that mess cleaned up immediately."

CHAPTER 10

On a sunny Thursday morning, Coop rocked on his heels holding a paintbrush, taking in the aromas of turpentine and fresh brewed coffee. The spacious parlor remained the best room in the house to turn his artistic muse free.

The blank canvas stared back at him on its wooden easel daring him to apply the first brushstroke. His muse held captive came to mind, putting an end to his plan of painting all day. He tossed the brush aside and left the room.

He wandered through several unexplored rooms in his new home. His uncle's library afforded cozy warmth he usually associated with distinguished gentlemen in silk smoking jackets puffing on pipes. Soft red and gold tones filled tapestries and heavy draperies in a room lined with oak bookshelves.

Although Uncle Eb had been a philosophy professor at a prominent university, he'd never walked the walk of a stuffy old fart with an attitude. Uncle Eb enjoyed football and a tall brew as much as he did Socrates and high tea. He fit well in both worlds. Coop had learned the hard way not to underestimate his scholarly uncle when he'd lost a Superbowl wager two years straight.

Rows of books, old and new, filled the walls surrounding rich cherry wood furniture and an elegant roll-top desk. Coop surveyed the titles as he ran a paint-stained index finger along the leather bindings. He discovered a diverse range of subjects; everything from auto mechanics to religion. Coop chuckled when he found the books arranged by topic instead of author. Uncle Eb had his own way of doing things, and a stickler for order.

Coop noted a large section on linguistics with an ample collection focusing on the Aramaic language. He pulled out a thick volume bound in gray leather with red lettering, and leafed through its worn and highlighted pages. Several folded notebook papers fell to the floor, containing Eb's familiar scrawl. Apparently, his uncle had studied the ancient language at length. Coop shook his head and replaced the note pages before re-shelving the book.

The man remained a mystery in so many ways, as a confirmed bachelor, part-time hermit, and learned scholar. Yet, Coop had come to accept his uncle's strange ways and found in him not only a savior, but also a good listener and true friend. Two more reasons why he couldn't refuse the old man's request to take over the property when the time came. *A promise is a promise.*

As he glanced through the last selections on zoology, his foot bumped a tattered cardboard box. He found it filled with clippings from The Knollwood Examiner, a local newspaper. The articles dated back as far as five years. He pulled them out and saw that many had yellowed over time, but remained legible. The first one read:

KNOLLWOOD KNIGHTS CLAIM BASKETBALL CHAMPIONSHIP

Coop frowned. Why had Uncle Eb kept a basketball article? When he read further, he knew. The story relayed how the academy's basketball team had gone on to win the championship amidst the tragic loss of one of their star players, who'd died after an unfortunate accident.

He pulled several other clippings out of the pile with more recent dates. They all had something to do with the academy. Each one reported some sort of bizarre accident or loss of a student. Coop couldn't understand why the school hadn't been investigated, until he reread them. In each instance, it appeared that the incidents had been an accident or self-inflicted injury. None of them had been fatal, except one. Still, it had become newsworthy in such a small town. Had anyone ever questioned the occurrences? He had a sinking feeling that his uncle had.

At the bottom of the box, he found a thin, leather bound book. When he paged through it, he realized it was his uncle's journal, started only the year before. Coop quickly flipped to the back page and found the last entry had been made only days before he'd died. Coop scanned the last couple of paragraphs...

I felt it pertinent that I go to the authorities with my findings. However, Knollwood's police chief, Lucas Koch, is "in the pocket," so to speak. I can feel it. His cold black eyes glazed over when I explained my concerns, even sharing my collection of articles about Knollwood Academy's accidents. He offered a patronizing reply that sounded rehearsed. No doubt, others have asked him the same series of questions. I don't like this man and realize my time spent in the suffocating office of the Knollwood Police Department was a full waste of time.

It might be best to take the matter to his superior, but I can't be sure how deep the evil root of the Knollwood Academy reaches throughout the town. I would be morally remiss to ignore the truths I've discovered and the culprit I suspect, therefore, I plan to pursue this to its end, even if it means risking my own life.

Coop closed the journal and headed for the door. He had some homework to do.

* * *

Coop realized he'd once again neglected his Jeep's tune-up. Good. He needed to pick Mitch-the-mechanic's brain. Mitch had said he'd been a student at the academy, so who better to ask? He wondered how to broach the subject with him because he'd clammed up the last time they'd talked. What would it take to get to the truth?

He pulled up to an empty garage stall at Bill's Auto and honked twice. After several seconds, Mitch waved him in, wearing his faded jumpsuit and a lop-sided grin. He lit an unfiltered cigarette as Coop pulled in and got out of the Jeep.

"I wondered what happened to you," Mitch said.

Coop nodded. "I've been kind of busy."

The mechanic popped the hood. "Yeah, I'll bet. Moving can be a bitch."

"You're right about that. I've been cleaning out some of my uncle's things and you can't believe the old stuff lying around," Coop led the conversation.

Mitch straightened from under the hood with the cigarette dangling on his bottom lip. "A real pack-rat, huh?"

"You got it," Coop said on his way to the soda machine. "But I *did* find something that might interest you. A box filled with newspaper clippings about the academy."

Mitch dropped a wrench, cursing under his breath. He cleared his throat. "The academy? What about it?"

"Well, that's what's so interesting. The school has quite a history of accidents and unusual occurrences."

Mitch sniffed. "Huh. You could say that."

"You don't seem surprised."

"Like I told you before, the place isn't right."

"Look, if there's something going on there, why doesn't somebody do something?"

The mechanic thought a moment, eyeing Coop carefully. Finally, he grinned and said, "I'll tell you what, Mr. Cooper..."

"Please call me, Coop."

"All right, Coop. If you want to spring for a couple of beers after we're done here, I'll tell you all about it."

* * *

Coop wondered if Smalley's Pit Stop could actually be an old pit stop surrounded by walls and a roof. Beer drenched gravel crunched under his shoes as he followed Mitch to the bar through a haze of cigarette smoke and loud music.

A blond waitress in a red mini skirt and white blouse brushed close to Mitch and whispered in his ear. Mitch grinned, nodded, and continued toward the bar.

"Hey, Smalley!" he called out to the stout, balding bartender. "My usual and a tall one for my friend."

The older man grunted and reached for a glass.

Mitch turned to Coop. "You know, on second thought, let's grab a booth. There's some big ears at Smalley's."

Coop shrugged and took his glass from the bar. They found a corner booth that still held the remnants of the previous patron's meal.

Mitch set to work clearing the mess by putting the dirty dishes on a nearby table. He swiped the area with a clean napkin and sat down. Coop brushed a greasy fry from the bench and slid in. He glanced around and noted the early American racecar driver motif, with photos of famous drivers and their cars plastered on every wall.

"Are you a race fan?" he asked Mitch.

"Not a big fan, but Smalley is." He lit another cigarette and after the second drag he said, "So, you want to know about the academy?"

"Whatever you can tell me." Coop took a draw of beer.

"Hell," Mitch said, and downed his whiskey shot.

Coop waited for more, but when he didn't elaborate, he said, "Excuse me?"

Mitch snorted a laugh. "Hell, man. Pure and simple. Knollwood Academy is hell."

Coop nodded toward Mitch's beer, which had sunken well past the halfway mark already. "I'm looking for more than that. How about another beer?"

Mitch's eyes gleamed. "Sure." He signaled the waitress for another round, and then continued. "Okay. Here's the truth about the school. I said its hell because it is. But not like you think. It's not because I have bad memories about how they made me tow the line and all that. I was there less than two years, but long enough to know the truth, and let me tell you, I was one of the lucky ones."

"What happened?"

"A lot of weird things. That's why none of the kids said anything. It's not like they abused us or anything like that."

"Can you give me an example?" Coop watched Mitch start on his second beer.

"Kids changed. That's one thing I remember. Sometimes, they'd go away for a while, a few days maybe, and when they'd come back they'd changed."

"How?"

"Just different. No life to 'em. Like zombies or something."

"You said they went away. Where did they go?"

"No one knows where they *really* went, but there was always a good reason for them to leave. That's where the accidents come in."

"What about the newspaper clippings?" Coop asked.

"I know about those. I read some of them when they first came out. But don't you see? Every one of those events can be justified as some sort of legitimate accident. It benefited the school that they became public because it got the academy off the hook."

Coop leaned forward. "Are you saying those articles were planted?"

"No. Not really. All I'm saying is that if the academy didn't want those stories to get out, they wouldn't have. Believe me, there's lots of secrets kept there." Mitch drained his beer.

"What about Chief Koch?"

Mitch chuckled and ran a grease-stained hand through his hair. "You mean, ol' crotch-rot?" He shook his head. "Everyone knows he's a real butt-kisser. He's in up to his eyebrows with the mayor and all his pecker-head cohorts. Even in a small town like Knollwood...*especially* in a town like this, the guys at the top like to stay there. So they watch each other's backs."

"What about the school? How is that involved? It's a private facility."

"Exactly. Money talks, my man. And Lucas Koch is a good listener."

"So you think he's been taking payoffs to make the troubles at the academy go away?"

"Wouldn't surprise me. He drives a new Camaro. You tell me how a small town police chief with a wife and two high school kids can afford something like that?" Mitch rubbed four fingertips against his thumb. "That's all it takes."

"Doesn't *anyone* try to stop it?"

"It's too powerful. It's..." Mitch stopped.

"What?" Coop asked

"It's just...I don't know...the academy."

Coop frowned. "You talk about it like it's alive."

Mitch's eyes were a little glassy, but still alert, and full of raw fear. "I won't argue with that."

CHAPTER 11

Artie Sikes sat before Mumsford's desk ready to pounce. He'd never felt this kind of rage before. He watched the headmaster writing out his detention with a gleam in his eye. The man seemed to enjoy his work.

"Here you are, Mr. Sikes." Mumsford handed him the green slip.

Artie grabbed it from him.

"As I told you, one more of these will put you out of the first game of the year. The school semester is still young, so I'd advise you to watch your behavior."

"I want an investigation." Artie glared at Mumsford.

"You have very little to say about it, Arthur. I will do what I think best."

"Something's going on here, and you know it. It's a sign!"

"*What's* a sign?" Mumsford looked puzzled.

"What they did to my hamster! Did you happen to notice how they gutted and pinned it like a sacrifice? There's something evil going on here!" Artie caught his breath, the vision of his pet still fresh in his mind.

"Calm down, Arthur. It was just a cruel hoax. Have you ever considered that your demeanor toward the other students doesn't win you any points? You have somewhat of a reputation."

"They can all go to hell."

"I don't think *they're* the ones who need to worry. Your behavior borders on hatred. Perhaps you need to work on your attitude."

"I wouldn't be so upset if I thought that was the only thing to fear around here."

"What do you mean?"

"Let's just say I've seen things. I *know* things. And if I ever catch anyone in my room, I'll wrap both my hands around their neck and—"

"And what, Mr. Sikes? Please tell me. You'll wrap both hands around whose neck?"

Artie knew he'd said too much. He had to get back to his room before he started to cry. The only thing he had left in the world had been brutally taken from him. His hamster had been his only friend at the Academy and Einstein hadn't deserved to die like that.

He didn't understand why the other kids hated him. His bullying had started only after he'd been attacked the first day, but what he wanted more than anything was a friend. Now thanks to Mumsford, the kids would avoid him more than ever.

He stormed out of the office crumpling the detention in his left hand.

* * *

Grant walked down the leaf-covered path from the school to the main house. His first week at Knollwood behind him, he'd managed to get through it without any weekend homework. The next two days would give him a chance to investigate his strange new home.

After the episodes with Artie, he'd become convinced something was wrong with the academy and the students could all be in some sort of danger. The whole incident didn't make sense. Most guys stayed clear of the bully. Why would anyone risk getting caught in his room slicing up his pet hamster? And what about Artie's thoughts? The kid had feared for his life. He knew Knollwood *felt* unsafe, but unfortunately, he hadn't seen anything blatantly dangerous, except the tunnel.

When he told his mother, she'd said, "Nice try. But it won't work. I'm not taking you out." He'd heard her soften saying, "You know this hard on me, too. I hate the idea of sending you away, but I really feel I have no choice."

He'd never seen her stand this firm before when it came to discipline and he worried that he'd finally crossed the invisible line from trusted son to potential felon. The emotional wall between them served as his prison and her protection. She didn't deserve any more hurt or disappointment in her life, but he'd provided it. His father's face surfaced in his memory as if to re-affirm his faith in Grant and his ability to do the right thing. He knew he'd never forgive his father for his hurtful actions against his mother, yet he longed for his approval—even from beyond the grave. With a sudden surge of confidence and a renewed determination to prove himself to his mom, Grant decided to start taking more responsibility for his actions.

"Grant?" an adult voice came from behind.

He turned to find Mr. Peterson hurrying to catch up, lugging his awkward leather satchel. Grant knew the tunnel lay hidden in the dead grass only a few yards away. He could almost see its cover from the sidewalk and fought the temptation to show the teacher.

Mr. Peterson's words were white wisps in the cold air. "I'm glad I caught you. I have a favor to ask."

Grant watched the man fumble inside his pack to pull out a folder. His high school ring caught on the handle and Grant noticed he'd graduated in 1993. The intricate carved gold surrounded a large red stone. He decided that if he ever got a class ring, he wanted something like that.

"I wonder if you'd see that Billy Parker gets this. He's been absent all week and I don't want him to fall behind." He handed over the folder with a wink. "How was your first week?"

"I survived." Grant glanced toward the manhole cover.

"Good. I think you'll do fine. In fact, I don't see you staying here longer than this school year."

"Me either."

"Well, I suppose I'd better get going. Have a good weekend."

Grant stammered. "Uh...Mr. Peterson?"

"Yes?"

"Can I ask you something?"

"Anything." He smiled.

"Have you noticed anything weird about this place?" His face grew hot.

The teacher stepped closer and frowned. "Weird? Like what?"

Grant looked around. "I'm not sure. It just feels wrong sometimes." He stuffed the folder in his backpack. "Never mind. Forget it. I'm not used to it, I guess."

"No, no. I know what you mean. I've only been here a little while myself. But I thought it was me. What have you noticed?"

Relief rained over Grant. He explained about the black beetles the day he'd arrived and about the blood-dripping bats.

"For one thing, bats aren't usually out during the day and what about the blood?" Grant asked.

"Maybe they were vampire bats," Mr. Peterson teased.

"I'm serious about this and no one believes me." Grant pulled up his backpack.

"Wait. Who else have you told?"

"My mom. She thinks I'm trying to find a reason to leave."

"Parents can be like that sometimes. Don't be too hard on her. This is probably an adjustment for her as well."

"Whatever. I don't need her help." Grant straightened.

"Don't say that, Grant. We can all use help at one time or another. Appreciate your family. Since my parents died, I'm down to a couple of distant cousins. I don't even remember their names.

"But back to your problem. I didn't mean to make fun of you. To tell you the truth, I've observed things, too." The teacher's expression grew serious.

"What things?" Grant asked.

"Well, I haven't seen any bats or bugs, except on Billy, but I am concerned about some of the students."

"What do you mean?" Grant's hopes soared.

"It's hard to say exactly. They change, but not necessarily for the better. It's as though they lose their spunk, or character." Mr. Peterson frowned trying to find the words.

Grant shook his head. "I don't know about that. But there's something else...something you should see."

"Hey, Taylor!"

Grant looked over to see Joe heading his way.

"See what?" Mr. Peterson said quickly.

"It's nothing. I'll tell you later." Grant started away. "I'll get this to Billy."

"I'll be in my office on Saturday afternoon if you need to talk," the teacher offered.

Joe came up beside Grant. "Hey, now's a good time to catch the football coach, he's in the field house. You better get over there before practice starts." He clapped Grant on the back. "Come on, man, let's go."

With that, he led Grant away with Mr. Peterson staring after them.

Grant turned back in time to see Mumsford had joined the teacher. As the two men headed off toward the school, Grant couldn't shake the fear inside. He wanted to warn Mr. Peterson, but didn't know why.

What did he fear?

* * *

That evening, Grant stalled in front of Billy's bedroom door wanting to slide the folder underneath and be gone, but his decision to take more responsibility made that impossible. Besides, he wondered about the boy's condition. He promised himself he wouldn't get too close.

He knocked and waited impatiently. His spirits rose with the idea that the boy might be out. Then he heard someone stumble inside and the door opened.

"Grant. What's up?" Billy said. He wore only a white T-shirt and faded gym shorts that exposed pale, bowed legs. The boy had recovered from the bite marks and Grant didn't see any bugs.

"This is from Mr. Peterson," Grant said handing over the folder.

"Thanks." Billy briefly leafed through the paperwork, and then tossed it on his bed. "Come 'ere, I want to show you something."

Please don't let it be a scab collection, Grant prayed.

"Look." Billy held up a football he'd taken from a bookshelf.

Grant stopped when he saw the scrawled autograph of Joe Namath. Cooties temporarily forgotten, he palmed the ball and faked a throw.

"Where'd you get this?" he asked Billy.

"My dad got it years ago when he worked the stadium where Namath played."

"How did he get it?"

"He said Joe gave it to him."

"Really?" Grant tossed the ball up and caught it.

"Yeah. My dad was janitor at the time. That was before he got fired and…"

Grant didn't ask. He had a feeling Billy's parental history explained the reason he'd ended up at the academy.

"I'll be in class on Monday." Billy forced a smile. "As much as I hate school, I can't wait to get back because I'm so friggin' bored."

Grant handed him the ball and turned to leave. "Right. Well, I have to go. I'll see you later."

"Wait," the boy said a little too loudly. "I mean, where are you going?"

"I need to get back."

Grant watched him pace a couple of times before asking, "Do you ever hear things at night?"

Grant frowned. "Like what?"

"I don't know. Voices. Whispers, maybe?"

"No. Do you?" Normally, Grant would have labeled the kid nuts and left, but he wanted to know what he had to say. After what he'd seen, the line between normal and crazy had become blurred.

"Sometimes. But I don't think my roommate hears it. He sleeps through the alarm every morning. Lately the voices have been getting worse and…never mind."

"What?" Grant wanted to know.

"Well, I think I leave the room sometimes."

"Why?"

"I don't know and I'm not even sure it's real, but I feel like I don't spend the whole night in my bed."

"Are you sure?"

"Yeah. One morning I woke up wearing only one sock and I found it in the hall outside the door," Billy shivered as he spoke. "I don't know what to do."

Grant ran a hand through his hair. "When did all this start?"

Billy thought a minute. "Not too long after I found out about the hole."

"The what?"

"The hole in the back yard."

Grant's stomach clenched. "Who told you about that?"

Suddenly Billy looked around like he wanted out of the conversation. "What's the difference? That's when the sleepwalking started."

"Did you tell anyone about the hole?" Grant cornered him. If word got out, Joe would blame him for it.

"No. No one would believe it anyway. You know how the guys are around me."

"Well, don't say anything to anyone."

"What am I going to do? I'm afraid of the voices I hear, afraid I'll walk away and never come back."

The boy's forehead shone with sweat. He looked ready to lose it.

That's when Grant heard Billy's frightened voice across the mental airwaves. *"Help me! I'm so scared. It's after me!"*

Grant shook the reverie from his head. "Okay. Relax, man. I'll come up with something, be cool about this and keep your mouth shut. Don't tell anyone, got it?"

He nodded. "What are you going to do?"

"Don't worry about it. I'll figure something out. Okay?"

"Right."

The whispers suddenly stopped inside Grant's head and Billy changed the subject as if he had found a savior, made his confession, and was on his way home.

"Hey, thanks for dropping off the papers. If you want to come by some time I have some great video games, even football."

"Yeah. Maybe I will." Grant closed the door behind him, and hurried to his room.

CHAPTER 12

Coop reread Uncle Eb's death certificate confirming the cause of death had been natural—a fatal tumble down the staircase. Not necessarily natural causes in his mind after reading Eb's final journal entry. His uncle had feared for his life and two days later, he'd died. Of course, Coop had been told there was no need to investigate an elderly man's demise after a fall like that, for it was a sad fact that people occasionally died alone in their homes. Not Uncle Eb, Coop told himself, not after reading the journal. He cursed himself for being too quick to have his uncle cremated.

He leafed through the leather-bound book and decided to start at the beginning. Guilt clutched his conscience when he turned to the first entry. He felt as though he were violating his uncle's privacy. Then he reminded himself that Eb had been a wise and methodical man, a man who had a reason for everything he did. Coop recalled the time he'd asked Eb why he kept his spare car key remote in the trunk of his car. His uncle had explained that if he became car-jacked and put in the trunk, he'd be able to get out. Eb certainly had character.

It occurred to Coop that Eb had purposely left a paper trail behind because he *wanted* his nephew to read it. With this in mind, he read Ebenezer Cooper's personal diary…

I'm happy to report that years behind a desk haven't dented my endurance or stamina and I am able to work with a landscaping crew without exertion—even at the prime old age of sixty-six.

Coop chuckled as he read, picturing his uncle on the job.

THE ACADEMY

I sit in the shade and partake of sack lunches with my Mexican co-workers who laugh at my accent and call me amigo. I find it unusual, that in my old age, I no longer desire philosophical stimulation. I crave adventure. It's odd that those inclinations didn't come in my youth; nevertheless, I believe my wish has been granted.

For several years, I've been following unusual events reported in the local newspaper about the Knollwood Academy for boys and it has come to my attention the school has a certain reputation for accidents and unexplained occurrences. I find it curious that in each episode the administrators have managed to clear the school of any involvement or responsibility. However, I've discovered a possible clue to the truth and it is with a heavy heart I report the unfortunate events surrounding my find.

Today was a cloudy Monday afternoon and the landscaping crew started its weekly work at the academy. I began behind the main house in preparation to mow the yard. My co-worker, Jose, reluctantly turned the job over to me due to a bad case of gout that had turned the muscular, hard-working Hispanic into a limping tin-man. I jumped behind the mower and started my passes when I noticed what looked like a manhole cover near the wooded area that backs up to the yard. The strangest sensation came over me when I bent for a closer look. I can only describe it as a severe sense of foreboding. My first impulse was to finish the job quickly and get away from the area, but the professor inside of me latched on to the cover's curious markings. I recognized the symbols as some sort of language, but of course I'm no linguistics expert and couldn't make them out. I will research the markings in hopes of understanding the language.

Coop nodded. That explained the language books in the library. He read further.

In addition, I found the size of the manhole cover extraordinarily oversized, estimating it at almost three feet in diameter. As I studied it, Jose hobbled up beside me carrying a rake. He leaned on it like an old man with a cane and asked me what I was doing. I pointed to the cover, expecting him to be as mystified as I, but he simply shrugged and told me to make sure I clear it with the mower. He said the boss would 'keel' me if I wrecked the blade.

Looking back, I should have left it alone and went on with my work. I wish to God I had. Instead, I got down on my knees and tried to open the damn thing. It wouldn't give and I realized then, there was more to it than a sewage system. Jose cursed in his native tongue, at least that's what it sounded like, and clumsily got down beside me. Together we worked to shove the cover from its base without success.

The clouds overhead had taken on an ominous gray and we knew our workday would be cut short. Jose nudged me and pointed skyward, forcing me to get back to work. While he kept working at the cover, I finished mowing.

When the job was complete, his forehead dripped with sweat and his shirt clung like sagging skin. The most frightening part of the whole scene though, was his eyes. They'd lost their brightness and had taken on a vacant stare, as if he was in a daydream. He mumbled something about bringing the right tool for the job next time. Suddenly, the skies opened up with a drenching downpour and we both headed for the truck.

He seemed to come out of his trance as we loaded our equipment and drove back to the shop. He sat mostly in silence though, which wasn't like Jose. I reasoned he was probably fighting down the pain in his swollen joints. When I looked at his hands, I noted they were badly scraped and his wrists were cut all the way around, as if someone had circled them with red pen. I'm no doctor, but I don't believe that's a sign of gout.

Later tonight, the phone rang and I was surprised to hear my boss, Harry Phillips, on the other end. He informed me that Jose was dead. Of course, the weather is blamed on the fact that his pick-up truck skidded off the road and rolled several times, finally stopping when it slammed into a large tree. Since Jose was nowhere near the academy, no one will consider the incident as anything but an unfortunate accident.

I can't help feeling it is partly my fault, as I drew poor Jose's attention to something best left alone. While some might say my guilt is unfounded, and that these things happen, there is one fact about the tragedy that leads me to question what really occurred. During the accident, both of Jose's hands were cut off at the wrists.

* * *

Artie let out a loud belch and tossed the empty soda can into the garbage on his way to the bedroom door. *Who the hell is knocking so late?*

He opened up to find Joe Blockman twitching with excitement, wearing a muddy T-shirt.

"Artie, you gotta come." Joe wiped his sweaty forehead.

Silent alarms went off in Artie's mind. Joe never called him Artie. It was always, *Arthur*, or other choice names. He crossed his muscular arms over his chest and cocked his head.

"What are you up to, Blockman?"

"Nothing, man. There's a cat stuck down the manhole, and I can't reach the damn thing!"

Artie stopped. A cat? Knowing Joe, *he* probably tossed the poor animal in for kicks. What an asshole.

"If this is a joke, I'll tear you up," Artie said grabbing his sweatshirt.

* * *

Joe had come prepared like the last time with a flashlight and rope. Artie stood beside the open manhole recalling his first time down the hole when Joe had struggled to bring him back up.

"You're puny," he told Joe. "You need to go down, not me."

"That mangy fur ball tried to scratch out my eyes. I'm not goin' near it. Probably has rabies or somethin'." Joe shook his head.

"How did it get down there in the first place?" He stared Joe down.

When Joe shrugged, he knew he'd been right. Joe had done it himself.

"I ought to throw *you* down there," Artie threatened. "Give me the damn rope."

The odor made Artie gag as he fumbled with the flashlight. Two opaque ovals gleamed below him in the tunnel. Cat's eyes.

Suddenly, he felt his left leg jerk downward.

He yelped, sure it had been pulled from the socket.

"Pull me up!" he cried.

Something grabbed his shoe and wouldn't let go.

"Joe! Get me up!"

Fire shot up his leg when his shoe ripped from his foot still tied. He felt something wet graze his heel and he struggled like a marionette on the end of the rope.

"Help!" he shouted, feeling the cord slicing his waist.

Joe's voice cut his panic. "I'm bringing you up now. By now the little bastard's probably dead."

Raised by inches, Artie finally climbed out of the hole, intent on killing Joe. But Joe had left, joke over. Artie seethed, making plans to get Joe back when he least expected it.

* * *

Grant squinted into the bright sun and threw a pass downfield. He loved playing football, even if the hope for a cheerleading squad remained nonexistent. Football made him feel good about himself, partly because he knew he could play well and partly because it made his mom proud. When he held the ball, he felt strong and in control, and those were feelings he longed to hold on to.

He'd made the team after a brief tryout with Coach Vargas and hoped to play quarterback like he had at his previous school. So far, today's practice had gone well and he was confident he'd play in the next game.

Coach Vargas blew his whistle and motioned the players in from the field. Grant jogged along, trailing the others when the ground suddenly shifted under his feet. Before he could gain his balance, he stumbled forward, landing on his stomach. Several teammates laughed and went around him as he lay on the field trying to catch his breath. The ground had bunched up like a twisted rug and tripped him. When he sat up and looked back at the field, it looked smooth. No ripples. No movement.

"C'mon, Taylor!" the coach called.

Grant jumped up and hurried toward the group, embarrassed and a little confused.

When practice ended, he sat on a bleacher listening to final instructions from the coach. His mind raced ahead to his impending meeting with Mr. Peterson. So far, the teacher accepted his fears about the school. No one else did, except maybe Billy.

As the group broke up, a tall shadow fell over Grant's line of vision and he looked up to see Joe palming a basketball.

"What's up?" Grant's stomach clenched.

"You almost done here?" he asked.

"Yeah. Why?"

"I'm on my way to basketball practice. Why don't you come? You can watch me in action on the court." He wore a sly grin.

"I can't. I'm going to see Mr. Peterson for a retest," Grant lied.

Joe's dark eyes narrowed. "A retest, huh? Is that all?"

"Isn't that enough?"

Joe sat on the bleacher beside him. He glared at Grant. "You wouldn't be going there for anything else, would you? Like a little chat about our secret?"

Grant's temper flared. He didn't like Joe's threatening tone. He leaned close to his roommate. "What's your problem? I said I wouldn't say anything, and I won't."

Their noses only inches apart, Grant refused to back down. Joe slowly pulled back.

"Sorry, man. Like I said before, you have to watch what you say around here."

Grant wondered if the boy's secrecy stemmed from fear. He knew he'd never admit it, but maybe Joe had seen or heard things too—things he preferred to keep to himself. Grant wondered what Joe would say about Billy's claims of hearing voices and sleepwalking. Better take his roommate's advice and watch what he said, he decided.

Then a fleeting thought struck him. A minute ago when he'd been locked in a stand off with Joe, he hadn't been able to read him. The boy had been charged with emotion, ready to pounce. So why hadn't he heard his thoughts? Thinking back, he'd never heard anything from Joe. He'd never been unable to read someone in such an angry mood before.

Joe turned abruptly. "I'm taking off. See you later."

Their attention turned toward the main house. Several emergency vehicles screamed up the circle drive, one of them a paramedic unit. The boys headed across the field toward the action.

When they reached the student house, Grant saw teachers herding classmates to the side of the building while Elias Mumsford pushed his way past the crowd. The paramedics rushed a stretcher inside.

"Who is it?" someone asked.

Grant strained to hear over the excited students.

"Mumsford's cat had kittens!" a tall boy in the front joked.

"Yeah, and Mums's the father!"

The students broke into laughter prompting Mr. Thompson, the shop teacher, to break up the group.

"Okay, guys. Let's move it back in the school. Show's over."

The boys grumbled, following orders. But Grant and Joe moved behind the ambulance to wait where no one would notice them, keeping out of sight from a nearby policeman.

Joe took out a cigarette and lit up.

"What are you doing?" Grant looked around nervously.

"Relax. You think anybody cares about *me* right now? I could blow smoke in Mumsford's face and he wouldn't even see it."

"Who do you think it is?" Grant asked.

Joe shrugged. "Don't know. Don't care."

"You're all heart." Grant boldly walked toward the main house.

"Don't count on it," Joe called after him.

A commotion near the doors grabbed Grant's attention. He watched the paramedics rush a sheet-covered stretcher toward the ambulance. Bloody gauze wrapped the victim's head and face and he couldn't make out the features. When he started for a closer look, a heavy hand held him in place to allow the paramedics by.

"Stay back, son," a police officer ordered.

Grant caught a glimpse of Billy's ravaged face poking out from the gauze. His cheek was a mass of shredded skin. The blood soaked sheet reminded Grant of his childhood visits to his Uncle John's butcher shop. This was much worse.

"What happened?" he asked out loud.

"The kid almost scratched himself to death," a teacher said. "I've never seen anything like it."

As the stretcher went by, a bloody hand shot out from under the sheet and clutched Grant's arm.

Billy's garbled voice pleaded, "You've got to tell them. Promise you'll tell them. We're all going to die!"

Grant pulled away as the paramedics lifted the stretcher into the back of the vehicle. He shuddered looking at the wet handprint on his arm. Across the yard, Joe pinned him with a dark expression. What did he think Billy had said to him?

After the ambulance turned off the road onto Route 41, Grant headed into the school to find Mr. Peterson before Joe could corner him. He hurried to the second floor office and found the door closed. He knocked several times before he pushed it open.

"Hello? Mr. Peterson?" he called, stepping inside.

The overhead lights and the computer were off, showing no sign that the teacher had been there.

Grant heard a sound behind him and turned to see Mr. Turner, the janitor, standing in the doorway leaning on a broom.

"What are you doin' in here?" he asked through a toothless sneer.

"I was supposed to meet Mr. Peterson. Do you know where he is?"

"Nope." The man eyed him skeptically. "Mr. Peterson never made it in today. You'll have to catch him on Monday, son."

The janitor waited until Grant moved out of the office, and quickly shut the door behind him.

Grant headed back down the hall, thinking Monday seemed a long way away, and hoping Sunday would truly be a day of rest at Knollwood.

CHAPTER 13

Monday morning, Coop entered the Knollwood Police Department. The redbrick building faced east at the end of a long stretch of shops and wasn't much larger than the floral boutique next door. Several officers pushed past him on their way out without bothering to ask if he needed assistance.

Seeing no one at the cluttered reception desk, Coop headed toward a large office enclosed by glass panels with the word Chief stenciled on the faded wooden door. Coop knocked once and waved at the man inside.

Police Chief, Lucas Koch, had a beak-like nose and dimpled chin. He wore his jet-black hair cropped like a marine's, a pencil thin moustache lined his top lip. He got up, offering Coop a penetrating look at the intrusion. His trim muscular build gave him an added air of cockiness, and Coop understood why Uncle Eb had disliked him.

"Yes, sir. What can I do for you?" The question sounded more like an order.

Coop extended a hand. "My name is Dreeson Cooper. I'm new in town and I have a couple of questions about the Knollwood Academy."

The man offered a painful grip. Coop wondered if it could be a subtle warning.

"What can I do for you, Mr...?" The man sat down without offering his guest a seat.

"Please, call me Coop." He sat anyway and looked him in the eye. "I want to know why there have been so many mishaps there and no investigations."

Lucas fingered his moustache, never taking his stare from Coop. He let an uneasy silence linger in the stuffy air before answering.

"You said you're new in town."

"That's right."

"Do you have children?"

"No."

"Then perhaps you can tell me why the school is a concern to you?"

"My uncle, Eb Cooper, worked there part time in lawn maintenance. He had safety concerns about the school no one wanted to address."

"Ahh. There it is." Lucas wore a self-assured smile. "Your uncle came to see me as well. I'll tell you the same thing I told him. There is no need for concern. The school's credentials and standing with the state are impeccable. The incidents *have* been investigated and found to be accidents. There's no foul play at the academy."

Coop firmly planted his hands on the man's desktop. "Don't give me that pat bullshit! There's something going on at that school and you're letting it go. Why?"

Lucas never moved. Apparently, it didn't faze him when people lost their tempers with him. "Sit down, Mr. Cooper. Before I have you removed."

"What's in it for you, Koch? Is that fancy Camaro out front compliments of the injured Knollwood students?" Coop shouted.

Now Lucas *did* move. His firm grip clenched Coop's collar. He pulled him close enough to smell the coffee on his breath. He growled through a tight grimace.

"Listen, *Coop*. I suggest you get back to your farmhouse and mind your own business, like your uncle should have done. Get a job to keep yourself occupied before you end up like him."

Coop didn't back down. "He's dead."

"I know. I was there."

* * *

Coop left the station with a heavy dose of adrenaline pumping through his veins. It had taken every ounce of restraint to keep from pounding the chief's bad attitude. He sat in his Jeep letting his anger die down. The words haunted him.

I know. I was there.

Of course, he'd been there, Coop reminded himself, he'd called the

Knollwood police when his uncle had failed to answer the phone on his birthday. It had been one of Koch's men who'd discovered the body.

He wondered if there'd been more to Koch's reaction than a cocky reply. The man's expression showed great satisfaction as the words slithered from his mouth.

Once his hands stopped shaking, Coop headed out onto Route 41 toward the Knollwood Academy, thinking about his uncle's description of Jose's last day. First Jose, then Uncle Eb. He frowned when he realized his vague suspicions could be easily dismissed as coincidence. He had nothing but a gut feeling, and a journal full of fears and questionable circumstances. That's exactly what Koch wanted. In Coop's mind, however, he had enough to launch his own investigation.

* * *

Coop pulled his Jeep into a parking space in front of the Knollwood Academy administrative building and mounted the concrete steps. Lucas Koch might be a condescending asshole, but he'd had a good idea. At least the visit hadn't been a total waste. Coop decided to take the man's advice and get a job.

Experience had taught Coop that a confident attitude could make or break any job interview, and that's what this visit amounted to, whether the administrator knew it or not. He grinned, thinking of his former boss, Art. He'd been wrong when he'd predicted Coop would be back behind a desk in six months—it would be far sooner than that.

He knew this time it would be different, though. In the city, he'd taught in order to pay the bills while struggling to pursue his art career. Now he desired chalk dust to turpentine because it fulfilled him like nothing else. It also proved to be the best way to find out the truth behind the academy.

Inside the administrative building, Coop followed the dark, polished floor tiles past office doors stenciled with titles like, Student Records and Department of Housing, until he reached the one marked Administrator. Coop took a deep breath, combed a hand through his hair.

When he knocked on the door, a firm voice said, "Come."

Inside the office of Nathaniel Jennings, Coop shuddered at the sudden cold permeating his pullover. The window curtains hung closed against the autumn sun. Behind the large oak desk, a pallid man in a dark suit stared back at him with sunken gray eyes. The artist in Coop decided if the man ever commissioned a painting of himself, the artist would need only black and white to capture his true essence.

The man rose to offer a bony, alabaster handshake. His long chin moved up and down like a ventriloquist dummy as his vacant eyes locked with Coop's.

"I'm Nathaniel Jennings, Administrator," the man said.

"Dreeson Cooper."

"Please have a seat, Mr. Cooper."

"Please call me, Coop." He sat down under the man's unnerving stare.

The desk lamp offered little illumination to the rest of the room and Coop wondered how the man could possibly see to do paperwork. The darkness did little to hide the decrepit condition of the room's furnishings, especially the bookshelves lining the far wall. All of the books looked identical. He couldn't see the titles from where he sat, but the lettering did not appear to be English. He concluded the extensive collection must be encyclopedias.

"What can I do for you, sir?" Mr. Jennings broke his thoughts.

Coop pulled his attention from the black, cracked bindings and forced his mind back to his visit. "I'm interested in a teaching position here at Knollwood."

The man forced a smile. "I'm afraid our staff roster is full at this time. What is it that you teach?"

"I'm an art teacher. Do you currently have an art program?"

"I'm afraid not. Our student body isn't really geared for that type of curriculum, unless you consider graffiti an art form."

Coop walked over to take a closer look at the man's library. "Yeah, I know what you mean. I taught inner city kids, and it was definitely a challenge. But I found it well worth the fight, because believe it or not, they really took to my class."

The gold lettering of the volumes had changed their shape entirely. He read the English titles of many of the classics and several language books, questioning his eyesight.

He rubbed his eyes and sat back down. "I think art gives the students a break from their regular classes which I'm sure are quite structured here. It allows them to let out their creativity in a positive way—instead of spray painting a wall."

"Very commendable." Mr. Jennings nodded. "But as I said, we're not looking to start that type of program here."

Without hesitation, Coop slid a checkbook out of his back pocket and grabbed a pen from the desktop. The administrator's gaze burned as he wrote. For several seconds, the only sound in the office was his pen scratching the paper and then the sudden ripping when he tore it from the booklet.

"In that case, I'd like to make a donation to the school because I feel there is a need for such a program and if money is your concern, I'd like you to know I work for free." He tossed the check onto the desk in front of Mr. Jennings and watched his frosty eyes gleam.

"This is a generous donation, Mr. Cooper."

"Coop," he corrected.

"Yes." The man smiled. "Uh, perhaps I can bring your suggestion to the board about an art program. You did say you would be willing to work without pay?"

"Absolutely."

"Forgive me, but may I ask why you would do such a thing?"

"I miss teaching. Frankly, you'd be doing me a favor."

"Of course. I understand."

Coop knew he couldn't possibly, and that was the whole idea.

* * *

Coop whistled on the way to his Jeep, confident he had a job *and* a way to find out what really happened to Uncle Eb. He dropped his keys near the bumper and stooped to retrieve them, his whistle dying on his lips when a large black beetle scurried across his hand. He jerked back as its needle-like legs beat a path to the grass and disappeared. He'd never seen a beetle that large before and hoped it wasn't a part of everyday life at Knollwood.

As he put the Jeep in gear, he caught a shimmering movement along the trunk of a large oak beside the administrative building. He squinted against the sun for a better look and realized it must be a heat mirage. Trees trunks don't move any more than dusty black books change their titles.

CHAPTER 14

Grant's hopes rose as he crossed the yard to the school. A man resembling Mr. Peterson pulled into the lot in a black Jeep. Then the man got out and he saw he stood much taller and wore his hair longer. He hoped Mr. Peterson had already arrived, and he hurried to catch him before class.

Moving along the dingy hallway, he avoided a mound of pink gravel where someone had puked up breakfast. It looked like the janitor had gotten an early start this morning. The creepy old guy showed up everywhere. Much like the day he'd found him in Mr. Peterson's office. It still puzzled him that the teacher hadn't made it to their appointment.

As he walked, Grant focused on his mother's visit the day before. He'd thought for sure she'd yank him out of Knollwood after hearing about Saturday's incident with Billy, but she'd only ignored his concerns, telling him the kid obviously had issues and she didn't think Grant would contract a contagious disease. He'd opted to leave out the part about Billy's thoughts. She wouldn't want to hear that he'd been at it again.

His mother seemed to think he could turn his *gift* on and off like a super power. Instead, he'd stuck to the facts about Billy, but it hadn't made any difference. When he'd explained about Billy's strange voices and sleepwalking episodes, she'd stared at him like he'd made it up.

"Jesus, Mom! What does a guy have to do? Die? Why won't you believe there's something wrong with this place?" Grant grabbed his lunch tray and headed to the far end of the long cafeteria table. His mom followed with her own tray of food and sat beside him. She unwrapped her silverware from the paper napkin saying, "You're acting like a two-year-old."

He shoveled a spoonful of lumpy mashed potatoes into his mouth and washed it down with chocolate milk. "Then take me home and punish me. I don't want to stay here."

"Can't do that and you know why." She looked away.

"Why won't you believe me? Is it because I'm just another disappointment in you life? Is it dad all over again?"

Now she did look at him. "You're treading thin ice, mister."

"I know about the affair."

She quickly gulped her lemonade.

"I'm sorry dad hurt you, but I've been paying the price ever since. I know I've screwed up, but I'm not going to turn into him."

Although tears formed in her eyes, he finished anyway. "That's what you're really afraid of, isn't it?"

"No." She swiped her eyes and pushed her plate aside. "I'm afraid of losing you, and I won't let that happen. Believe it or not, I love you."

"But everything that's happened to get me here has been a mistake. That knife wasn't mine and you know it. I don't deserve this place."

"What are you going to do, Grant? Stay at home and waste the school year? You'll never catch up. You don't have a choice and neither do I. At least you can earn credits until you can get back into your old school next year. It's the best I can do." She grabbed her purse. "You going to walk me to the car?"

He couldn't believe it. "You're *leaving*?"

"Yes. I'm not hungry and it's getting late."

"Wait. I need to tell you something else. It's important." He followed her toward the doors. "There's a hole in the back yard behind the school. A tunnel. I think there's something dangerous about it. I'll show you."

His mother stopped outside on the top step and put on her sunglasses. "I'm not falling for this, Grant. You'd better stop before I put you in therapy on top of everything else."

"Good! I need someone to listen to me. You don't!"

She reached over and kissed his cheek before he could turn away. "I'll call you next week. Love you." With that, she headed toward the parking lot, leaving him staring after her.

Grant slammed his locker closed now at the memory and headed off to his first class. Maybe Mr. Peterson could help him.

When the classroom door opened, a young skinny man in black trousers and a white button down shirt hurried to get behind the podium.

Grant recognized the man as a substitute teacher he'd had once before in science by the name of *Mr. Denus*. The guys had had a field day with that one. The teacher's voice cracked as he shifted his papers from the left and then back to the right. He wiped his sodden forehead with a hanky and quickly shoved it back into his pants pocket.

"I'm Mr. Denus, your teacher for today and most likely for the rest of the school year."

A round of whispers filled the room. Grant's stomach knotted into a ball. His hand shot up.

Mr. Denus nodded at him and shifted his papers once more.

"What happened to Mr. Peterson?" Grant asked.

"That is a private matter, but please be aware that I am capable of teaching you the required materials of World Geography and the only way you will not receive credit for this class, is if you fail to do the work." He mopped his face with the limp hanky and turned to write on the blackboard.

* * *

When World Geography ended, Grant passed Mumsford's office on the way to his next class. The hallway remained relatively deserted because of the headmaster's annoying habit of standing outside his door watching the boys go by. He never failed to find a reason to call over a student and waste their time with something as trivial as a fanning shirttail. For this reason, Grant usually avoided the hall, but since he couldn't afford another tardy, he took a chance with the short cut.

He slowed when he heard lowered voices coming through the open door of the headmaster's office.

"You're a fool. How could you let this happen?" an unfamiliar voice asked.

"I assure you our World Geography studies will not suffer. Mr. Denus is more than qualified and far less likely to befriend any of the students. He's terrified of them." Mumsford answered.

Grant listened outside the door, wondering whom Mumsford was talking to.

When he peered around to see, footsteps neared the door and he quickly pulled back. If caught, he planned to say he was waiting to see Mumsford. The footsteps stopped short and suddenly the door closed. He leaned closer hoping to find out what happened to Mr. Peterson.

The other voice carried through the door. "This never should have happened. Peterson knows too much. You'll have to deal with this like the others."

"I suppose you're right. Things have come too far to end over the likes of Peterson. I'll take care of it before the open house."

"Yes, you will. Remember your reward will be great when my goals are fulfilled. I will not forget my promises to you."

"That's most reassuring. And you know you can count on my devotion to the cause." Mumsford sounded reverent.

"You don't have much choice, although I see your heart is truly in your work." A snide chuckle wafted toward the door and Grant ducked around the corner.

The door opened and someone headed down the glossy tiles in the other direction. When Grant glanced around the corner to see who had the upper hand on the headmaster, he stared down an empty corridor.

* * *

Grant sat in shop class staring at the back of Artie Sikes's greasy, black hair. Artie slammed down his books and started setting up his workspace. It looked like ol' Artie was having another bad day. Since the day he'd found his slain hamster, he'd taken plenty of guff from the other students and had laid low.

As a testimony to his true bullying self, he scowled at a skinny kid in the front row, sending the kid sinking into his chair. When Artie's foot caught a nearby desk leg, he sent it slamming into the workbench with a solid kick. Grant hoped the workshop teacher would appear before the guy started sawing people in half.

Grant wondered about Mr. Peterson's sudden disappearance. The guy could have left for any number of reasons. Perhaps there'd been a family emergency, except Mr. Peterson said he didn't have anyone. Maybe he'd been transferred to a better job in the city. Grant wondered if he'd ever know the truth.

Artie slammed a cabinet door, making Grant jump. Ignoring it, Grant took out a piece of wood he'd been working on this week. The finished project would be a small shelf for his bedroom at home, if he ever returned. His mother's words burned in his brain like an unshakable tune. *I'm afraid of losing you.*

Grant knew that was a crock. Knollwood was dangerous and she could easily lose him to the place she thought would save him. She just wouldn't see it.

Suddenly, Artie bellowed out a curse and stuffed a piece of paper into the waste can beside him. Grant recognized the green slip as a detention form. That made three for Artie and meant he'd be sitting out the first football game of the season.

The other students watched in silence while Artie put on his goggles and started up the saw. Several boys in the back nudged one another. It was a strict rule of shop class that no one operated any equipment without supervision. Artie didn't seem to care. He slid his economics book into place under the spinning blade.

The new kid, Tom Smithers, headed to the front of the room to find another seat. He glanced back at the six-foot bully about to break all the rules, and most likely saw his way into yet another detention.

Everyone cringed at the high-pitched whine as the blade sliced through the thick book. Grant tried desperately to think of a way to stop him. The bully's hands shook like an old man when he reached into his satchel for another book. Before Grant could act, it happened.

A stuttered grinding sound caught everyone's attention. Blood sprayed over the workbench, splattering a kid nearby, sending the screaming boy out the door. Artie stood motionless in front of the spinning blade.

Grant jumped up, rounding the table. His foot slid on a puddle of blood causing his hands to land on the smeared tabletop.

The rest of the class fled the room; as Grant tried to coax the giant into his seat before he fainted and cracked open his skull. He tugged at Artie's shirt sleeve saying, "C'mon, man. Sit down. It'll be all right. Just sit down."

The boy's eyes remained fixed on something in front of him.

"Sit down before you fall." Grant followed the kid's gaze.

Artie's left hand lay palm up on the table beside the whining machine. It looked like a bad movie prop with blood-speckled fingers curled into a claw. Wrist skin hung loosely over exposed bone. Grant looked away to keep from losing control.

"Hey! Get some help in here!" he called.

With that, Artie crumpled to the floor, banging his head hard enough on the tabletop to cause it to bounce twice. His eyes rolled back in his head leaving only white orbs staring back at Grant.

Several staff members rushed in, including the tardy shop teacher, who clutched his stomach and threw up in the wastebasket at the sight of the severed hand. Medical help arrived, forcing Grant aside. He watched helplessly as they bandaged the stump and dumped the severed hand into a plastic baggie. He thought of Billy on the ambulance stretcher making him promise to tell someone they were all in danger. *I tried, but no one believes me.*

CHAPTER 15

Knollwood's open house and first basketball game of the season brought out the school spirit in everyone, including Mumsford. He paraded down the hall feeling like a proud parent on graduation day. Wearing his dress clothes, he belted out orders to the janitor, Mr. Turner.

"We have important visitors to impress, you know! Let's make sure the floors shine bright."

"Yeah, let's," Mr. Turner mumbled as he stopped mopping long enough to wipe his brow with a hanky.

"Chop. Chop," Mumsford said and clapped his chubby hands for emphasis before heading off toward the main house basement.

Behind the large staircase leading to the upper rooms, he took out a large silver hoop of keys and opened the basement door. A musty puff of air made him blink as though the room had coughed in his face. He hurried inside, closing the door behind him.

His feet scuffed the damp cement steps that ended in the belly of the darkened room where a multitude of unused items dwelled, such as old desks, abandoned science equipment, and empty chalk boxes. Mumsford kicked an eraser box in his path sending it flying over a warped, wooden podium.

When he reached the far wall, he glanced behind at the debris of countless generations of Knollwood students and teachers. It served its purpose in hiding his secret. He moved several boxes and found the place in the wall he sought. It slid open easily. Mumsford entered the hidden room.

* * *

Far above the basement on the second floor of the main house, Mumsford's quarters reeked of stale incense and dirty socks. Grant closed the headmaster's bedroom door behind him and moved ahead in the dark. A wide ray of yellow moonlight bled through the tall windows making it easy to move across the room. His eyebrows raised at the spacious accommodations of a bedroom area twice the size of his own, an adjoining master bath and a tidy kitchenette. Too nice for Mumsford, he decided.

Stacks of books and papers cluttered a rickety desk, some spilling onto the floor beneath. Grant flashed his penlight across the faded book titles held loosely together by cracked bindings. He carefully paged through the top book feeling the brittle paper beneath his fingers. The title, *Ancient Remedies of Souls* was written in gold script. What kind of title is that? Another read, *The Art of Satanic Worship.*

Grant dropped the book and moved to the dresser. He had no doubt he would find what he came for. Ever since Mr. Peterson had *disappeared,* and he'd overheard the conversation in Mumsford's office, he'd been unable to stop the niggling feeling that something wasn't right, and that Mumsford had to be involved. It bothered him he'd been unable to figure out who Mumsford's mysterious visitor had been. Still, he wanted to know more about the strange headmaster who wielded so much power at the academy.

The phrase "breaking and entering" sailed through Grant's head as he riffled through the man's personal things. He chose to ignore it. There was something dangerous about the man. Even his book choices revealed a twisted mind. There had to be a clue.

His fingers brushed against a polished stone-like object in the bottom of the top dresser drawer. He fished it out and examined the orb under the penlight.

"Shit!" He dropped it.

A marbled testicle rolled to the corner of the drawer.

"Oh, God." He forced himself to pick it up. "Can't be real," he whispered.

Real or not, the mud colored object had been coated with some sort of varnish to preserve it. He dropped it when his fingers grazed the wadded clump of skin where it had been cut off.

He dug through the rest of the man's dresser afraid he'd find more body parts. The bottom drawer held cardboard boxes containing powders, metal trinkets, and a multitude of partially burned candles. In the middle drawer, he pushed aside the man's boxer shorts and found a weighty round object wrapped in black silk. His fingers shook as he undid the covering.

His breath caught when he saw a man's class ring. The red stone glistened under the penlight's glow and he recognized it as Mr. Peterson's.

"What the hell is Mumsford doing with this?"

He shoved aside unfolded socks and gasped. A carved wooden pentagram sent chills up his arms. Mumsford was practicing witchcraft.

* * *

Later, the gym stood nearly filled to capacity as Grant made his way along the bleachers past a long row of parents waving hand-held Knollwood flags. Thoughts of his earlier findings in Mumsford's room circled in his head. If the man was a warlock, they were all in danger. He had to get his mind off the possibility.

Tonight signaled the school's first basketball game as well as its open house. He dreaded sitting alone, until a group of Joe's friends called him over to sit with them. His mom had to work tonight, and although he could tell she'd felt badly over the phone, he couldn't shake the idea that she could have switched with someone at work if she'd really wanted to come. After her last visit, he could hardly blame her for not wanting to make it. He knew he'd acted like a jerk in trying to make her feel bad about leaving him here. Maybe she'd been right and he'd overreacted to a few coincidental incidents.

As far as he knew, Billy would be returning soon and word had it that Artie seemed to be making a fast recovery. Accidents happen when carelessness is involved, and Artie had definitely asked for it. Still his mother's reaction to the news about Artie had surprised him. She'd broken her cold silence on the other end of the phone only to tell him she didn't want to hear his complaints again. He knew she didn't believe him.

The crowd suddenly jumped to its feet as the music started and the Knollwood Knights ran onto the court by introduction. Joe Blockman entered the gym to an explosion of cheers from the Knollwood students. The star of the team. He watched as the Treybelle twins, Terrence and Thomas, joined him on the court with a series of high fives. The rival team known as the Taber North Titans was announced with far less fanfare and soon the starting whistle blew.

Grant watched in amazement at the speed and agility of his roommate and how he anticipated the other team's moves before they even got the ball. No wonder Knollwood treated him like a basketball god. The Treybelle twins followed hot on Joe's heels playing their guard positions well enough to gain a three-point shot before the Titans made it halfway down the court. The twins' double image blurred into one combination of sleek moves and fast action as they ran back and forth. By half time, the Knights had a twenty-point lead and showed no signs of slowing down.

Then it happened. Thomas Treybelle lost control of the ball to the Titans on the way down the court. The Knollwood crowd went wild with cruel gestures and calls as the other team scored a three-pointer. Joe pinned Thomas with a glare as the team headed off court for a time out. The kid shrank from his six-two stature as Joe verbally pummeled him.

Grant looked over to see Joe's friends beside him encouraging their hero as though he could hear them. When the buzzer signaled the start of play, Terrence rudely elbowed his brother as they trotted back onto the court.

From there, Thomas's performance grew worse. He couldn't catch up with the game's pace. The Titans were fast moving ahead, leaving the home team with only a two-point lead. The Knollwood crowd went wild when Coach MacIntyre finally pulled Thomas out and replaced him with John Carter. Grant watched the defeated guard return to the sidelines, eyes lowered.

Grant sympathized with him. In the team's big chance to shine in front of parents and other important visitors, he'd blown it. Thomas should have been on top of his game tonight more than any other, and for that, Grant could see how his teammates, and even his brother, could hold him accountable should they lose. He could only imagine the repercussions if they did.

* * *

Deep in the bowels of the main house, Mumsford moved about in the damp darkness of the small lower room of the basement. He'd lit several large lanterns along the floor to create enough light to see what he'd come to see and to pay homage to the one who could save him. He'd taken care of the geography teacher as promised.

His eyes beheld the large glass case that entombed the beating

THE ACADEMY

heart. Its rhythmic dance offered him the comfort he'd longed for and the reassurance that it was still there. He watched the throbbing red muscle in awe, his hand resting gently on top of the glass as if to caress the precious life inside. Sweat streamed down his temples as he fought the temptation to shatter the glass and take the contents. After a moment, he forced himself away. The master had promised it to him; after all, it belonged to him. He had to trust in order to survive the times ahead. Patience had served him well so far and it wouldn't be much longer before the prophecy would come to pass.

Mumsford backed away slowly and turned to face the makeshift altar draped in black. He raised the sleeve of his favorite brown dress shirt then clutched the sacrificial dagger tightly with his other hand. The first cut burned like fire; always fire, along his pudgy flesh. He felt the familiar warmth of blood trailing down to his elbow. He breathed deep allowing the metallic aroma to fill his lungs. It smelled of life and the new order to come. The blood dripped into the golden chalice beneath with a melodic plopping sound and he closed his eyes as the lightheaded feeling consumed him. The longing in his loins reached a frenzied peak and heated throbbing made his balls ache.

He pumped his fist open and shut urging the blood to flow faster. Finally, the desired level of cherry colored liquid filled the small cup. With a shout of praise to his master, he closed his eyes at the sudden release between his legs and rode the wave of ecstasy as he climaxed into his new dress pants.

* * *

Grant jumped to his feet when the final buzzer rang. The game ended with a score of seventy to fifty-five after a fast comeback by Knollwood. Joe rode the shoulders of his teammates as they moved across the crowded gym toward the locker room chanting his name. Grant looked for Thomas, but he'd left.

Joe smiled and waved like a celebrity. He seemed to expect this kind of treatment. He caught site of Grant and motioned him to follow into the locker room. By now, Grant had become grid locked into the crowd of spectators and couldn't move. He shrugged at Joe and signaled that he'd meet him later. He watched Joe duck as his teammates squeezed through the doorway and disappeared, still cheering.

Grant shuffled along with the crowd until it broke up enough for him to get outside. The autumn air felt refreshing after sitting in the stuffy gymnasium for the past hour and a half. He watched parents and other guests walking the grounds in the moonlight and wondered why he thought of Knollwood as anything but a school for boys. Although each boy—each family, had its issues to hash out, they were all a part of a greater plan. Nothing evil or treacherous in that.

Everything appeared normal with colorful team flags, and clutches of families making their way to the refreshment table in the cafeteria. It dawned on him that maybe there wasn't anything wrong with the school at all. Perhaps it had been his twisted perceptions forming an ugly picture of the place that could actually help him. Suddenly he realized the academy could provide a way to mend his ways and start over next year. Even the crazy events with Mumsford and Artie and Billy blended into a picture of rationality. He'd been the one who'd forced himself to see the events as threatening because he wanted a reason to leave.

He thought hard about his time at the school. Had he been harmed? Couldn't each incident be drawn back to a case of carelessness or neglect? Even his concerns over the manhole began to fade, melding into a case of poor engineering on the part of the builders.

Tom Caruthers from science class headed his way with a young woman. Their likeness was remarkable.

"Hey, Grant," the boy said.

Grant caught the woman's motherly tone remarking about Tom's open jacket. Suddenly he missed having his own mom's participation in tonight's open house.

Guilt gripped Grant at the idea of her working late tonight, and all the other times. She'd done it all for him. Until now, he'd considered his placement at the academy a form of revenge to make him pay for all the hell he'd caused her. But that wasn't it at all, he realized. It had hurt her just as much to put him here because she thought she'd failed as a parent. So far, he'd only proven her right at every turn.

He made the decision that those days were over and he'd make her proud from now on. He'd failed his last attempt. His eyes briefly scanned the spot where the manhole cover lay enveloped in the black syrupy night between the school and main house.

"Bullshit." He mumbled under his breath. "It's just a metal plate." He kicked a rock on the walk and watched it sail into the grass and disappear.

*   *   *

That night, Grant dreamed he walked in total blackness, his arms stretched out helplessly for protection in an effort to get his bearings. It reminded him of the nightmares when he tried to stop himself from falling down a bottomless pit, and he'd awaken out of breath in an icy sweat.

His feet trudged along a thin carpet that reminded him of the main house foyer and he willed himself to wake before he plowed into something and had a coronary in his sleep. He knew dreams could be cruel enough to send you into madness, or so they'd said on a television show he'd watched.

A sliver of golden light glowed across the floor and he slowly moved forward. It bled out from under a doorway only a few inches away. His hands pressed against the blessed solidness of a wooden door and he groped for a knob. The cool metal tingled against his fingertips, but his hopes fell when he found it locked. Turning back into the darkness, he wished he could wake up.

Sharp screams crept through the wall behind him and Grant pounded on the door. The cries grew louder then trailed off into a series of faint wails. The light from under the door blinked off. He stood frozen in the dark.

A heavy hand spun him around. Grant opened his mouth to shout, but nothing came out. He saw no face or body, only a vice grip around his throat. The pressure intensified, as he tore at the icy presence cutting his breath.

He kicked at his invisible attacker, connecting with air. Then something hit him hard and he fell to the floor.

Grant struggled to his feet, head on into the blackness from where he'd come. He ran toward the staircase, but before he'd gone more than a few feet, he slammed into a barrier and fell back. Rattled breathing grew closer, and he backed away with his hands behind him like a back pedaling spider. He stopped when his head hit the door. He pushed against its wood trying to keep a distance between himself and the unknown thing drawing steadily near.

A tail-like whip shot out of the darkness and gripped his chin. He fought with both hands, but it clamped tighter, cutting into his skin. The presence lifted him high into the air then threw him against the door. He fought for breath, and terror seized him when he thought he'd die in his sleep.

His eyes bolted open and he heard his own ragged breaths as he came out of the dream. Finally, he'd awakened.

The blackness still held him and he squinted to see his room. Slowly his vision cleared to a slice of light under the doorway. He sighed in relief knowing he'd survived the nightmare and he scrambled to get out of bed for a drink. His hands felt carpet instead of bed linen. Fully awake now, he saw he was in the main house foyer behind the staircase. Dim wall sconces lit the large room as he firmly pressed up against a wooden door. His heart raced when he realized it hadn't been a nightmare.

CHAPTER 16

On his way home from work, Mitch gunned the Harley as he approached his old alma mater, taking only a brief glance at the grounds. Once again, he noticed Coop's Jeep parked in the faculty lot and wondered why it sat there for the third time this week. He reminded himself if he could see the cars that clearly, he needed to speed up going past the academy. Before he could kick it up a notch, he caught sight of Coop heading for his Jeep. Mitch pushed past his better judgment and decided to catch up with him. He turned the Harley off Route 41 and headed down the stretch of pavement that led to the school.

He ignored the slick black trees along the paved road and kept his eyes ahead.

Every part of the school's landscape exuded evil. In his opinion, Knollwood was diseased. The whole scene gave him the creeps and he half expected decaying zombies to burst from the manicured lawn and crawl after him. Not that his imagination needed any help. The pool episode flashed in his mind and he fought a wave of nausea. Even that incident couldn't compare to the horrible secret he'd discovered late one night—the truth he'd tried so desperately to keep hidden, even from himself. His discovery had come unexpectedly during Jake's last moments.

He still pictured Jake's face right before he died, or at least Mitch hoped he'd died. The boy's pale freckled hand had reached up one last time and Mitch had clutched it tight. He pulled hard against the tide pulling Jake down. His biceps burned as he yanked the boy's face up from the bloody waters.

"Mitch! You've got to leave," Jake panted.

"What are you talkin' about? C'mon, I'll pull you out." He tugged on the boy's arm.

"No! It's too late. Get away from the school before it gets you, too!"

Jake's head jerked under the water and Mitch had to pull harder this time to bring him up. "Jake!"

The boy breathlessly sputtered his last words. "The academy is alive...it's a living thing. It's going to take us all!"

With that, Jake disappeared beneath the crimson red causing Mitch to lose his grip.

He tried to force the memory down. But there was no escape. It resurfaced as the one dark truth he could never expose because it would most likely get him killed, or worse.

The realization that he'd never told anyone what really went on behind the Knollwood gates had become his walking nightmare. His list of excuses had grown over the past five years, as he tried to sooth his conscience. Among his favorites... *No one would care. No one would believe it. They'd just cover it up.* Still, when the night surrounded his beaten down little shack and he settled beneath his dingy bed sheets, the voices spoke with great volume in his brain. *Kids are still suffering and it's your fault!*

Seeing Coop ahead, he pushed back the memories and swung in beside the Jeep. He let the bike idle, as he straddled the Harley.

"What are *you* doing here?" Coop cut his engine.

"I guess I could ask you the same thing. What's going on?"

Coop grinned. "I couldn't take the retired life any longer and decided to get back behind the desk."

"Not smart, man. I told you about this place."

"You really believe all that doomsday stuff? I know you had a bad experience here, but look around. Does it look evil to you?"

"Nope," Mitch said lighting a cigarette. "But neither does Satan. They say he was the most beautiful angel, you know. But he's a real asshole." Mitch spat onto the grass. God how he hated this place.

"I guess." Coop didn't offer anything more.

Mitch switched gears seeing Coop either didn't get it or didn't want to. "How's the Jeep runnin'?"

"Fine. No problem. Thanks again."

THE ACADEMY

"Yeah. Well, if you have any more trouble, come see me." His skin crawled and he longed to be on his way. He revved the engine and glanced over the redbrick buildings with sleepy shutter eyes penetrating his mind. His uneasiness grew when he spotted the vacant yard between the main house and the school building. A cold sweat broke out under his shirt.

Coop interrupted the silence. "Where you headed?"

"Home. Maybe Smalley's. You gonna stop by?" Mitch flicked the half smoked cigarette across the lawn.

"I doubt it. I have to plan next week's lessons."

"You really want to do this? I mean, here at Knollwood?"

"Why not?" Coop shrugged. "It's a good school and I've met a lot of great kids. Although sometimes you have to scrape the surface enough to see their potential."

Mitch could tell Coop had made his decision. He'd never see the truth until too late. "Well, good luck, man. And remember, if you have any trouble, call me."

He backed up the bike, hoping the teacher caught his offer. He knew Coop would soon need all the help he could get.

* * *

Coop watched Mitch turn off the road and onto the main highway. His fingers tapped a nervous tempo on the steering wheel as he contemplated Mitch's warning. That's what it had been, although he hadn't come right out and said so. Nevertheless, he'd already decided he wasn't going anywhere until he found out the truth about the school and his uncle's death.

A cold flush washed over him when he considered how quickly a teaching position had opened up. Mr. Jennings had called on Tuesday morning to ask if Wednesday would be too soon to start. It was almost as though they'd been waiting for him.

The first few days went smoothly. He'd made points with the students by allowing them to drop the formalities and call him Coop. He found the kids weren't as hard to handle as he'd expected, especially a kid by the name of Grant Taylor. His story didn't differ much from a thousand others he'd heard. With one or both parents out of the picture, the kids seemed to fall into corrupt situations. But he sensed something unique about Grant.

They'd hit it off right away and he could tell by the look on Grant's face, he wanted to talk. Coop arranged to let the kids out of class a few minutes early as a reward for their full cooperation in an attempt to draw the Mr. Peanut model he'd brought in. He preferred that to the usual bowl of plastic fruit that never looked real in the first place. At least the peanut model became something to joke about and break the ice between teacher and students.

After class, Grant had lagged behind and they started talking about Knollwood. It didn't take long before the boy spilled his concerns about several strange incidents involving accidents, including a small breaking and entering confession. He knew the kid had taken a great risk in trusting him not to say anything, especially about Mumsford's incriminating conversation and what Grant had found in the man's room. The incident confirmed his own suspicions that Mumsford had sordid intentions, but he'd never expected witchcraft.

Coop's blood had turned to ice when Grant mentioned the manhole cover. It sounded like the same one in Uncle Eb's journal. If nothing else, it confirmed his suspicions that his uncle had been on to something, something that might have gotten him killed.

Coop grabbed the keys from the ignition and took off for the main house feeling he probably wouldn't be seen in the dusky evening light. If anyone questioned his presence, at least now he could honestly say he belonged here. A brisk wind picked up as he started between the buildings and headed toward the unlit back yard.

With the sun sinking fast, Coop hurried to find the mysterious cover. He stopped abruptly when his foot hit metal, and looked down to see that the cover was indeed larger than a typical manhole lid. He bent for a closer look. A sudden wind gust pushed him back. Perspiration covered his forehead at a heavy scraping sound coming from under the metal disk. He moved closer and willed his heart to stop skipping beats.

After several moments, he pressed his ear to the cover and listened. No scratching. Probably a rat, he convinced himself, and reached inside his jacket pocket for a pen and paper. The eerie markings resembled some sort of language, but the script was unfamiliar.

He quickly copied the markings exactly as written, and shoved the paper into his pocket. Then he noticed the disk lay slightly askew from its base. How had he missed that? He knew with no flashlight, it would be impossible to see down into the hole, but he shoved the cover to the side anyway. To his surprise, it slid off easily and he squinted down into the darkness for a better look.

The putrid stench made his nose burn and reminded him of sulfur. The odor changed with each breath he took. He winced at the familiar smell of feces and urine, then the smell of decay and heavy smoke. When he leaned deeper, his fingers touched a moist fleshy interior. It resembled human muscle or skin.

Suddenly, the inside of the tunnel gave a tremor and he pushed away from the edge. The fading sunset provided just enough light to see the beefy inner lining rippling with contractions. Coop kept a safe distance until the movements ceased, then moved the lid into place and took off toward the parking lot.

The sun had become a red sliver in the sky's veneer by the time he got back into his Jeep. As he started down the long stretch of road toward home, he wasn't quite sure of what he'd seen or what it meant. He *did* know his find could well be the key to the mystery of Knollwood.

* * *

The great demon, Malik, watched the little man scurry like a rodent from the yard to his car. He stroked the smooth muscles of his biceps and wondered at their form. How small the creature called *man*, he mused, how fragile its short life. How is it that its soul is the most powerful force in the great span of existence? It is the most unappreciated gift man owns.

"They know not how to use it," he sneered. He knew humankind had been kept in ignorance awaiting someone to teach them. Just as well for his cause, he contemplated.

After God's defeat, Malik would stand in charge of mankind. He would teach the lowly humans how to harness the true power of their souls. Then the final battle against Satan would be his greatest challenge, and supreme victory.

He transformed to his true form and waited in the dark for the main house to quiet. Soon the students would lose themselves to the realm of sleep and dreams. Only a few more souls were needed to advance his plan.

His army would not fail in the final battle of Armageddon. Soon his soldiers would arise according to prophecy and win the victory. He moved inside his lair, examining the large cocoons. The encapsulated souls thrashed about seeking their freedom. Their cries rose with the smoke of the nearby fire pit. Soon the souls would be released and the war would begin.

CHAPTER 17

Amanda Taylor's thoughts drowned in the black abyss of her chaotic mind as she drove from work. She couldn't stop the reverie of Grant's concerns that Knollwood Academy wasn't safe and her own nullifying rebuttals. She winced at the memory of his knowledge of Mick's affair. It shouldn't have surprised her, everyone had known, except her. Then she recalled she'd suspected Mick's betrayal all along, but had chosen denial. Pride can be an ugly foe.

It hurt her to think Grant didn't want to be like his father and he thought she would prefer it that way. Nothing could be further from the truth. His father had been a good man, just a lonely trucker on the road for weeks at a time. It happens. She pushed past her bitterness and decided if Grant turned out anything like Mick Taylor, he'd be ten steps ahead of the world.

Her guilt grew daily over her decision to place him at the academy, yet she knew her choices had been limited. Until now, she'd thought Grant's ranting had been a ploy to get his way and leave the school, but now she had doubts.

Tonight at work, the 3-11 shift had gone quickly because the new ICU nurse turned out to be a good worker, full of experience and energy for the exhausting job. On a short break, they'd talked about past jobs at various hospitals and the woman mentioned a patient she'd cared for shortly before she left her most recent position at a small hospital just outside the town of Knollwood.

Amanda choked on her coffee when the woman described the

severe, self-inflicted wounds of a boy about Grant's age. She'd said the boy had nearly scratched himself to death after a battle with little black bugs. They'd been unable to identify the type of infestation, but had treated it like scabies. Fortunately, the treatment worked and he showed remarkable improvement.

The nurse had never seen the bugs, only the results of the boy's digging which landed him in ICU because he'd lost so much blood. They'd managed to save him and as far as she knew, he would soon be moved to a regular room. While she'd never said the boy's name, Amanda knew it had to be the same boy Grant had told her about, Billy Parker.

A quick glance into the rearview mirror confirmed her suspicion that she looked like holy hell and would probably feel like it before this night ended. After her extra shift at Fontaine General Hospital, she was on her way to the facility the new nurse had told her about only thirty miles away in Knollwood. She wanted to see Billy Parker for herself.

She parked in the visitor's lot and released her hair from its holder, watching it spill around her shoulders. It showed no traces of gray, but at thirty-four she knew the age clock stopped for no one. She'd come to terms with her widowhood and figured there would probably never be another man in her life. Right now Grant was the only person she wanted responsibility for.

She finger-combed her bangs and checked her look once more. Her pale oval face showed the telltale signs of a double-shift. Amanda knew she'd fit right in with the other staff members.

Still wearing her nurse's uniform, she had little trouble getting in after visiting hours and conned the night nurse working Billy's case to allow her five minutes with the young boy. It had only cost her a can of soda and a turkey sandwich from the cafeteria vending machine.

The room held a soft glow from the wall lights close to the floor and she made her way to his bedside. His black hair lay slicked back from his pasty looking face. He slept without any signs of discomfort as the IV dripped an antibiotic solution into his system. No one bothered her as she watched him for several minutes before gently touching his arm.

"Billy?" she whispered. "Billy, can you hear me?"

The boy's eyes opened slowly, looking bewildered.

"Billy? My name is Amanda Taylor, Grant's mom."

"Who?" the boy's dark eyes narrowed.

"Grant Taylor, from Knollwood Academy? He's a friend of yours."

Billy showed no trace of recognition.

He sat up slowly and frowned. "Why are you here?"

"Do you remember Grant?"

"Yeah. I guess." The boy glanced past the curtains toward the wall clock.

"I'm sorry to bother you so late, but I need to ask you something."

"Okay."

"You told Grant you heard voices and that you'd started sleepwalking shortly before your accident. Is that true?"

"What accident?"

She didn't know what to say. What had he been told? Surely, he remembered scratching himself to shreds?

"Well, uh, the reason you're here," she finally said.

"A rash." His eyes stared past her.

She turned to find the doorway empty.

"Now think, Billy." She looked at his blank expression. "You told Grant about hearing voices in the night, and that you thought you'd gone out of your room once, but couldn't remember doing it. What happened?"

"I don't know what you're talking about. Are you sure you've got the right room?"

Amanda fought her anxiety. The kid must be heavily sedated, or he truly had no recollection of anything.

A shadow in the doorway told her she'd overstayed her welcome, turkey sandwich or not.

"I'm going now, Billy. I hope you feel better soon."

"I'll tell Grant you were here."

"You do that," she said with a heavy feeling that poor Billy would have no memory of her visit after tonight. The kid didn't seem to have a solid thought in his head.

* * *

Saturday afternoon Grant finished the last play of football practice by taking an unexpected hit that landed him on the ground. As the cloudless sky faded in and out of focus, he tried to make out a gray shadow overhead.

"You okay?" a familiar voice asked.

Grant forced his lungs to expand and closed his eyes. "Yeah."

"C'mon then, I've found something." The new art teacher extended his hand.

"I'm up." Grant tried to shake off the nausea.

Coach Vargas shouted from the sidelines as he collected his clipboard and jacket. "You all right, Taylor?"

Grant waved him on.

"Tough practice?" Coop asked.

"The usual." Grant shrugged and removed his helmet. "What's up?"

"You have time to meet me in my office?"

"Sure. Let me shower first."

"I'll be there."

A short time later, Grant knocked on the classroom door and pushed inside. Coop sat at his desk scanning something not bothering to look up when Grant sat in a front row desk.

"I'll be right with you." Coop traced the page with a finger. "There." He tapped it hard.

"What?" Grant moved closer.

"Take a look." Coop turned the paper around for him to see.

Grant looked at a blueprint of the school's main house.

"Where'd you get this?" he asked.

"You'd be surprised what one can find in the mechanical room."

"How'd you get past ol' Turner?"

"Let's just say he appreciates fine cognac." Coop grinned.

Grant turned back to the blueprint. "What's with that?" He pointed to the spot where Coop's pen rested.

"I'm trying to see where the manhole cover leads to. From what I can tell, it goes straight into the main house basement. It would have to."

He pulled out another page that showed the school's blueprint and moved the two pages side by side. "See, between the two buildings, right here," he placed a hard candy on the designated spot, "is where the manhole cover is. If you follow the building plans, the hole should end up in the basement somewhere."

"Cool. Now we know where it goes, but what does that mean?" Grant swiped the hard candy and unwrapped it.

"It means we can locate its end in the main house. But there's something that bothers me."

"What's that?" Grant popped the candy into his mouth.

"It's not written in on the ground blueprint. Technically, it doesn't even exist."

"Maybe they put in after the plans were drawn?"

"Good call, but if this tunnel serves any real purpose, like for sewage, it would had to have had approval when they built the place."

"So, what do you think it's for?" Grant shoved away from the desk.

Coop frowned. "I'm not sure. But there's a way to find out."

Grant grinned. Coop seemed all right, as adults went. He wasn't all caught up over right and wrong, and Grant sensed his sincerity about wanting to help him. "And that is?" he questioned the teacher.

"We'll go see for ourselves."

* * *

Grant and Coop were careful not to arouse suspicion as they moved through the main house. According to the blueprint, there was a door in the foyer hallway behind the stairs, leading into the basement. Grant wiped his palms at the sight of the dark paneled walls of the large entryway. His nightmare haunted him as he fell behind. Coop motioned for him to hurry.

"What's wrong?" Coop worked at the lock.

"Nothing. This place gives me the creeps."

"This old lock is probably just a spring latch. Won't take long at all." He turned to look at Grant. "You're soaked with sweat. Are you sure you're okay?"

"I'm fine. Just hurry up." He watched his teacher maneuver the knob.

Coop looked like he knew what he was doing, and Grant wondered about his background. He didn't know the man well enough to ask such a personal question. He did, however, feel he could confide some of his own personal history—like the recent nightmare that had landed him in front of this door.

The lock clicked and they both gave a sudden look over their shoulders. Coop opened the heavy wooden door and they went inside.

Grant followed, wincing at the strong mildew odor. "Man, when's the last time anyone was in here?"

Coop kept silent as he negotiated his way in the darkness.

When Grant touched the cement wall beside him, his fingers came away slimy. Not what he'd wanted to find in a mysterious room that most likely ended at the bottom of the writhing sinewy tunnel.

Coop found the light switch and suddenly the room filled with gray light from a single dingy ceiling bulb. Grant followed his teacher down the stairs, taking in all of the abandoned items piled high in the crowded basement.

"I don't see anything but junk," Grant stopped on the bottom step, unsure if he wanted to go any further. He recalled the invisible force that had stalked him and threw him against the upstairs door in the foyer. He knew he had to tell Coop.

The teacher waded through the basement's clutter, heading toward the far wall. "It has to come out somewhere in here."

"Hey, Coop?"

"Yeah?"

"I guess things have been kind of quiet since Artie left, except for Billy Parker's roommate leaving."

"Oh? Why did he go?"

"Family illness or something. Anyway, he looked okay when he left. But now it's *too* quiet. You know Billy mentioned sleepwalking right before he ended up in the hospital."

"Right. You told me."

"Well, I think it's happening to me, too."

Coop stopped and stared. "What happened?"

Grant's anxiety lessened as he explained the nightmare. Coop let him finish without comment.

"So, what do you think? Am I losin' it, too?"

"I doubt that. You say you woke up in the foyer upstairs?"

"Yeah. And something was there, breathing hard. It picked me up and threw me against the door. I can't believe it didn't wake up the whole house. And those screams I heard, I know they came from down here."

Coop looked around once more. "Listen, from now on you have to try to keep something in front of your bedroom door so you'll wake up if you try to leave. Tell your roommate you're afraid of sleepwalking. He won't know the difference. You've got to watch yourself."

"Then you believe me?"

"Why wouldn't I? We both know there's something going on here and right now I don't think either of us can be too careful." He lifted another box and set it aside to expose the damp cement wall behind it.

"Listen. I think there's something else you should know if we're going to work together."

Coop smiled. "Is that what we're doing?"

"I'm serious, Coop. You're gonna think this is weird, but after everything else, maybe it's not."

The teacher stood, brushing his longish hair from his eyes. "I'm listening."

"Sometimes I can hear what people are thinking." When Coop

didn't laugh he continued. "It's not all the time, only when people are really upset or emotional. Like right now I don't have a clue what you're thinking, but I kind of wish I did."

"It's not so uncommon, Grant. It's a form of mental telepathy."

Grant felt relieved. Not only was it common, it actually had a name. "I heard Billy and Artie before they got hurt and they were frightened of something coming after them. I didn't tell anyone, because they wouldn't have believed me."

"You did the right thing. Anything else?"

"Yeah. I *can't* read Joe Blockman. We're roommates, don't you think I'd have gotten something from him by now?"

"I'm not surprised." Coop moved another box aside.

"You're not?"

"Your ability is based on strong emotions, and Joe is the kind of guy who is able to keep his well guarded."

"I guess." Grant went over to see what Coop had found, feeling much lighter now that his burden had been shared and someone other than a fellow student, believed him.

"Did you find it?"

Coop sighed. "No. But there's one more wall over there, if I can get to it. God, this place is a firetrap." He began shoving boxes and old desks out of his way.

Grant helped and before long they'd created a narrow path to the wall and Coop suddenly stopped.

"What is it?" Grant asked.

"I think it's the door to a crawl space."

Grant took one look at the faded whitewash of the wooden hatch. "That's got to be it. Open it up."

"Can't." Coop frowned. "The lock is completely rusted. Look at this thing; it must have an inch of rust on it."

"Bust it open."

"I can't just break the lock."

"Why? We've come this far. Don't tell me you're getting all righteous on me now. Just add destruction of property along with our breaking and entering."

Coop's eyebrow lifted. "No wonder you're here," he teased.

"Not funny."

"Why *are* you here, anyway?" Coop looked around for something strong enough to break the lock.

"Got caught holding a knife for a friend at school and they expelled me."

"Yeah. That'll do it. C'mon, help me find something to bust this open."

"Will this do?" Grant held up a rusty sledgehammer.

"Perfect."

The lock broke off in two swings. Grant edged closer as Coop opened the hatch.

"Anything?" he asked as Coop poked his head inside with a penlight.

"Nothing. It's an empty crawl space."

"So what does it mean? Where's the tunnel end?"

"According to the blueprints and our little tour here, it goes nowhere."

CHAPTER 18

Monday morning, Grant pushed through a crowd of shouting students in the science hall to find Thomas and Terrence Treybelle rolling on the floor throwing punches. Thomas flailed on the bottom with a bloodied fat lip and cut eyebrow.

"You fucked up, man. You almost cost us the game. Why can't you just do what I say?" Terrence hauled back his fist to send the message home.

Thomas rolled, avoiding the hit causing his twin's knuckles to meet the tiles. He seized the moment and jumped on Terrence, gaining the upper hand.

"Ain't that why we're here? Yeah, I fucked up. I listened to you, *big bro. We're* the reason Aunt Betty cries herself to sleep at night. I'm sick of followin' you straight to hell!" Before he could connect with Terrence's face, a strong arm grabbed and held his wrist.

"That's enough. Both of you, in my office, now!" A heavyset man dressed in a security uniform pulled Thomas up by his collar and Terrence by his arm. The crowd started to break up and head toward their classes as the man escorted the boys to the office.

Grant heard his name called above the hallway din. He turned to see Parker Boggs from his science class.

"Hey, did you hear Billy's back?" The boy almost dropped his load of books, sneezing into his hand.

"No. Have you seen him?"

"Yeah. He's still butt-ugly, but at least he doesn't have bugs."

Parker sniffed at a stream of glistening snot edging its way toward his top lip.

"Right," Grant said moving faster. "I'll catch him later. Thanks."

"I still wouldn't get too close to him," Parker called out.

* * *

Billy had returned all right. But which Billy, Grant wondered? He looked like him, had zits like him, dressed the same, but something was missing. After partnering up in art class for a small project together, Grant finally figured out what had come up missing—his personality. The already too quiet, shy boy had slipped away completely leaving only a greasy-haired, glassy-eyed zombie in its place.

Coop noticed the strange behavior too, offering Grant a questioning look. When Grant considered what the kid had been through, he realized Billy was entitled to act a little weird. His skinny arms still held the telltale signs of scarring from the deep wounds he'd inflicted. His vacant expression reflected his flat tone.

"Hey, Billy," Grant had said coming into class. "How's it goin'?"

The boy stared past him. "Fine."

Later, as they'd worked together, Grant had to keep reminding him what they were to do with the large white paper.

"So, how are you feeling? You on any medicine or anything?" Grant finally asked.

"No." Billy laid his paintbrush aside and stared straight ahead.

Grant leaned closer and spoke low. "Heard anything at night?"

The boy looked puzzled.

"You know. Any more voices or midnight walks?"

"I don't know what you're talking about. Are we almost through?" the boy asked.

"No, man. We've got another half hour. What's your problem?" Grant felt his frustration rising.

"No problem. I'm fine."

"Don't you remember when we talked in your room about weird things going on here?"

Billy frowned and shook his head.

"You said you started sleepwalking after learning about the hole."

"What hole?"

Grant shoved his chair back and sighed as the boy sat in a daze beside him. He resembled an empty shell. What had happened to him?

Grant tried one last time to shake him out of it.

"You know I made the football team. Mind if I stop by your room later to have another look at that Joe Namath pigskin?"

Billy's hand tightly gripped his brush making rote circular movements on the page. "I don't have a football."

"Sure you do. You showed it to me. Said your dad got it from Joe Namath."

"No football." He dipped his brush into the paint again.

"I think you have enough on the brush." Grant watched the glistening tempera splatter across the table in large drops.

Billy pressed harder on the page, continuing the same motion. The dark red splotch bled through the surface and the paintbrush began to shred the paper beneath.

Grant grabbed his hand. "Stop it!"

He focused his mind and tried to hear Billy's thoughts, but the only whispers Grant heard came from nearby students wondering what happened. He heard nothing from Billy.

Coop looked up briefly from his desk. "Problem?"

"No. We're okay." Grant kept his hand firmly over Billy's, feeling it tense and release, tense and release as if in a spasm.

When Coop went back to his work, Grant let go and watched in horror as the boy's hand restarted the mechanical motion. Billy's dark eyes locked straight ahead.

After class, Grant lagged behind to talk to Coop. He didn't much care if he turned up late to his next class. In fact, he wanted to go back to his room for the rest of the day. Billy's actions had been upsetting. What had they done to him in the hospital, and why had they released him when he obviously still needed treatment?

Coop collected the wet pictures from the tables, hanging each one on a thin wire at the back of the room with clothespins. "What's up?"

Grant sat on a tabletop, picking the paint from his nails. "Billy's up. Did you see him?"

"He's a little backward. Maybe he's just getting into the swing of things again."

"No. There's something wrong with him. He's not right. He didn't remember anything we'd talked about before he went to the hospital, not even about his prize football from Joe frickin' Namath."

"He must have had some kind of counseling in the hospital. What he did bordered on suicide, although that's not the scuttlebutt in the teacher's lounge. They all seem to think he's just acting out for attention."

"That's not all. I can't read him," Grant said.

"What do you mean?"

"I couldn't hear his thoughts. It's like his hard-drive is blank."

"I see. But you don't usually get readings on everyone, and you said you have no control over it. Maybe his emotions weren't strong enough to send a signal." Coop shrugged.

"Maybe. I don't know. This time it's different. I usually get *something*. A vibe at least."

Grant collected his books, then stopped. Coop's posture had gone suddenly rigid beside the table where Billy's picture lay.

"Look at this." Coop held up the soggy paper by its ragged edges.

Paint bled down the page, dripping onto the floor from the large round circle in the center. Grant recognized it immediately, but had no idea what it meant. Billy had painted an identical impression of the manhole cover, complete with its perimeter markings.

* * *

That night after lights out, Grant lay awake in bed, hands clasped behind his head. He couldn't get Billy's blank expression out of his mind and the painting he'd created without even looking. The kid had seemed hypnotized. Grant had been unable to hear anything in his head, just like the time with Mrs. Bobis.

In the third grade, Grant had been forced to walk to school every day because of his mom's work schedule. It was a ball-numbing walk in the winter, but he tagged along with a large group of boys who whipped insults and snowballs at one another to keep warm.

The crossing guard was an elderly woman named Elizabeth Bobis, who looked older than dirt to Grant and his young friends, but he found out later, she was only seventy. Not nearly Neanderthal after all. She stood about four-foot-nine with thick white curls poking out from her hooded parka, over a beak-like nose and pudgy cheeks. She looked as though she might topple over any minute from the multiple layers she wore to keep warm. She'd sit on a small folding chair to rest, making her look like one of the Eskimo elders waiting to die out in the snow.

He often wondered why no one bothered to bring her a thermos full of hot chocolate. It seemed the least the parents could do while she risked frostbite to cross the Fontaine Elementary brats.

The kids all liked Mrs. Bobis or Mrs. Bo, as she allowed them to call her. She always had a warm smile, and Grant figured her dentures were probably frozen to her gums by the time she crossed her last set of kids. No need for adhesive.

He noticed he could *always* read Mrs. Bo's thoughts, and it disturbed him. That had never happened before. Over the years, he'd gotten to know the ol' girl quite well, even though they'd never said more than hello.

He knew she had a daughter in Poughkeepsie, divorcing a man Mrs. Bo had never liked, and she'd unknowingly shared her struggled over whether or not to redecorate her bathroom because she needed to save her money for Christmas. He'd also come to know much more than he ever wanted to about her overactive bladder. Grant didn't understand until much later why he could read her on a daily basis.

One January day, he trudged along with his friends, wishing he could go back home because in his mind, they should have called a snow day. He couldn't see two feet ahead and the blizzard-like, whipping winds forced traffic to crawl slower than he walked. He stumbled twice, nearly losing his sack lunch in the tall drifts along the way. To make matters worse, he hadn't studied for his math test. He tried to come up with a good reason to leave school early today. Then it happened.

As his group reached the corner, Mrs. Bo waited for them, bundled up in her chair. Something was wrong. Grant focused on her thoughts, trying to hear something—anything.

He raced ahead of his friends through the heavy drifts. Frigid ice flakes stung his eyes as the boys ran shouting to catch up.

When he reached her, Mrs. Bo's eyes stared ahead. Her blue tinged mouth hung open under a stream of iced snot. She didn't move or acknowledge the boys when they slammed into one another behind Grant.

"What it is, Grant? What's going on?"

"Oooh, shit," one of the boys said.

Grant tentatively reached out his gloved hand and touched her snow covered shoulder. "Mrs. Bo? You all right?"

Randy Blanchard jerked Grant back, his eyes mere slits against the sleeting snow. "Jesus Christ! She's dead!"

The group pressed closer for a better look, hanging on to one another for balance and courage. Several of the boys backed away.

"She's frozen! Look at her eyes," a kid said.

Grant stared at the purple hue under her chin. He tried to pretend it was all a joke. She couldn't be dead. He'd come to know her as his silent friend. Her thoughts had been entertaining and sometimes sad, but he knew her on a more personal level than any of these boys. Now she sat here in the cold, an empty shell.

"Maybe she's just sleeping," someone suggested.

"She's probably drunk. That's what my dad looks like every Friday night," another boy smirked.

Grant barely heard them. He'd known she was dead before he reached the corner. There'd been only silence in her mind.

Silent like Billy.

He watched Joe across the room sleeping with one arm hanging off the bed and the covers balled up in a wad at the foot. He'd been restless tonight, flipping and turning frequently. Quietly, Grant slid from the bed and into his slippers. He removed the chair he'd bolted against the door after Joe fell asleep, and turned the knob. The hall's dusky light slithered across the floorboards as he slipped outside. Closing the door behind him, he took a deep breath and headed toward Billy's room.

The old sleepwalking excuse might just come in handy if he got caught, and it wouldn't be far from the truth. He tried to come up with a reason to give Billy when he awakened him in the middle of the night, but his mind came up blank. He'd have to figure that out when he got there.

His slippers scuffed along the threadbare hall carpet to the end of the hall. He stopped briefly when a loose floorboard cried out in alarm.

Finally, he reached Billy's door and looked around. No one knew he was up. He raised his knuckles to knock, but stopped when he heard the sound of giddy laughter coming from inside the boy's room. His heart sank when he realized Billy's roommate had returned. They sounded like they were having one hell of a good time.

After coming this far, he couldn't go back and decided he'd pretend to want in on the fun. If Billy had returned to normal, he could make an excuse after a few minutes and leave. From the sounds of the racket going on inside, Billy had not only snapped out of his stupor, he'd learned to lighten up and have fun.

Grant knocked and waited. The laughter stopped suddenly and he heard hushed whispers and bare feet padding. He grinned when he pictured Billy and his roommate rushing to get into bed to pretend to be asleep.

He knocked again and said in a loud whisper, "Hey, Billy. It's Grant. Open up."

Silence. He waited.

"Billy?"

Suddenly he heard a dog growling near the door and he backed away. He'd been chased once by a pit bull on his way home from school and had harbored a fear of growling dogs ever since. He listened and waited until the sound stopped. This time he knocked harder.

"Let me in. What are you guys doing?"

After several moments, Grant decided to swallow his fear and try the door. He didn't hear the dog anymore and wondered if the boys were playing tricks on him. He wiped his sweaty palm on his pajama bottoms and turned the knob. It opened easily and he waited for a vicious charging canine, but nothing happened.

"Billy?" he asked moving into the room.

His eyes stung at a strong urine scent. He coughed and fanned the air before him. "Hey. What's going on in here?"

The roommate's bed remained neatly made. No one was there. Grant scanned the dimly lit room, and gasped. He fell back, catching his balance on a nearby chair. It couldn't be! Icy sweat drenched his body as he slid along the wall toward the door. It had to be a joke.

No one was in the room but Billy, but he wasn't sure the *thing* he saw, was Billy. Grant's eyes trailed upward where his friend hovered three feet above the bed like a giant spider. He moved closer looking for strings, or wires, or anything that would hold the boy's weight.

Billy's arms stretched out as though he'd been nailed to an invisible crucifix, his lips stretched into a tight grimace. Sunken ebony sockets stared above protruding cheekbones, sharp enough to pierce the skin. Urine stained briefs exposed skinny, scarred legs that hung crossed at the feet.

A barrage of rapid whispers swept past Grant, sending chills along his neck. He whirled around to see nothing there.

Another cluster of low voices brushed his ears, this time loud enough for him to catch what they said.

"Join us..."

Billy's head tilted as they spoke. His gravel voice shifted into that of an old man's. "You are chosen. Join us."

Grant watched in horror as a fresh trickle of urine bled down Billy's crossed legs.

"You are chosen!" Billy's garbled voice broke into croaking laughter and he slowly descended toward the bed.

Grant turned and bolted. His lungs fought for a breath. He raced down the hall praying Joe hadn't locked the door. The sight of his room just a few feet away spurred him faster. He pushed inside the room and slammed the door behind him. He closed his eyes, breathing hard as he pressed his back against the solid wood.

Joe jolted up, turning on his bedside lamp. "What the hell are you doing, Taylor?"

Grant couldn't talk. His breath came in short rasps.

"Jesus. You look like you've been in a fight. What happened?"

Finally, Grant moved to his bed and sat for a moment with his head between his palms. "It's Billy."

"What about him?" Joe said.

Grant jumped up. "We've got to tell someone. Where's the floor chaperone?"

"Whoa, man. Sit down and tell me what's going on."

"You wouldn't believe me."

"I've been here a long time. Try me."

Joe listened without comment, lighting a cigarette. He didn't interrupt as Grant told what happened. When he finished, Grant waited for a response, or sound advice. If what he'd seen *had* been Billy, the kid needed help, if not, they were all in danger.

He watched his roommate snub out the cigarette and blow the last smoke stream into the air. "Man, I told you that kid was weird, but that must have been one hell of a nightmare. Remember what I told you the first day?"

Grant shook his head, unsure of anything.

"I told you to mind your own business." With that, he turned out the light and lay back down.

Grant sat in darkness listening for something at the door, wondering what to do next.

"Joe?" he tried.

No answer.

"Joe! I think we should tell someone."

"You hear anyone gettin' murdered out there? If there was a naked wet kid levitating down the hall, don't you think ol' Mrs. Franklin would be screaming for the marines? Now shut up and go to sleep!"

He knew Joe had to be right. By now, one of the chaperones would have heard or seen something. Could it have been a nightmare?

Grant forced himself to get into bed, pulling the covers close. He lay in the dark thinking and listening for a long time. Once again, he found himself alone and no one believed him.

CHAPTER 19

After class the next morning, Coop listened carefully as Grant explained the previous night's events. He'd noticed the strange look that crossed Grant's face when he saw Billy in class. Now, he understood why Grant had looked like he'd wanted to jump out of the window when the kid sat down beside him.

He wasn't sure he completely believed what Grant said, but throughout his teaching career, he'd learned to spot a tall-tale when it came his way. By the look on the boy's face, he knew Grant believed it. Given the strange events he'd witnessed personally and those described in his uncle's journal, he decided to let him finish before coming to any conclusions.

"He was floating above his bed!" Grant paced before the desk. "What the hell could it mean?"

Coop shuddered at the image of a Christ-like Billy levitating in the dark room. No wonder Grant looked pale. He hated to ask his next question, but had no choice; he had to know if Grant had hallucinated. "Are you sure you weren't sleepwalking again?"

"No way. It was too real!" The boy shoved a chair with his foot, sending it across the polished tiles. "Why won't anyone believe me?"

"Okay. Slow down, Grant. I believe you saw something that scared you. You're sure it wasn't some kind of trick?"

Grant pinned him with a look. "For one thing, Billy isn't evil enough *or* smart enough to come up with a stunt like that. And two, there were no wires or anything—believe me, I checked. Anyway, how could he have rigged himself up there like that? There was no one else in the room."

"Sometimes in the dark, our eyes play tricks—"

"Then how do you explain the voices and his eyes...Jesus, those eyes!" Grant started pacing again.

"What did the voices say?" Coop studied him carefully.

"At first I couldn't really understand them, they spoke too fast. Then finally Billy said—but it wasn't Billy's voice—that I should join them because I'd been chosen."

"Join *them*?"

"Yeah. Like a gang or something. But I couldn't see anyone else there."

"Have you told anyone besides Joe?"

"Are you kidding? This is between you and me."

"Did you go back and check on Billy after you told Joe?"

"I couldn't make myself go near his frickin' door and Joe didn't seem too worried about it. I don't think he really believed me. I wussed out."

"You're no wuss." Coop tapped a pencil against his teeth, thinking. "Maybe it's better that Joe doesn't accept your story for now. Let's try to figure this out before it gets out of hand." He leaned forward. "I wonder if Billy would have been okay if you'd gone back."

"Yeah like in horror flicks when the person finally gets someone to come with them and everything's back to normal. You saw Billy this morning. He's fine. If I'd ask him about it, he'd deny it like all the other stuff he conveniently can't remember."

Coop knew something terrible had happened in Billy's room and if it had happened like Grant said; only an exorcist could help them now. "Listen, Grant. I've made an appointment to see a friend of mine this afternoon about those manhole markings. He's a linguistics professor at Harper University. I can't help thinking that all these events are somehow tied to the tunnel. Meantime, you need to make sure you stay in your room at night, no matter what. Got it?"

A fresh rush of sweat drench Grant's forehead.

"No problem. I'm not goin' anywhere."

"Good." Coop scribbled on a piece of paper. "Here's my cell phone number if you need me. I'll leave early this afternoon and be back for class tomorrow."

Grant pocketed the paper on his way out the door. "I hope so. The last time a teacher told me that, I never saw him again."

THE ACADEMY

* * *

Coop relaxed in the comfortable leather chair, waiting for Dr. George Batten. The professor's office would be the envy of any librarian with walls of dusty leather bound books filling every available shelf and spilling into neat stacks on the floor. Coop took note of the mounds of paperwork on the large oak desk and wondered how a man of seventy-something managed to teach, guest lecture, and play racquetball on a regular basis. *He* got winded taking his morning twenty minute jog.

He recalled his days as Dr. Batten's student. Even then, the man had been a powerhouse of energy and drive, always pushing his students to accept nothing and question everything. Although a linguistics professor, he had proven his talents as a great historian, with a strong interest in religion.

He'd managed to keep in touch with George after his own teaching career took off, with many late night discussions about the ways of the world and his role in the lives of so many troubled inner city kids. The man became his friend and mentor as he struggled to find his niche in the world of education. In Coop's mind, George was the perfect man for this job, on a professional level, as well as personal.

The door opened and closed behind him and he heard his friend's low chuckle.

"Well, well. Is the world finally coming to an end?" George rounded the spacious desk and took a seat. His crystal blue eyes sparkled under the office light as he placed a liver spotted hand to his snow-white beard.

Coop shrugged. "I hope not. Why? Do you have some insight, Professor?"

"Not at all. But what other reason could there be for Dreeson Cooper to come calling on an old scholar like me?"

Coop offered a thin smile.

"Ah. I see it is far more serious than I'd imagined. I'd hoped you were simply here to tell me the good news of your engagement, or perhaps a promotion." His stare lingered on Coop as he waited for an answer.

"No, George. It's bigger than either of those and far more dangerous."

The man shoved aside a small pile of papers and clasped his hands before him. "Let's have it. I'm turning seventy-three in a few weeks. Considering the laws of nature, we should probably proceed quickly."

His playful grin put Coop at ease. He knew he could tell George anything—no matter how bizarre.

Coop pulled out the paper with the manhole markings from his jacket pocket, and tossed it onto the desk. "What do you make of that?"

George slipped his rectangle shaped glasses onto the bridge of his nose and furrowed his fuzzy brows. Coop thought of Santa looking over his naughty-nice list.

"Yes, yes, yes," the man said.

Coop waited in silence giving the man all the time he needed to translate the mysterious symbols.

"Uh-huh," George mumbled as he copied the markings onto a separate sheet of paper.

Coop fidgeted in his seat trying to be patient. The wall clock's ticking only made the wait seem longer. Finally, his old friend removed his glasses and sat back in the plush leather office chair.

"Well? What's the verdict?" Coop asked.

"First of all, where did you find this phrase?"

"So it *is* a language. I knew it."

"Absolutely. Where did it come from?"

"That's the hard part. It doesn't make sense."

The old man chuckled. "Now that's a good one. Why don't you try me?"

It took only a few minutes for Coop to relay the details about his uncle's suspicious death, the weird occurrences at the academy, and finally the manhole cover. When he finished telling him the most recent events, George merely lifted his eyebrows and nodded.

"Well? What is it?" Coop asked again.

"The markings are Aramaic, one of the world's oldest forms of written language. The language of Jesus Christ, if you will. But I must tell you that this language has undergone some evolutions from its original style, which is thought to be around the ninth century B.C. This form of the language was, in fact, used long before the birth of our good Lord."

Coop wondered how the markings got on a manhole cover at a boy's school only a century old. Someone had gone to a lot of trouble to carve them into a steel plate that would remain more or less hidden from sight. Why?

"My question is what is it doing on a manhole cover at a boy's academy?" The professor cleaned his glasses with a hanky.

"Can you translate what it says?" Coop asked.

THE ACADEMY

"Oh, yes. Of course. I've already done that. The phrase means nothing out of context, but it says—quote—Judgment savors the purest souls—end quote. Mean anything to you?"

Coop repeated the phrase over several times, trying to make it fit into the crazy puzzle. "Nope. You said it's out of context. Do you think there's more to it?"

"Oh most definitely. This didn't just drop out of the sky. It's most likely part of a longer text, perhaps a lost scripture of some kind. There are many such documents all over the world. The general public is naturally unaware of their existence due to the political and religious fallout it would cause."

"How in the world did someone at Knollwood Academy get a hold of something like this?" Coop asked.

"Not by accident, I can assure you. I'd be most interested to see the rest of the text, if you should come across it."

"You'd be the only one I trust."

"What about the boy?" the professor asked.

"Grant? What about him?"

"You might warn him not to mention this to anyone until we know what the implications are. You've said he's experienced several paranormal occurrences since discovering the cover. Perhaps he is in danger."

"Well, like I said, he didn't really discover it. His roommate showed it to him and made him promise not to say anything."

"If I were you, I'd look into just how many other boys have knowledge of this tunnel. It could prove deadly if you don't."

"Why is that?"

"The phrase itself is unclear, but if I understand its meaning correctly, it sounds like a warning."

* * *

On his way back from Harper University, Coop thought long and hard about his mentor's last words. He didn't know what kind of warning it could be, except to keep the boys away from the tunnel for safety reasons. But what good would that do when it's written in an ancient language that no one can read?

He'd hoped to have a better understanding about the phrase and what it might mean for Knollwood when he left Dr. Batten's office, but now he had more questions than answers. None of it fit. Not the accidents, or the paranormal incidents of young Grant. Maybe they weren't related at all, and he had wasted his time. If he hadn't let his overactive imagination take over, he would have contacted some sort of authority besides Koch the minute he'd read his uncle's journal. Perhaps he could have spared Billy or Artie the grief they'd suffered.

As a new faculty member, he had to be careful not to ask too many prying questions. He'd taken a chance in securing the blueprints by bribing the janitor—a move that had assured an unspoken trust between the two of them. Mr. Turner would lose his position for drinking on the job, and Coop had no business with the school's blueprints. Still, any further inquiries to Mr. Turner might arouse suspicions and send the man straight to Mumsford, or the administrator. He couldn't afford to get fired before he found out the truth. This dead end slowed his investigation, making him helpless to act.

He startled when his cell phone buzzed in the seat beside him. His pulse jumped at the number.

"Grant? What's up?" he answered.

"Coop, you've got to get back here now," Grant sounded breathless.

Coop's foot pressed the accelerator. "Are you all right?"

"Yeah. But they just found Thomas Treybelle slam dunked underneath a basketball hoop."

CHAPTER 20

Coop's blood ran hot when he learned there'd been another *accident* to add to the school's list. He made it in time to see the janitor and his crew cleaning up. He hadn't been prepared for the scene. When Grant told him they'd found Thomas under the basketball hoop, he'd figured the boy had fallen and hurt himself. Coop pushed past the onlookers to find the boy's twin, Terrence, surrounded by teachers. Mr. Turner, the janitor, stood near the bleachers in shock.

Coop learned the two boys had been serving their detentions by helping Mr. Turner in the gym. When the man had gone into the back to raise the hoops electronically, the boys had started shooting baskets.

According to Terrence, Thomas had barreled down the court trying to outdo his brother's last shot. He'd slam dunked the ball and hung on to the rim, swinging hard as the hoop rose. Terrence had yelled for him to get off when he heard a loud creaking sound coming from the motors above. As Thomas swung, the whole device broke loose, coming down on top of him, pinning him underneath.

Mr. Turner wiped the sweat from his paste colored forehead and sat down. "I can't believe the boy wasn't killed."

Workers had begun cleaning up the mess and Coop watched as the string mops turned bright red. It sickened him to know he'd been unable to prevent another tragedy. His anger ignited at the sight of police Chief Koch standing across the gym interviewing a teacher. Coop shot him a searing look.

The chief offered an arrogant smirk.

Coop stalked over to Lucas.

"Hey, Koch!" he called.

The man turned briefly from his conversation and frowned.

Coop came up beside him keeping a tight reign on his clenched fist. "Tell me this didn't happen. Tell me this is just another *accident*. How many does that make altogether, or can you count that high?"

The gym teacher Koch had been interviewing moved away from the stand off.

"I'm in the middle of an interview. I should arrest you for hindering an investigation," the chief said.

"You won't arrest me. There's no money in it."

The chief sucked in a breath as if he'd been cut.

Coop continued, "Why don't you get to the bottom of these attacks and stop them?"

An officer came up behind him. "Everything all right here, Chief? This guy need to go in or somethin'?"

Lucas shook his head. "No, Paul. The new art teacher was just leaving. Weren't you?" His eyes narrowed.

Everyone stared at Coop. He knew he could leave it alone and get out of it by claiming he was upset. If he didn't back off he'd probably lose his position at the school *and* his chance to find out what was going on. Koch knew he had him.

He left the gym feeling all eyes following him.

Later, when he talked to Grant, Coop caught on something the boy said.

"Wait. What did you say about voices?" he asked him.

"When they fought yesterday, Terrence yelled at Thomas about hearing voices and how he needed to pay more attention to the real world."

"So Thomas had been hearing voices?"

"I guess. Just like Billy…and me." The terrified look in Grant's eyes spurred him past anger to confront the one person who could explain the truth about the academy.

He strode toward the gym doors with Grant on his heels.

"Where are you going?"

"I'll be back soon. I need to have a little talk with my mechanic."

* * *

Coop's Jeep came to a grinding halt on Mitch's gravel driveway in a cloud of dust. His first stop at Bill's Auto in town had been a waste of time when he learned that ol' Mitch had taken the day off. Mitch's boss looked disgusted about it.

"Asshole's prob'ly nursin' another hangover," he said shoving his horn-rimmed glasses back up his sweaty nose. "Try 'im at home." He flicked a cigarette butt out the window.

Coop's ire grew fierce when he pictured Mitch sitting at home relaxing while kids dropped like flies at the academy. He fumed with the desire to rearrange the lazy grease monkey's attitude, but not before he got some answers.

He had a strong suspicion the little jerk knew more than he was telling and vowed Mitch would spill his guts today, one way or the other. His fingers clenched against his sweaty palms in anticipation of meeting the mechanic's stubbled cheek. He would make Mitch pay.

He pounded hard on the faded wooden door, receiving several splinters in the process. The dilapidated porch swayed and creaked under his boots.

No answer. He looked around at the beat up Harley in the drive beside the battered garage. He kicked at the door with a few selective curses, and a threat to tear it off its rusty hinges if he didn't open up. Finally, he heard a lazy click and the door opened a crack. Coop pushed his way inside.

Mitch stepped aside in his underwear, eyes and mouth wide open. "You can't just come in here like that! What's your problem?"

Coop didn't miss a beat. He slammed the mechanic against the paint chipped wall causing Mitch's head to bounce. "Listen, asshole. You'd better come up with some fast answers about the academy."

Mitch's Adam's apple bobbed helplessly up and down against Coop's forearm. "I don't know what you mean, man."

"Sure you do." Coop pushed him onto the couch. "You've been hinting and warning me about the place for weeks, and now suddenly you don't know what I'm talking about?"

Mitch straightened and raised his bony chin in defiance. "No. I don't."

"We'll see. I have a pair of brass knuckles in my Jeep just waiting to engrave themselves on your face. Wait here and I'll get them."

Mitch shot up in a flash. "Hold on, Coop. Let's talk about this." He ran a hand through his disheveled mane and headed to the kitchen. "Want a beer?"

"I want answers. Now." Coop leaned against the kitchen counter and waited for Mitch to pop open a beer for himself. He watched him gulp down half the can before he belched and took a seat at the kitchen table.

Coop moved a chair away from the overflowing garbage can and sat. "Let's have it."

Mitch chugged the rest of the can and tossed it into the kitchen sink. "Guess this calls for some reinforcements," he said on his way to the cupboard where he took out a half empty bottle of whiskey.

"Join me?" He raised the bottle.

"No. Just get to the story."

"Have it your way." He uncapped it and took a long swig. "Mutha's milk for the damned."

His bloodshot eyes fixed on Coop.

Mitch lowered his voice as if someone might hear as he pinned Coop with his gaze. "This is no bullshit."

"For your sake, it'd better not be." Coop leaned forward.

"All right. This here's the story of Knollwood Academy, otherwise known as Hell.

Coop knew the man was telling the truth by the fear in his eyes. Rivulets of sweat formed on his forehead, as the mechanic picked at his grease-stained fingernails. He listened as Mitch relayed his experiences at Knollwood. His blood turned to ice when Mitch told him about a pool incident involving a student and how he'd seen the kid a few nights before out in the yard standing beside the manhole cover with Mitch's roommate, Cliff Travis. They'd argued when the kid, Jake Connally, had refused to go down into the hole. Finally, Jake had stalked away giving Cliff the finger. The next time he saw Jake, he'd been surrounded by blood and bones in the pool.

"I knew something was up with that hole in the ground then, but I tried to chalk it up to coincidence. But I *knew*. And it's a good thing I did, because not too long after that, ol' Cliff tried to get me down there, too."

"What happened?" Coop asked.

"By then I knew my time at the academy was running out. My parents had died, and I was almost eighteen. I had no real reason to stay." Mitch leaned in as if to share a secret. "I'll tell you what. I believe that's the only reason I'm alive today. If I'd have seen that hole, I'd either be dead or missing."

"Why is that?" Coop asked.

"Because once you've been introduced to it, you're chosen."

The words made Coop sit up straight. "Chosen?"

"Yeah. I saw it one other time when a new kid went missing shortly after he'd come in. Cliff had mentioned he was going to show the kid around one night, and a couple of days later, the kid disappeared. Everyone thought he went back home or something, but I knew better."

"Whatever happened to Cliff?" Coop asked.

"See that's just it. After I left, I tried to make contact, and he never got back to me. I've never been able to find any of the guys I knew well. It's like they fell off the earth. Everyone but me. Guess I'm the lucky one." He tipped the bottle to his lips once more and suckled like a babe.

"Why didn't you tell anyone you selfish prick?" Coop pressed.

"Who the hell would have believed me?"

"Do you know how many boys have been victimized? How can you live with yourself?"

"Look. Don't judge me until you know what it's like. I've lived with the guilt for years, but there's nothing I can do. The place is evil and it controls those inside. If you don't get out, it will get you, too."

"Maybe. But I'm willing to take a chance and try and stop it."

"You can't stop it! Don't you see? It's Satan, man! He's in control. Get out while you can."

Coop knew the booze had finally caught up with him. His glassy eyes tried to focus as he yawned, belched, and finally laid his filthy head onto the crumb-ridden table. He left him like that, letting the screen door slam behind him.

On his way home, Coop reviewed what Mitch had revealed, trying to put the pieces together. It all seemed too unbelievable, yet the fear in Mitch's eyes had been raw. Perhaps he had every right to spend his free time pickling his liver. He'd barely escaped the mouth of hell.

Coop slammed on his brakes and pulled to the roadside. Mouth! That had to be it. Grant's description of the moist lining of the tunnel and its white muscular probe finally made sense given the translation! "Judgment savors the purest souls" meant only one thing—the hole was a giant mouth.

* * *

The next afternoon, Grant found himself in Terrence's room at a loss for words. The boy sat on his bed, cradling his basketball and staring off into space. Awards, trophies, and photos lined the walls and shelves of the room he shared with his twin.

"Any word on Thomas?" Grant turned a chair backwards and sat facing the bed.

"He's holdin' his own. A lot of internal bleeding," the boy stopped.

"Sorry about that. Are you going to stay here?"

"Got to. It's that or I'll end up on the streets again and that would kill my Aunt Betty. Thomas was right. We *are* the reason for all her problems." He looked past Grant and out the window at the gray skies. "It should have been me under that hoop. He didn't deserve this."

"That's not true. No one deserved it. It was an accident," Grant tried to convince him.

"I don't know, man. All his talk about hearing voices and then he started losin' his game. I could see it at practice. He just wasn't right. I even caught him trying to get out the door of our room one night, like he was in a trance or somethin'." Terrence shook his head. "He must have had a lot on his mind. That's why I got so angry when he nearly lost that game. He'd been out the night before instead of practicing, and it almost cost us."

"Where'd he go?" Grant asked.

"I think he went out with Joe. I don't know for sure, but he came back talkin' some mess about a hole in the ground and I told him the only hole he should be worried about was the one he kept missin' on the hoop," Terrence's voice broke.

Grant nearly squirmed off the chair. "What hole? Where did he say it was?"

"I told you I didn't pay attention to what he was sayin'. He wasn't making any sense and I didn't want to hear it. I should have listened though. Should have done a lot of things."

Grant knew exactly what Thomas had been trying to tell him, and now he wondered if Billy and Artie had seen it, too. Had Joe warned the others not to tell as well?

Bad things happened to the boys that knew about the hole. Sooner or later, they all had accidents. Everyone except himself, and Joe. Were they different for some reason, or would it only be a matter of time before they got theirs?

CHAPTER 21

The afternoon sun cut a wedge across the floor tiles between Mumsford and his audience in the small meeting room. Coop thought the rotund little man's occipital hairline resembled a clown's grin as he turned to step up to the podium. The headmaster was full of himself today rambling on to staff members about new guidelines to ensure student safety.

"And, therefore, I'm calling for an investigation into the string of unfortunate accidents. We'll all sleep better, knowing Knollwood has, in no way, been negligent or responsible for the recent tragedies."

Coop coughed. Everyone turned to stare.

"A comment, Mr. Cooper?" Mumsford's eyes narrowed.

"Uh, not really. I suppose it's more of a question."

"Please feel free."

"I'm new here, so I'm wondering how long these *accidents* have been going on and why they haven't been investigated until now?"

Coop ignored the shocked stares of the other teachers and locked gazes with Mumsford.

The little man cleared his throat. "There have been other incidents in the distant past, but I assure you they've been thoroughly investigated and the school's good name cleared. You must understand, Mr. Cooper, that in an environment such as this, the old adage 'boys will be boys' applies. Certain occurrences are simply unavoidable."

Yeah, like my uncle Eb and Jose.

As Mumsford droned on through the rest of his meeting notes,

Coop's thoughts drifted to the manhole and how dangerous it had become. In Coop's mind, the tunnel was no longer just a mysterious icon; it had become a direct path to pain and death.

If Mitch had told him the truth, Grant and countless other boys were in danger. Who could tell how many of them had been exposed to the manhole and what the consequences would be when they either accepted or declined the invitation to explore it. He had to find a way to warn them without drawing attention to himself, or he might end up like his uncle.

Both Jose and Uncle Eb had known about the hole, but they hadn't been *chosen* as Mitch had put it. Common sense told him that could be the reason they'd been killed. When poor Jake Connally had refused to enter the hole, he'd sealed his fate by knowing too much and not cooperating. However, cooperating with what, or with whom, was the question. Someone was killing and maiming the boys of Knollwood, and Coop decided he wouldn't stop until he found out the truth. Perhaps his first step should be a short chat with Joe Blockman, who like Mitch's roommate long ago, was the one who found the tunnel and for some reason didn't fear it.

* * *

Later that afternoon, Coop caught Grant in the hallway and pulled him inside an empty classroom.

"Is everything okay with you?" he asked the boy.

"Yeah. Any word on Thomas?"

"Not yet." Coop went on, "Mumsford is planning an investigation into the accidents, but meantime you need to be careful."

Grant nodded and said, "Looks that way. I found out more about Thomas."

Icy daggers of sweat sliced down Coop's back as Grant relayed his conversation with Terrence. Thomas had been introduced to the tunnel not long before his accident.

Grant paced. "Something tells me Billy and Artie knew about it, too. It's like a curse or something."

He told Grant about his conversation with Mitch and watched the boy's mouth twist into a dark frown.

"How come he never told anyone?" Grant wanted to know.

"He was afraid no one would believe him. And he was probably right. At any rate, he might have ended up dead or missing like the others. But he said something else that bothers me."

"What's that?"

Coop met his look. "He said the boys had been chosen."

Grant stared at him. "That's what Billy said that night. That I'd been chosen. What the hell does that mean? Chosen for what?"

Coop sighed, unsure how much to tell him. "Look, I spoke with my friend at Harper University. He translated the markings."

"What do they say?"

"Judgment savors the purest souls."

"What does *that* mean?"

"Remember when you went down the hole? You said it seemed alive with some sort of probe at the bottom."

"Yeah. So?"

"Grant, I think the tunnel is a mouth."

At first, the boy grinned, but when Coop didn't laugh, his expression faded.

"I don't believe it. How could it be a mouth? A mouth has to be attached to something...something alive!" Grant said.

"Exactly. I don't know the details, but it's dangerous and you need to stay away from it."

"No kidding. But what do we do now? If that thing *is* a mouth, then we have to find out what it belongs to. There has to be a way to reach the end of it and I still think it's in the basement. We missed something last time."

"You're not to go down there, got it? Not without me," Coop said.

"But—"

"Got it?" He placed a heavy hand on the boy's shoulder. "I mean it, Grant. Don't do anything until I can get more information."

"How are you going to do that?"

"I need to talk to your roommate. Any idea where he might be?"

Grant dropped his notebook and scrambled to pick it up saying, "Don't. Leave him out of this."

"Why? Doesn't it seem strange to you that he's showed at least two people the cover and then they had an accident? He's doing what Mitch's roommate did years ago with some of the same results. Joe is the only one who knows about it, except you, and he hasn't been affected. It could all be coincidence, but I intend to talk to him. Now you've got to promise me you won't go near that basement, or the hole."

"Okay. I won't. I have too much homework anyway. I'll be stuck in my room all night."

THE ACADEMY

"Good. I'll see you tomorrow in class."
"Right."
Coop watched him blend into the hallway crowd and disappear.

* * *

Grant ignored the guilt as Coop's warning repeated in his head. He knew the basement could be the answer to everything. To his surprise, the door opened easily, as if it hadn't even been locked. He crouched behind a group of boxes when Mumsford unexpectedly came in. He watched the man carefully.

An annoying grating sound filled the room, and Grant craned to see around a stack of boxes. His eyebrows shot up. *So that's how it works.*

When the headmaster removed a loosened piece of wall, he pulled on a metal ring. A closet-size niche became visible, as a partition grated back. Amber light bled outward from two wall sconces inside. As Mumsford raised both palms upward, he began to chant.

Grant couldn't understand the words, but suspected they were the same language as the manhole markings. He listened in sick fascination as the headmaster's voice reached a pitching crescendo.

Suddenly the room fell silent and Grant strained to see what Mumsford fumbled with. *Come on,* Grant silently pleaded. *Move so I can see.* Taking a chance, he quietly inched over, butting up against a nearby box.

He watched as Mumsford undid two strings from around a black cloth. Grant watched in shock as the man stood before a small altar and lifted an item from the material. He began to chant once more as he held a book high above his head.

The room smelled like worms, and a gray haze formed along the damp floor around Grant. He backed further into his corner as it curled around his ankles. The heavy mist covered his legs, seeping through his pants.

Suddenly, Mumsford's voice broke from his chant to speak to someone.

"Master. Our work is nearly complete. The time is near."

Grant heard no reply and then the headmaster spoke again, as if in reply to an unheard response.

"Yes, Master. I understand. Your will be done." With that, he backed out of the narrow alcove and pulled the hidden latch again. The wall creaked back into place and Grant scrambled to avoid being seen.

Relief filled him when the putrid smelling mist dissipated, leaving miniscule crawling fragments over the floor. He waited until Mumsford climbed the basement steps and firmly closed the door. He bit his lip as his shaking fingers wrapped around the hidden latch.

* * *

That evening at home, Coop finished his dinner and tossed the frozen food container into the trash. Some customs die harder than others, his bachelor habits among them.

He moved to his art studio and examined his latest painting attempt still staring blankly back at him from the dusty easel. The aroma of oil paint and turpentine usually stirred his desire to produce a masterpiece and fulfill his creative need, but not tonight. Most likely, his brush would merely bring to life the frightening images that threatened his imagination the most.

His hand reached for the tube of burnt umber, for the darkest tones possible, realizing that his efforts would be a complete waste of time and energy. In the morning's light, he knew he would hastily remove the oily drab mood from the canvas. The idea that his uncle had been murdered had triggered his downward spiral into a murky pit of dread. He knew the academy was the real culprit, dragging everyone in its path straight to Hell.

He couldn't shake the uneasy feeling that something explicitly evil dwelled among the vines and bricks that made up the century old school, something ancient swelling to life even as he paced in the quiet safety of his uncle's home. He shook his head. He hadn't come to think of this house as his own yet and he imagined it might be some time before he could put his uncle's murder behind him

His inability to locate Joe Blockman earlier in the day ate at him and he wondered how a boy who lived at the academy could disappear so completely. No one knew his whereabouts, not even his coach. The whole situation struck Coop as odd, but he'd let it go when Mumsford started questioning him about why he'd become so interested in Joe. There's always tomorrow, he told himself. The kid would have to turn up eventually.

The phone jarred his thoughts and he hurried to answer.

"Coop? I need to see you right away," Grant's voice garbled through heavy static.

"What's happened?"

"…meet me…Knollwood Road…as possible…"

"Grant? Are you there?"

For a moment, Coop thought he heard the roaring sound of distant winds as though a hurricane coursed through the lines. Then the phone went dead.

* * *

As Coop drove, a vicious current coughed up whirlwinds of fallen leaves in front of his Jeep. Tattered veils of dense fog, hung across the unlit road. Ancient trees lined the path as if beckoning him toward the academy grounds. He cut his brights and slowed to see any sign of Grant along the road. His head pounded with a tension headache that had started the minute the phone line cut out. He sped too fast for the wet conditions in a rush to find the boy in hopes that he wasn't too late.

A sudden white flash swooped across the windshield and he swerved to miss it. The Jeep veered off the slick pavement and he hit the brakes, barely missing a huge oak tree. He cut to reverse and pulled back onto the road.

"What the hell was that?"

The Jeep idled while he searched overhead and saw nothing but a hazy night sky. His wet palms gripped the steering wheel as he squinted past the windshield. Ahead, a figure wearing light colored clothes, ambled toward him. Grant.

Coop pushed open the door. "Get in."

The boy complied, his cheeks tomato red from the brisk night air. He clutched a tattered black book close to his chest with one arm and held a can of soda in his other hand.

"Dinner?" Coop nodded toward the can.

Grant flushed. "Yeah. It's all I had time for."

"C'mon. Let's grab something with nutritional value. How about pizza?"

* * *

Back at home, Coop carried in the steaming pepperoni pizza he'd picked up in town. He tossed it onto the kitchen table, and watched Grant tear open the box and bite into a slice before he could offer him a paper plate. The boy held the book tight as he ate.

Coop reached across the table and tapped the old volume. "May I?"

"That's why I called you," Grant muffled around a large bite.

"What is it?"

"I don't know. It's written in that funky language on the manhole cover."

"You mean, Aramaic?"

"I guess." Grant reached for another piece.

Coop opened the frayed cover, and noted it resembled some sort of hardened skin. As he leafed through it, he recognized the same script Dr. Batten had described as Aramaic and frowned at the dark brown ink. Goose flesh chased up his arms as he paged through the manuscript. What had Grant found?

He searched for a publisher name or copyright date and found the book simply started with text. The unusual columns of script reminded him of the Bible and he wondered if it could be some sort of religious document. He knew by its condition the book had to be old. It felt like hardened dust in his hands and he was careful to touch only the edge of each page as he turned.

"Where did you get this?" he asked.

"Never mind." Grant helped himself to a soda from the refrigerator.

"You went into the basement. Damnit, Grant. I told you not to go down there!"

"Look, I had to, okay. I had to for Billy, and Thomas, and even for that jerk, Artie. Don't you get it? For some reason, I haven't been hurt yet. Maybe I'm immune or something. Maybe I tasted lousy when that tongue touched my leg. I don't know, but I had to do something. We both know it's just a matter of time before that thing comes after me."

Coop knew he was right. "Do you mind if I keep the book? I want to take it to Dr. Batten and have him translate some of it. This could be the key to the whole thing, but you can't tell anyone about this. Where in the basement did you find it?"

Coop listened as Grant delivered the details about the hidden niche and Mumsford's latest behavior. Apparently, the man was mentally ill enough to hear voices. The man could be far more dangerous than originally thought.

Grant sat back, and belched. "I'll be in deep shit if anyone ever finds out I took it."

"Then it would be better not to take it back with you."

He noticed Grant's appetite had suddenly halted. "You filled up already?"

Grant shoved the pizza aside. "That's not all I found down there. I heard someone crying...no, more of a high-pitched moaning. I nosed around and finally heard it the loudest when I put my ear to the niche wall. It's like someone's behind it."

"It's probably the pipes."

"I don't think so. It sounded too human."

"Well, don't worry about that now. I'm going to get the book to my friend tomorrow. Meantime, I hope I'm not wasting my breath again when I tell you to stay clear of the basement."

Grant grinned and reached for another slice of pizza.

CHAPTER 22

Grant's sneakers squeaked as he crept toward the main house basement. If he'd learned nothing else at Knollwood Academy, he'd greatly improved his breaking and entering skills. *Mom will be so proud.* He slid inside quietly closing the door behind him.

His ears strained to hear the cries he'd heard earlier.

What if Coop had been wrong? What if somebody needed help?

By now the placement of boxes and stored furniture had become a memorized floor plan in his mind and he snaked among the ruins without running into anything. He moved to the place where the cries had been loudest. Suddenly, he heard someone coming in.

He ducked behind a tall group of boxes and squatted. His heart pounded a beat in his head making his ears throb. He worried it would echo in the silent room. The sound of footsteps and heavy breathing came closer, then stopped. He hoped one of his unruly black curls hadn't given him away. He held his breath. Maniacal laughter broke the solitude, causing him to cringe.

Stubby fingers narrowly missed his face and tugged at a nearby box.

"Ah, hear we are," he heard Mumsford say.

The headmaster giggled and groped with both hands.

When the box of Mumsford's choice caught on an overturned coat rack, Grant carefully nudged the container along. He couldn't risk being caught.

Mumsford's labored breaths rattled as he set the carton on the floor.

Grant peered around to find the man digging inside with both hands.

"Oh, the master will take pride in this and I will be rewarded." He lifted a hamster wheel from the box. "Each token will bring the appropriate element."

Mumsford removed several items and held each one up to the dingy basement light for inspection. Grant realized the man was obviously crazier than anyone knew. *Look at the poor twisted jerk whispering to himself.*

The man examined one piece in particular and smiled. Grant stifled his response when Mumsford cradled a football with a black marker scrawl along the side. It was Billy's treasured Namath football. Could Mumsford be involved in the so-called *accidents*? Why would he keep personal items that would link him to the boys?

Mumsford's nasal voice echoed softly in the room. "Soon my heart will beat joyously in my chest when all prophecy is fulfilled and I am rewarded! Oh, what a glorious day!"

Grant fought the urge to shift his position as a cramp burned up his thigh. He knew he couldn't stay down much longer.

Finally, Mumsford replaced the items as he hummed an unfamiliar tune and shoved the box back.

Grant bit his lip as the pain in his leg shot higher. Finally, heavy footsteps ascended the rickety stairs and the door shut with a bang. Grant let out a long breath and leaned back to stretch his legs. As he massaged his aching muscles, his hand brushed the container of personal items.

When he opened the cardboard flaps and peered inside, his stomach churned. Artie's hamster wheel lay next to Billy's football. Digging deeper, he pulled out several other items that belonged to other boys in the school, including one of Thomas Treybell's smaller trophies. How many victims *were* there? The box's contents reached the top. His mind tried to rationalize what it could mean.

His hand shook when he lifted out his father's lost key chain.

* * *

Coop watched Dr. George Batten's eyes, large behind his rimless glasses. The man sat at his desk, tracing the decrepit book cover with an index finger. His thin lips parted as if he couldn't find the right words. His gaze traveled methodically along the passages inside.

"Well?" Coop leaned closer when he heard the man whisper something. "What's that?"

"Rumors," the old man replied.

"What rumors?" Coop asked.

George stared at him. "For many years there have been stories, rumors, if you will, about a black bible. Many scholars have called the idea absurd and have written it off as an attempt by anti-Christian groups to undermine the true importance and meaning of the Christian bible."

"I've heard of that. It was written by a guy named Lavey."

"Wrong. That was man-made. The black bible I'm referring to was written by Satan himself."

"So what exactly *is* the black bible?"

"Well, if it's everything history claims, it's the anti-bible. Supposedly, it is the exact opposite of the Christian bible. In it, Satan gives counter reasons for everything in God's word to tell the true story of the fall of angels and man alike. Until now, no real proof has substantiated any claim that such a manuscript exists."

"You said, *until now*. Are you saying this is the black bible?" Coop's heart pounded in his ears. *Demons?*

"I'm not sure. I'm afraid it would take years to *officially* prove its authenticity. Remember, there is no real proof that it truly exists."

"Unofficially?" Coop asked.

"It most likely is. I've never encountered anything like it. For one thing, this isn't papyrus or rice paper; it's some sort of skin. I suppose it would make sense, for Satan to sacrifice one of God's creatures in order to write his own story. I'm just not sure which of God's creations it is."

Coop swallowed hard. "It's not human…"

"Like I said, I'm not sure. The ink is unusual as well. The color tells me that is isn't ink at all."

"What is it then?"

"I'd venture to guess it's blood. But then, it will have to be tested to say for certain.

"There's something else of interest. The book appears to be a complete text, which is unusual if it is some sort of bible. Most religious manuscripts are incomplete, usually found in bits and pieces. It takes years to locate the smallest fragments to put together even one full page.

"And look at this." He opened the book and began paging through it. "Although it is written in Aramaic, you can clearly see it holds the exact number of pages as the original bible, even down to the same number of chapters in the first book, which by the way I'm sure, will translate to Genesis. It's as though whoever wrote it, knew exactly what our Bible of today would say. However, I'm positive it is not a modern day document created as a hoax. Based on what I've seen, I would guess this book is at least two thousand years old."

Coop's mouth had gone dry. What were the writings of Satan doing at Knollwood Academy? "George, is there any way to find the rest of the phrase you translated?"

The doctor carefully leafed through the pages. "It might take some time to find."

"I don't think we *have* a lot of time. We need to know what it says before something else happens."

"Right," George said staring ahead in thought. "It translated to, 'judgment savors the purest souls.'"

"Is there anywhere in the Christian bible that might talk about the purest souls and their judgment?"

"Of course. Revelation. It speaks of end times and the battle of Armageddon."

"Then that's a good place to start."

As George opened the book and traced down the verses, Coop paced before the desk with his thoughts running wild. If this book were truly Satan's bible, it would have dangerous implications not only for Knollwood, but for the world itself. He'd never considered himself a religious man, but Coop found the sudden urge to pray as his friend combed through the ancient book.

The minutes ticked as Coop waited. Finally, he grew tired of pacing and sat.

George's voice broke the painful wait. "Here it is." His eyes sparkled at the find. "The original passage is right here, and there *is* more." He frowned and started writing down symbols and letters on a pad of legal paper.

Coop came around to stare over his shoulder, trying to decipher the words for himself. After several minutes, George sat back, wiping the sweat from his brow.

"What does it say?" Coop stared at him.

The man sighed. His face had gone suddenly pale beneath his facial hair.

"Jesus. What is it?"

"It's *not* Jesus. After reading this passage, I'm thoroughly convinced this is indeed Satan's black bible."

"George. Tell me what it says!"

The man avoided Coop's eyes as he spoke the translation. "Judgment savors the purest souls for the chosen soldiers of Armageddon."

"What the hell does *that* mean?"

"It sounds like Satan is building an army for the final battle with God. Like I said, I'll have to go over it slowly to be sure of the translations, and even then, it is subject to diverse interpretation. The Bible itself has many. So much more with this, I would imagine."

"There's that word *chosen*, again. The kids are being singled out. But for what? Some sort of army?"

"It looks that way, Coop. You should get out of there while you can. Who knows what this will bring? You could be next."

"I don't think so. So far, the kids have been the only ones harmed. But the use of the words 'purest souls' doesn't make sense. I mean, these kids are at a boy's academy because of bad behavior. None of them would be considered pure. Why are they chosen?"

"Perhaps I can learn more by further study. I think we should try to discern the manuscript's age. That would be a step in determining if it could possibly be Satan's bible. I have a scientist friend, Johannes Pearlman, who does radiocarbon dating. I'm sure he'd love to get his hands on this."

"Don't take this the wrong way, George, but what difference does it make if it *is* the black bible? The kids at Knollwood are in danger."

"It would make all the difference in the world. We'd know if we're truly dealing with the powers of the dark side, or simply a sick headmaster with delusions of grandeur. It will ultimately show us the right course of action in dealing with the situation."

"*You* believe in demons and the supernatural?" Coop couldn't believe it.

"Of course. In my line of work I would be foolish not to. I'm a university professor. If I'm not open to contemplating the unexplained, I will stagnate and die as a teacher as well as a human. So what do you say? Shall I call him?"

"Won't the testing take months?"

"It used to. Now days the procedure can be done in two or three days. Pearlman owes me a favor or two. I'm sure I can get something back to you shortly. But for now, I'll repeat my warning to you. Get out before it's too late."

* * *

Joe sat on the end of his bed smoking a joint.

Grant waved a hand to fan the smoky haze. "Jeez. Do you have to do that right before bed?"

"It'll help you sleep. Sit down, we need to talk," Joe ordered.

Grant wasn't in the mood. He had many questions he wanted to think about, not discuss. He plopped onto his bed face down, and hugged his pillow. The smell of weed started making him nauseous and he wished Joe would at least have the decency to crack the window before indulging.

"Hey." Joe's voice cut the silence. "You listening?"

Grant's patience grew thin. He longed to be back home in his own room where no one ever bothered him when he needed privacy, not even his mom. A sudden thought intruded, but he forced it back. He was *not* homesick.

Turning over to face his roommate, he said. "Can this wait? I can barely see you through all that goddamn smoke."

The boy's chuckle infuriated Grant more.

"Goin' through mommy withdrawal?" Joe taunted.

Grant stopped. How in the hell had he known that? It had been a fleeting thought and nothing more, a thought he couldn't accept. So why had Joe brought it up?

"What's it to you? I told you, we'll talk later." With that, Grant turned over and closed his eyes.

Suddenly he sat up, gasping. His tongue felt too big for his mouth, blocking his throat. He couldn't breathe. The room became a blur through teary eyes. They burned inside his skull. When he tried to talk, he made only a gruff croak.

He coughed once and managed to take in a gulp of air. His lungs burned as he forced them to fully expand. The feeling eased as he forced another breath. His veins pulsed with hot anger while Joe sat calmly on the end of his bed, finishing his joint.

The boy's dark eyes penetrated Grant's searing gaze making him want to sink into the mattress. The nausea hit him again, but this time he couldn't fight it down. He took off for the bathroom and lifted the lid in time.

His sight blurred again, but he could see well enough to know it wasn't his lunch in the toilet. Black tar poured from his lips as he retched for a third time. He wiped his mouth on a towel and sat on the floor with his back against the wall. White dots spotted his vision and his stomach muscles ached. A bitter, bile taste filled his mouth and he fought back the urge to vomit again.

A shadow moved inside the doorway as Joe leaned casually against the frame. "Feel better?"

Grant sat panting, trying to fight down another wave. He shook his head.

"Too bad. I really wanted to talk to you."

"So talk. I'm not going anywhere," Grant managed, wiping his forehead with a washcloth.

"True." Joe grabbed the desk chair from outside the door and turned it backwards inside the doorway. He rested his elbows on its back and folded his long fingers as if he were about to pray.

"Listen, man. I've been thinking about your situation."

"What situation?" Grant asked.

"You don't belong here. But before you can ever hope to get home, you're going to have to prove yourself. Make amends."

"And how do I do that? I'm here till summer. Then, if I haven't screwed up, I'll probably be able to go back to my old school. You can relax, Joe. You'll have the room all to yourself again."

"That has nothing to do with it. I'm trying to help."

"So what do I do?"

"Think about it. You've failed your family, your mom. You have to make amends."

The words cut sharp. Grant knew he was right, and wondered why he would bother telling him this. Everyone at the school had earned a place here because they'd failed their parents, or the schools, and even themselves. He sat up straight, feeling a little better and stared at his roommate. Joe's excited expression looked as if he'd discovered a world-altering concept. He wondered if the kid was doing more than weed.

"Okay. I'll bite. What should I do?" Grant inched away from the toilet.

"Nothing. Just think about it. I've been giving it some serious thought myself. I'm screwed for life, but you don't have to be if you make the right move when its time."

"And how will I know when that is?"

"You'll know. And when it comes, I bet you'll make the ultimate sacrifice if necessary. You'll do it for your mom."

Later that night, Grant couldn't sleep. He lay in bed listening to Joe snore wondering what their little talk had really meant. He knew Joe wouldn't remember it in the morning. Whatever he'd taken had briefly turned his personality. *Ultimate sacrifice?* Since when did a kid like Joe care about anyone but himself? All the talk about making amends and sacrifices made Grant think of his pastor, Father Bennigan. The guy was definitely fire and brimstone, along with quite a bit of communion wine. But the one thing he'd stressed had been forgiveness of sin and how to get it. Joe must have had a revelation.

Grant settled under the covers and tried to force recent events from his mind. He'd have more than amends to make if the evil loose in Knollwood got to him.

CHAPTER 23

Saturday morning Grant awoke to an empty room. He'd never seen Joe hang around much on the weekends when most kids visited with their parents or guardians. Joe didn't seem to have anyone, and Grant had never brought up the subject. For all he knew, Joe's parents were dead.

He got dressed, wondering if his roommate remembered what he'd said the night before. It had been heavy stuff for a guy like Joe Blockman. The basketball star slash tough guy had never shown that side of himself, and until last night, Grant would have thought it impossible. He decided to forget it. If he brought it up to him, Joe would most likely deny it.

He hated to admit it, but the kid had been right. If Grant ever straightened out, it would be for his mom. She deserved better, no matter what the cost. He'd just have to try harder.

Grant headed down for breakfast with a hollow stomach. He'd never seen a bout of stomach flu come and go so quickly and wondered if it had something to do with Joe's smoking. He'd been around dope for years, starting as young as fourth grade. It had never made him sick before. Maybe Joe had concocted his own mixture, laced with something. Grant decided to leave next time his roommate indulged.

* * *

Grant straddled the Knollwood yard sign as he watched for his mom's car. His shoe kicked the marble at an even pace. He watched several cars pull in to the visitor's lot and the occupants make their way to the main house. Visiting day at the prison. What a life. He tried to burn Joe's words from his mind, but they resurfaced. *You failed your family, your mom.*

It angered Grant he'd even listened to the guy. Joe's pep talk only served to make him feel worse.

Fortunately, his mom was the forgiving kind; he thought about what his father had done and how she'd taken him back. The look on her face when she discovered he'd been cheating burned permanently in his memory. Yet, she'd taken him back. She always took him back.

Then he'd died two years ago, abandoning them both forever. Although Mick Taylor hadn't been the ideal man in either of their lives, they'd both experienced the void of his absence. Grant wondered why he always weighed the actions of other men against his dad, and if he'd eventually turn out like him. He didn't want to be another disappointment in Amanda Taylor's life.

He jumped off the sign, resisting the urge to run, and met the familiar Chevy rambling up the drive. He wanted to go home.

* * *

Amanda cut the engine and sighed. Although the academy had an impeccable reputation rehabilitating young boys, not to mention beautifully landscaped grounds, she squirmed as guilt twisted around her heart like an angry vine. She knew Grant needed to be *somewhere*, she just wasn't sure it was *here*. Maybe Jill had been right that Grant played on her softhearted nature and she needed to stick to her guns. But deep inside, she struggled for peace over her decision.

Although Grant had brought on his own unhappiness, her motherly instincts wanted to quell his disappointment. It amounted to a tug of war, and she'd never been good at games. Amanda wished she could find some solid emotional ground to stand on and fight the drawing tide threatening to wash her and her son over the edge of uncertainty.

It annoyed her that she'd been thinking of Mick lately—asking him what she should do with their Grant. He'd never been there for her during their marriage, why would he help her now?

As Grant approached, she blinked hard in the rearview mirror. Now was not the time. Tears were reserved for her pillow.

He rapped on the passenger window and she smiled, opening the door.

"Hey, handsome. What's up?"

"You're on time." He grinned.

"Why is that a surprise?"

He shrugged. "Just making conversation."

"Actually, I thought I might be a little late. The oil light came on and I had to stop at the auto shop in town. The guy topped it off and gave me hell about needing an oil change. I'll put that on my to do list."

The silence bled into several long seconds. Finally, Amanda forced a smile. "Want to get something to eat?"

Grant's face lit up. "You mean we're leaving here?"

"Just for lunch, buddy."

Grant's expression faltered slightly, trying to hide his disappointment.

"C'mon. Let's go sign you out." She led the way.

* * *

As they passed through the foyer, Grant had an idea. If seeing is believing, his mother couldn't deny the truth any longer. He'd prove his theory by showing her Mumsford's strange collection of personal items in the basement.

He grabbed his mother's hand telling her, "I want to show you something."

An audible sigh escaped her when they stood before the locked basement door. Grant jiggled and maneuvered the stubborn knob to no avail.

"I'm telling you this door is never locked. It's *supposed* to be locked, but I get in all the time." He frowned.

"Grant, the fact that it's locked means you're not *supposed* to be in there. You want to get kicked out of this school, too?"

She grabbed his arm. "C'mon. Let's get going before we both get in trouble."

Grant tried once more, but the knob wouldn't budge. It seemed as if the door had a will of its own.

* * *

They stopped in Grant's room to grab his jacket. The fall air had taken a sudden chill under sunny skies, making Amanda wish she'd brought her heavier coat. Suddenly, the bedroom door burst open by a tall boy with piercing green eyes and a coal black buzz cut. He looked angry.

Grant spoke first.

"Hey, Joe. This is my mom."

Amanda watched the boy turn as if he'd just noticed someone else in the room. His gaze fixed and held on her face. She shuddered. Her breath caught as though she'd swallowed wrong. She opened her mouth, but couldn't respond. A stabbing fire in her chest caused her to break out in a sweat.

Joe's voice broke through her pain. "I'm Joe Blockman."

The burning ceased. "Nice...to meet you, Joe."

Suddenly freezing, she huddled inside her thin windbreaker, her eyes checking the thermostat. Teenage boys and their hormones, she rationalized.

Amanda continued to shiver as he went on with his business. She couldn't wait to leave. Why did she feel terrified? She directed her attention to Grant's dresser, absently fingering various trinkets on top. Her knotted stomach made lunch less appealing and she tried to relax.

"Ready?" Grant asked.

"Yeah." She shook herself from the feeling. Turning back, she called to Joe, "I'll see you next time." But he'd left.

* * *

Coop had never particularly enjoyed research or homework, but in this case, it had become unavoidable. When he'd tried to put all of the mysterious academy pieces together, he'd come up lacking in the evidence department. If the police refused to do their job, then he would.

For starters, if he wanted to know how Satan's bible reached the boy's school, he needed background information. He wondered who'd established the academy and his question led him to the Knollwood Public Library. It beat sitting around waiting for another deadly twist of fate.

One of the Knollwood reference librarians turned out to be a walking history book on the town and various details of the school. The academy's long-deceased founder, Caleb Rasmusen, established the school in 1905 after the tragic loss of his youngest son, Harry. Coop learned that the fifteen-year boy had been accidentally killed when a gang of hoodlums robbed him on the street one night. Caleb had mourned his son deeply, vowing to do something in his son's memory. Two years after Harry's death, Caleb opened the academy with hopes of giving troubled boys a solid foundation to mould their lives. He'd taken on a crusade to save the children.

Coop thanked the elderly woman who'd sent him on his way with the name and address of Caleb's remaining Knollwood relatives. He pulled up beside the curb in front of a raisin colored, brick, Tudor on the town's outskirts, thinking the meticulous landscaping would certainly have impressed Uncle Eb.

At the door, he cupped a hand beside his face and peered through white lace window sheers. The heavy oak door swung open and a petite woman in her fifties tilted her head in question.

"Yes?" Her eyes darted toward his Jeep.

"Sally Martinson?" Coop smiled.

"Who wants to know?" She smiled back.

"My name is Dreeson Cooper and I'm looking for Porter Rasmusen. I'm a teacher at the Knollwood Academy."

"Oh. I see." Her expression became uneasy and she toyed with her blouse collar. "My father is resting now. I'm afraid he can't be disturbed."

A wiry voice called out from behind her.

"Who is it, Sally? Stand aside and let me see."

"But Dad..."

Coop watched the woman jump out of the way as a wheelchair barreled up to the screen door. A frail old man brought the buggy to a sudden halt, white tufts of hair fanning out from the side of his head. He leaned forward to give Coop the once over and asked, "What do you want, son?"

"My name is Dreeson Cooper, and I'd like to speak with you about Knollwood Academy. I'm a teacher there."

The man rolled back a bit to allow Coop entrance. "C'mon then."

Sally stepped forward. "But, Dad, you don't even know this man. It could be dangerous."

"Not nearly as dangerous as the academy," he said wheeling past her.

Sally calmed when Coop entered without incident. She even offered to make coffee after they'd settled into a nearby parlor. Coop declined and apologized for any inconvenience.

"I'm sorry if I disturbed your rest, Mr. Rasmusen."

"Ah, think nothing of it. I'm eighty-five. Pretty soon I'll be sleeping all the time." The man's blue eyes sparkled at his own joke. He resonated an unbeatable spirit under the layers of wrinkles and twisted arthritic joints.

"What is it you want to know about the school?" he asked.

Coop remained careful not to let on about the mysterious book. He explained what he'd learned from the librarian and began his questioning with the harmless topic of ownership, hoping to stumble onto something as he went. Porter Rasmusen was most likely his only living link with the truth behind Knollwood Academy.

Sally helped her father with his coffee, an action the old man didn't seem to care for.

"I have to have help with just about everything since my stroke last year. Thank God, it didn't affect my mind. Now let me tell you what I can before it goes, too.

"You seem to have the facts straight about my grandfather, so I'll go on from there. He continued to add buildings to the grounds until 1925. The place grew into a small town in itself. By 1935, his health began to fail and he turned everything over to his remaining son, Peter."

"Peter would be your father then?" Coop accepted a cup of coffee from Sally.

"That's right," she answered for her father. "Then in 1945, my father took over..."

"Who's telling this story?" Porter interrupted. "Let me finish."

Coop grinned at the old man's spunk. No wonder he'd made it to eighty-five. Sally turned abruptly and left the room.

Porter continued. "Now I can speak freely." He lowered his voice, "You see, the place is cursed."

"Excuse me?" Coop sputtered coffee down his chin.

"You heard me. It all started after my grandfather brought in that damned Knollwood mascot. There have been too many incidents to be bad luck, as some believe. *I* know better."

Coop leveled his gaze at Porter. "I'd hoped you'd be able to tell me more than historical facts."

The old man nodded. "Now that we're on the same page, I know you'll understand. Caleb started a crusade to save troubled boys, and with that in mind, he came up with the idea for a Knight in armor to stand as the school's mascot. He finally managed to obtain the knight you see in the main house foyer from a private collector named Barnabas Archer.

"The man claimed he'd had nothing but misfortune since taking possession of it and so my grandfather got it for a steal. Ol' Caleb scoffed at the man's paranoia saying he'd already received his share of bad luck when he lost his son.

"So like Sally said, I took over the school for my father in 1945, but I couldn't wait to get rid of it. My whole life I'd watched tragedy after tragedy happen at the school and in our lives. Too coincidental if you know what I mean."

Coop nodded. He did indeed. "Didn't anyone ever question the mishaps?"

"Naturally. But they always came up legitimate. Labeled as accidents. So a year after my father passed away, I sold the place to a private party based in another town and I've never looked back." Porter broke into a fit of coughs and grabbed for a hanky.

Coop could see the man's energy waning. He would have to be direct. "Mr. Rasmusen, have you ever heard of a black book at the school?"

The man furrowed his eyebrows into a long white caterpillar. "Hmm. Yes, I recall a story about a book. Let me see…"

"Dad?" Sally rounded the corner with a glass of water and a medicine bottle. "It's time for your pill."

"Sally, what was that tale about the book they found at the school?" Porter coughed again.

She held the glass and watched him swallow his medication. "Oh, I remember." She sat on the couch beside Coop, eager to enter the conversation.

"The day they brought the suit of armor into the main house, a workman knocked the whole thing over causing the helmet to come off. When that happened, a black book fell out of it."

"Interesting." Coop nodded.

She continued. "But that's not the weird part. The workman committed suicide less than a week later. I get chills just thinking about it."

Porter stared at her. "Would you turn up the thermostat, dear?"

Sally frowned. "I know when you're trying to get rid of me, Dad."

"What kind of book was it?" Coop broke the tension.

"I heard my father tell the story many times. He said the writing was foreign. No one could read it. So Caleb ordered the book boxed up with a bunch of junk and as far as I know no one's seen it since."

"I see. Have you any idea what the manhole plate behind the main house covers? It's quite unusual."

Porter frowned. "Manhole? I have no idea. Didn't know there was one. I'd guess it has something to do with the sewer."

The man yawned and closed his eyes briefly before stopping

himself.

Coop caught Sally's pleading look and said, "One more question and I'll leave you to get some rest."

"What's that?" Porter said straightening.

"Do you know where the armor originally came from?"

"I can answer that for you, Mr. Cooper. I'm the history buff in the family and I researched it as far back as I could. I've traced the piece's sale history from Barnabas Archer back through a series of private owners in England."

Sally's eyes gleamed. "The piece was originally brought from the Jordanian city of Petra, when the city was rediscovered in the 1800's."

"What do you mean, *rediscovered*?" Coop frowned.

"The city of Petra was built in the third century B.C., but lost after the fall of the Roman Empire. Apparently the suit of armor had been discovered in the 1800's with the rest of the city."

Porter had no comment because he'd fallen asleep with his chin resting on his chest.

Coop excused himself, thanking Sally for her hospitality and information.

"You must think me a total bore, Mr. Cooper. I don't get out much, taking care of my father and all. Reading is my connection with the outside world and whether it's fiction or real life, I love a good mystery."

* * *

Coop arrived home late and headed straight for the living room phone. He cradled the receiver between his jaw and shoulder as he sunk onto the couch and peeled off his socks and shoes. A craggy voice came over the line.

"Yes?"

Coop grinned at George Batten's greeting. He greatly respected the unusual, but brilliant man.

"George?" Coop leaned back against the cushions.

"Coop. I should have known." The old man laughed.

"Were you sleeping?"

"Actually, I'm having a nightcap. Care to join me?"

"It's been a long day. But I *could* use your expertise. Do you know of an ancient city called Petra?"

"Ah, yes. It's in Jordan, and has claimed its share of Hollywood fame from one of the Indiana Jones films. Why do you ask?"

"That's where the book came from."

"Petra? Are you sure?"

"It was found in a knight's armor when the school opened. The armor had been bought and sold several times due to a string of bad luck, until it ended up at Knollwood when the founder decided to use it as a mascot."

"How do we know it's the same book?"

After a brief explanation about his visit with Porter Rasmusen, Coop waited for George's response.

"Well? What do you think?"

George cleared his throat is if preparing to lecture. "The city of Petra, also known as Sela in the Bible, was built around the third century B.C. The city held a great number of mountain carved tombs, which of course provided the perfect place to hide valuables and perhaps Satan's bible.

"The crusades made their mark there after the fall of Rome and so it is feasible one of the knights found the book and hid it in his armor. The hero in question most likely gave his life in an attempt to safely bring the book to his king where it could be properly destroyed."

Coop grinned. "I knew you could help me."

"I can't help you if you won't listen to me. I told you the book is dangerous."

"Did something happen? You're usually not this dramatic," Coop said.

"Don't give me that. This is serious business," his mentor warned.

Coop let the man's pause hang. Finally, the doctor gave in.

"Yes. Something did happen. I went on to translate other areas of text."

"And?" Coop asked.

"The more I read, the more I'm convinced this is truly Satan's bible. The outlook is quite grim."

"Give it to me."

"It's no secret there will be a final war between good and evil. It's the events leading up to the battle that have remained shrouded behind the secrecy of symbolism. This text, however, describes it fully, without any reserve."

"What does it say?"

"I told you this manuscript has the exact number of books as the original bible. I translated other areas where the battle of Armageddon might be mentioned and the results are frightening."

"How frightening?"

"You'll see me in church this Sunday."

George interrupted Coop's chuckle.

"I translated a large section entitled, BUELL, whom I'm assuming wrote the text, much as the new testament books are named after the disciples who penned them. I chose this particular book because of its placement. It coincides with the book of Daniel in the Christian bible where the prophet refers to a vision about the final battle involving a demon and Michael the Archangel.

"The black book's message is clear that the battle of Armageddon will be spiritual, not physical. It went on to explain that the Prince of the Persian Kingdom, and his *chosen army,* will fight against Michael."

"So when is all this supposed to happen?" Coop asked.

"Unlike the Christian bible, the black bible gives away the ending. I've used timelines, maps, and even astrological charts to come up with my best estimate. According to my findings—and mind you I did the translations in an awful hurry, I'd say it's less than a week away. All Satan needs is to complete his army.

"Listen to me, Coop. Leaving the academy would be your best course of action." The man sighed into the phone. "But then that's not an option for you, is it?"

"Nope. I'm not going anywhere as long as the kids are in danger."

"I was afraid you'd say that. Well, I'll push for the carbon dating and hope Dr. Pearlman can put an end to this mystery. If it *should* prove to be Satan's bible, I can't see how that will change much. It seems you've already made up your mind to stick it out until the end. Whatever that might be."

CHAPTER 24

Grant had a renewed dread for Mondays when he left his last class of the day with more homework than hours to do it in. He stopped by the art room where Coop sat hovered over his own pile of paperwork looking worn and tired. It looked like neither one of them had managed much sleep.

He dropped his books on a nearby desk and plopped down in the seat.

Coop looked up over a five o'clock shadow at three in the afternoon. "What's up?"

"Homework. You?"

"Homework." He scribbled a large red D on the top paper.

Grant had become familiar with their verbal drill. When they had something important to discuss, they went through a few lines of everyday B.S. first to make sure there would be no interruptions. A moment of silence hung over the room before Grant spoke.

"I found my key chain."

"Great. Where was it, lost and found?"

"Sort of."

Coop looked up with a twisted frown. "What does *that* mean?"

"Look, I know what you said about the basement."

"You didn't!"

"I did. And wait till you hear."

"Grant. I don't care. You could be in danger. You promised."

"Yeah, well, never trust a juvie." His smile faded when Coop didn't laugh.

"You're not a juvie. That's a term for delinquents. Sorry. You'll have to do better. So, tell me what happened."

Grant finished his tale on Mumsford's actions, the creepy mist, and finally the personal items. "That's where I found the key chain."

Coop studied him for a moment. "You're sure it wasn't some sort of lost and found box?"

"Why would the lost and found be in a locked basement?"

"Maybe the items have gone unclaimed so long they put them away."

"Coop, I held Billy's football in my own hands a few weeks ago. Those things weren't lost. They were taken. Besides, from what I saw they belonged to boys who've had recent accidents. It's almost like the crazy bastard is keeping trophies."

"It reminds me of some sort of magic, like voodoo where a personal item is needed to perform a spell on the person."

Grant stopped. He hadn't thought of that. "You think that's why they come back to school like zombies?"

Coop shook his head. "Just throwing it out there. It doesn't mean I'm right. But it is strange."

"You think Mumsford is some kind of witch?"

"Warlock. I think a male witch is called a warlock. As you can see I know little about it. But you need to stay out of the basement until we find out. What if he'd caught you?"

"I would have come up with something, I guess. You know, 'boys will be boys' or something?"

"Yeah. I know how you juvies are." Coop winked at him.

Grant left the office feeling lighter, except for the stack of books he carried. At least someone else knew about Mumsford. If something did happen, the headmaster would be the first place they'd look.

* * *

That evening, Coop downed the last of his brandy as he stared into the roaring fireplace. His bones ached tonight, as if all of fall's dampness had settled into his body. He'd turned up the thermostat twice in the last two hours, and still felt chilled. Perhaps the furnace needed maintenance. Who knew how long it had been since the filter had been changed?

His mind wandered back to earlier in the day when he'd finally cornered Joe Blockman about the tunnel. He'd waited as the boys filed out of the locker room after basketball practice and called him over. Joe's cocky saunter sparked a deep annoyance in Coop. It looked like he already knew what to expect and had the answers tucked away like crib sheets for an exam. The kid was good, Coop decided. He hadn't flinch at the insinuation he knew something, and he didn't deny knowing about the tunnel, making Coop feel as though he'd overreacted. But he knew better.

"Mr. Cooper, I'm not saying it isn't a little weird having a manhole cover planted in the backyard, but what's the big deal? As far as I know, no one has ever fallen in. Not many kids know about it."

"That's not what I heard. I know at least one boy who went down there, thanks to your prodding, and that could be dangerous."

"Oh, you mean Grant? Yeah, I tricked him into going down. I wanted to see what he was made of. No harm. Just a stupid prank."

Coop fumbled with a temporary loss for words. He'd expected to catch the kid in a lie, but he hadn't faltered. *This kid has balls!*

"Look, I'm warning you not to take any more boys back there. I know you know more than you'll admit. So I'll be watching. Stay away from that hole."

For a split second, an unreadable expression flashed in Joe's eyes. A shiver crept through Coop as though he'd been touched by an invisible force. He couldn't understand it, couldn't prove it, but somehow he knew he'd received a strong warning. Then the feeling disappeared and he watched Joe Blockman heading toward the gymnasium doors.

He drew his robe tighter over his clothes, still unable to keep warm. Even the brandy hadn't done the trick and he considered the possibility that he might be coming down with something. It had all started with the icy shiver in the gym. He just couldn't shake it. Time for the hard stuff, he decided, and he headed into the kitchen to make some hot tea and whiskey.

A short time later, his empty teacup sat on the small table beside his chair. The fireplace flames had long ago died, turning the living room air to black frost. Coop lay sprawled across the small divan, huddled under a thin crocheted throw. One foot rested on the hardwood floor while the other hung over the end of the small couch. His robe lay open with the tie on the floor like a terry cloth snake.

Coop grunted awake at an unfamiliar sound. He listened in the still darkness, trying to focus his eyes. Silence.

He sat up, pulling the scrap of blanket around him, feeling his head pounding. He'd never been a drinker and knew he shouldn't have tried the whiskey. His binge only served to remind him that his plan hadn't worked. He still shivered under the coverlet.

Coop heard the sound again. His heart pounded in his ears at the thought of someone in his home. He tried to convince himself it was impossible, but jumped when something scraped along the floor. The intruder drew closer, from the living room entryway.

He reached for the portable phone on a nearby table, but stopped when he heard the sound again. It sounded like a mouse. He grinned at his own paranoia. *You inherit a farmhouse, you inherit its occupants.* Coop's eyes had adjusted enough to see the room's furniture silhouetted against the pale moonlight bleeding through the blinds. He retied his robe and made his way toward the kitchen to try to find the unwanted houseguest.

"God!" He jerked up his foot when it sunk into something warm and slimy. He hopped on one foot toward the light switch.

He examined his toes, gagging at the smell. A gray, jelly-like substance dripped from his foot. A watery puddle lay on the floor beside him and he knew he'd never eat chicken dumpling soup again. It resembled the same substance he'd found on Uncle Eb's foot, and every nerve quickened. The intruder couldn't be a mouse.

He wiped his foot with the blanket and moved toward the kitchen. His stomach churned from the overwhelming bitter smell in the room.

He sidestepped another mound of slime as he rounded the corner into the foyer. What kind of animal would leave such a mess, he wondered? The answer came unexpectedly.

A thick black whip lashed out at his head. He ducked in time, rolling into the darkened living room. A tall black figure flashed across the room.

He inched toward the light switch. A low scraping sound grated against the hard wood floors as the creature neared. Coop kept his back to the wall, searching the darkened room.

Before he reached the light switch, something grabbed his ankles and pulled. He landed hard onto his back and slid quickly across the room. Coop sped too fast to grab onto anything. He saw he was headed toward the basement door. Something told him it would be the end of him if he ever reached it.

Coop quickly removed his robe tie, lassoed it around the foot of Uncle Eb's antique hutch, and held on tight. He yelped in pain when he jerked to a sudden stop.

The creature's scream was deafening.

Coop strained to see the thing that held him. In the darkness, he made out a snake-like form with a large fanning cobra head. The beast's stone white eyes fixed on him drawing closer. Pinned by its tail, he watched the giant head loom inches from his face.

"No!" Coop watched in horror as the face changed shape and melded into Uncle Eb's. The serpent's body writhed as his uncle's voice pleaded with Coop.

"Please, help me. Dreeson, I need you. Come with me."

He saw his uncle's last moments played out in his mind.

He closed his eyes trying to erase the images, but the beast had complete control over his thoughts. The creature's grip held him in place as he helplessly watched.

Eb moved cautiously near the top of the staircase, checking left and right. A shadow moved suddenly and his uncle raised both hands in defense as it engulfed him. He heard Eb's screams and a loud wrenching crack of bone. The man flopped down the stairs like a rag doll, his limbs never attempting to break the fall. Coop knew he'd been paralyzed before he'd even started falling. The dark presence slithered after him stopping midway down the stairs to belch out a wretched pile of vomit.

Mercifully, the images in his mind shut down. But just as quickly, he heard his mother's voice cooing softly into his ear. Coop opened his eyes.

"Oh, Dreeson. It hurts so much. Why do you make me suffer? Why must you be such a rebel? Do the right thing and make the pain stop."

The cancer ravaged body of Terry Cooper filled his sight. Losing her in his twenties, to leukemia, he'd never been able to shake the sense that his youthful misdeeds had somehow triggered the cancer cells within her tiny frame. The creature knew it.

He fought the desire to succumb. He wanted to tell his mother how he regretted all the pain and trouble he'd caused, especially when she'd been silently fighting a battle with an overpowering foe. Instead of making it easier for her, he'd made things worse.

Coop forced himself back to reality. This couldn't be happening. His family was gone. His mother rested in peace and he intended to protect her memory. This supernatural entity was treading on personal turf, and on the streets of his youth that was cause for retaliation. He decided to fight.

"If you want me, you'll have to do better than that. You want a battle, you got it."

The creature had shown him his most painful and weak moments, trying to wear him down. He had to counter them. Coop brought up images of his work with the inner city students, who'd gone on to graduate and become productive adults. He focused his thoughts on one of his former students, Jeremiah Miles, who'd broken away from gang life and started helping others to do the same. Eventually he'd gone on to teach. Jeremiah had personally named Coop for his success during his college graduation speech.

Coop replayed the young man's words. "Dreeson Cooper is the greatest mentor in my life. If not for him, I wouldn't have had the courage to break out of the street life."

Coop turned his head as the rancid stench of the creature's breath heated his face.

He heard a low rumble deep inside the beast's swollen belly and Coop covered his face as a smoldering stream of froth engulfed his head and hands. The ooze seeped behind his fingers and into his nose. His screams cut the frigid air as his eyes began to cook in their sockets. He lost all rational thought as his brain began to boil inside his skull. Then the darkness took him.

CHAPTER 25

A buzz of excitement emanated from the small crowd outside Coop's art room. Grant pushed his way through, to see. He heard someone say, "Man, too bad. I knew it wouldn't last. Things will probably be like before."

Had something happened to Coop, Grant wondered? He craned to see over the group. Someone grabbed his arm and he turned to find Parker "Booger" Boggs, standing too close.

Grant backed up a step asking, "What's going on?"

"Artie's back. There goes *my* peace and quiet."

"Where's Mr. Cooper?" Grant's heart raced.

"Got me. Guess he's late."

As Grant moved through the crowd, he saw that Artie had indeed returned. He knew the boys gathered around him weren't the welcoming committee; no one had missed the bully. Instead they showed great interest in his stump. They stared at the gauze-wrapped stub sticking out of Artie's arm sling. The dirty bandage looked like it hadn't been changed since the day he'd left. The worn dressing looked spotted with crusted black blood. Yellow-green pus stains bled through the gauze. Where had the boy received such poor care? Grant didn't need to get too close to know the bandage reeked like something that needed burying. Several boys gagged and quickly turned away.

"Jesus, Artie! What's that smell?" One boy staggered back.

Grant forgot all about the foul-smelling bandage when he looked at Artie's eyes. They looked pasted into their sockets. He suspected the vacant stare registered nothing but the space beyond his group of fans. He'd changed.

Once again, he focused and tried to gain access to Artie's mind and thoughts. "C'mon," he whispered to himself.

He frowned, coming up with nothing.

Grant wished Coop could see this. Was this his imagination? No one else noticed anything wrong with the bully. The kid looked like he always had, with his junk food paunch and greasy mop hair. His thick uni-brow no longer furrowed into an angry snake, but perched like a shelf across his acne-covered forehead. Still, Grant knew the boy wasn't the same. Something was different.

"Time for class," Artie said, and he strode off into the art room.

The boys looked at one another in dead silence. Their questioning expressions followed him as he went.

Trailing behind, Grant wondered for the second time where Coop had gone.

* * *

Mumsford's lily-white potbelly swallowed the elastic of his boxer shorts. He gazed at his reflection in the bathroom mirror with the razor poised to strike. He was one step closer to the night of nights; his long awaited reward. But first, he had to prepare.

He quickly lathered his chest with shaving cream and began the tedious task of removing his body hair. The sink full of water grew milky white as dollops of hair-sodden foam floated in its warmth. Long lines of newly shaven pink skin formed along his torso as he shaved from neck to belly. Everything had to be perfect.

He chanted, feeling his sense of euphoria rise. After years of preparation, the master's ultimate goal would soon be fulfilled and he, Elias Mumsford, would finally receive the recognition and promised reward he deserved. He stopped abruptly at a terrifying thought. The razor dripped on the gray tiles below.

"No!" he shouted to his reflection. "The master wouldn't do that! I am the keeper. He promised me!" Betrayal had never crossed his mind. There'd been no reason, until now.

He fought to shut down the fragmented thoughts he knew couldn't be true. Malik would never forsake or deny him. He'd kept his word so far. Still, an edge of doubt lingered. What if?

He took several deep breaths to force his hand to stop shaking and continued his work. When at last he finished, he wiped off and admired his reflection. His skin shone against the bathroom light and he knew he'd done well. He let his boxers drop to the floor and kicked them aside as he replaced the dull blade with a new one. Standing naked before the mirror, he reached for the shaving cream again and lathered his buttocks and groin.

As the razor trailed a sharp track, Mumsford's mind traveled down its own twisted path. He needed a back up plan to insure his advantage should the master choose deceit. His years in the dark arts served him well and he knew what powers he dealt with. Caution could not be underestimated. Service to the great one would indeed prove beneficial, but not if he was dead.

A sly grin twisted his pale lips when he considered the surprise on Malik's face if the occasion should arise to turn the tables. The upcoming event would surely prove interesting, one way or the other.

* * *

Coop bolted into the art room to a class full of questioning looks, including Grant's. He regretted he couldn't stop to explain his tardiness, and started the lesson. What he had to tell Grant couldn't be said within earshot of any of the students, and must be explained with the greatest of care.

His telephone conversation minutes before with George Batten had been the reason for his late appearance, and he'd raced to his class hoping to find Grant unharmed. Regardless of Coop's responsibility to his class, the doctor's news could not be put on hold. It had confirmed that Grant's life was in serious danger.

Once the class started working on their daily project, he settled behind his desk and pretended to grade papers. He allowed his mind to catch up with the events of the past few hours, starting with his surprise at awakening alive this morning on his living room floor. Even now, the pain in his head pounded his temples causing him to move slowly. Waves of nausea pitched in his stomach as his mind replayed the scenes of the previous night.

He'd awakened to a mind-numbing headache and a quiet house. There'd been no signs of steaming puke or snake-like creatures, as he'd slowly pulled himself onto a nearby chair. What had happened? The last thing he remembered, he'd been sitting by the fire sipping spiked tea. While he knew his drinking skills couldn't match Mitch Blair's, he also knew he hadn't overdone it. Not enough to cause hallucinations.

He made his way into the kitchen cautiously looking around for any signs that the event had been real, but found none. The sight of the basement door caused him to shudder. What had he feared downstairs?

Coop filled the coffee maker and let it brew as he wandered back into the living room. He winced at a twinge in his bare foot and found a small object stuck to his skin. It was the size of his thumbnail and translucent in color. Pulling it free, his breath caught when he saw it was a reptilian scale.

Someone sneezed in the classroom and he snapped out of the memory. Because he'd been allowed to live, he knew the attack had only been a warning. If that thing had wanted him dead, he wouldn't have been able to fight it. He hadn't understood what it all meant until he'd arrived at work and found the message to call Dr. Batten immediately. After speaking to him, all of the pieces fell into place, painting a dangerous picture.

Finally, the bell rang, and Grant lagged behind as the other students left. He scribbled him a pass knowing Grant would be late for his next class.

"What's up?" Grant asked.

"Shut the door, will you? We need to talk."

* * *

Amanda Taylor eyed her reflection in the mirror. Her blue eyes shown like crystals, a feature she'd always been proud of. She ran a brush through her shoulder length hair and thought about adding color for a slight makeover. Perhaps some blond highlights or even a bold change to deep auburn would do it. She laughed at herself, knowing she would probably do neither.

She stepped back to admire her new work uniform and smiled. *Not bad.* Sometimes she found herself wishing she'd gone into a different profession. Why hadn't she chosen to be a bank teller or secretary where she could work normal hours and have weekends and holidays off? It would be nice to wear smart, stylish clothing instead of nursing white. She quickly tucked that wish in the back of her mind along with her others. Nursing paid extremely well, and she couldn't afford to give it up.

"Speaking of which," she absently said to Milo the cat, "I better not be late again, or the unit manager will be all over me."

She fought to ignore the phone when it rang as she headed toward the door, but something told her it might be important. It could be the school.

"Hello?" she answered.

"Mrs. Taylor?" a man's voice asked.

"Yes."

"This is Dreeson Cooper from Knollwood Academy."

She inwardly groaned. "Did Grant do something wrong?"

His brief hesitation made her stomach churn. *Not now. I'm going to be late for work!*

"Not really. But I need to talk to you about him. It's important," his tone sounded cautious.

"Is Grant all right, Mr. Cooper?"

She heard the tension ease in his voice. "Please call me, Coop."

"Well, Coop. I'm on my way to work right now. Can we talk tomorrow?"

"No. I'm afraid not."

Amanda's cheeks burned. She didn't like games. "Look, either he's in trouble or he's not. If he's not, then why can't we talk another time?"

"Mrs. Taylor, Grant *is* in trouble. But not the kind you're thinking of. You need to get Grant out of here as soon as possible."

"I don't understand!" Her anxiety grew as she glanced at her watch. "What has Grant done that I need to take him out?"

"Listen. I know you don't have time for an extended explanation, but please promise me you'll take him away from here tonight."

Suddenly she understood. Grant had this poor man snowed.

"Has Grant been telling you stories about weird happenings at the school? He can be quite convincing."

"What do you mean?"

"I know he wants out of there and it sounds like he's gone to great measures to get his way. I'm sorry he's putting you through this, Coop. But he needs to stay there no matter what he tells you."

"Mrs. Taylor, please."

Amanda knew she couldn't avoid being late. Her temper flared. Grant continually made her job as a parent tougher. This time he'd gone too far. She could lose her job.

"Look, Mr. Cooper. You tell him for me, that I will not take him out of Knollwood. I don't know what he's been telling you, but if he doesn't stay, he'll end up in more trouble than ever before."

"I doubt it."

"Why's that?" she asked.

Her blood turned to ice at his response.

"He'll be dead."

CHAPTER 26

Grant stared up at the bedroom ceiling from his bed. He didn't know where his roommate might be, but it didn't matter. Right now, he had a lot to think about.

Coop's revelations about the black book frightened him. He never would have guessed the ratty old thing could have been such a big deal, but now he feared if Coop's professor friend was right, he'd be in more trouble than ever. He'd stolen Satan's bible!

His stomach churned and he jumped up to pace the short length of the room. He had to find a way to put it back before Mumsford realized it was missing. But that was impossible because Coop had left the book with Dr. Batten. To make matters worse, the doctor had translated other verses and learned Satan's plan for winning the war of Armageddon. Coop's expression had been serious, as he'd explained.

"As far as we can tell, Satan is building an army for the final war with God. That's why Billy and Artie are acting like zombies. They've been robbed of their souls.

"Satan plans to use the captured souls of those with the potential to do good. He wants good souls, not bad. However, one of the translations states that a soul cannot be taken, it must be freely given. That tells me his power is limited. And that could be a good thing for us."

When Grant had questioned what it all meant, Coop hesitated.

"Think about the boys who have been chosen. They all have certain qualities that separate them from the average boy who ends up at the

academy. They have the potential to do good and get away from this life. For example, Billy isn't a bad kid. He's just a victim of the system. And, while Artie might be a bully, he has a soft spot for animals and plans to be a vet.

"According to Dr. Batten, Satan's bible explains there are seven good souls needed to lead his army. I've gone back through my uncle's newspaper articles and there were three recent incidents, before Billy, Artie, and Terrence. That makes six. Grant, I think you're the seventh soul."

Grant sat on his bed mentally exhausted from trying to digest what he'd been told. How could he ever be considered good? He'd done nothing but cause his mother grief and had even told his father he hated him only days before he'd died. How did that give him potential?

He wished he could ignore Coop's findings, but they made too much sense. Something evil lurked inside Knollwood. He'd already seen too much to deny it. They were heading for an unpreventable disaster.

The translation about a freely given soul baffled Grant. If true, then the boys had willingly offered their souls. He didn't know any of the kids well, but he knew Artie Sikes wouldn't let go of his soul without a fight. Unless he'd been made an offer he couldn't refuse.

Grant felt his body wearing down. His thoughts wandered to his mother and how he wanted to hear her voice. She'd be at work now and had warned him not to bother her there except for an emergency. He wondered if being chosen for Satan's personal army would qualify. Her responses to his concerns so far hadn't been taken seriously. She'd probably have him committed if he told her his latest fears.

He lay back on the bed and closed his eyes to think. His mind reviewed the facts, trying to find a logical explanation. How could he avoid his fate?

It occurred to him that Thomas hadn't returned yet, and it meant there were only five boys available. If Satan needed seven to lead his army, Grant still had time to get away from Knollwood before his turn came.

He decided to sneak out after house rounds and walk to Coop's house. They'd never miss him until morning—until he was already safe. Together he and Coop would come up with something.

More pacing. Palms sweating.

What am I waiting for?

He went to the door and listened for footsteps. Joe hadn't returned, but that could change at any moment. He had to act *now*. But what about the others?

Grant knew he wasn't the only one at risk and if he left there wouldn't be anyone to warn them.

Grant sat on the bed. "Shit."

He pushed the plan from his mind. There had to be a way to get to the others without drawing the wrong attention. Once united, the students stood a better chance of survival.

Grant rested his head on his pillow, thinking of ways to reach potential victims. He fought heavy eyelids as his mind conjured every possibility. His last thought snuffed like a candle flame as sleep won out.

* * *

Mitch let out a loud belch as he plopped down on the tattered living room couch. The television screen flashed as he channel surfed across the vast network of cable stations. What an invention. He scanned the monotonous array of reruns without blinking and began to relax after a long day at the shop. In less than two hours, he'd be licking the sweat from sweet Sandy's titties after one of their power sessions. Maybe he could con her into a little massage as well.

The phone rang disrupting his daydream. He grabbed it up, annoyed.

"Yeah."

"Mitch?"

He cringed at the sound of Coop's voice.

"Mitch, listen. I might need your help tonight."

"*My* help? You wanted to tear me up a couple of days ago, and now you need my help? I don't think so." He started to hang up, but stopped when he heard Coop mention something about the academy.

"What's that?" He listened this time.

"I said, I think something's going to happen there soon. Maybe tonight. Can I depend on you?"

Mitch found he couldn't speak.

"Mitch?" Coop broke the spell.

"Yeah, yeah. I'm here. What do you mean, *happen*?"

He listened as Coop tried to explain about a black bible and a prophecy involving the Knollwood students. Although he didn't fully understand, he knew it had to be pure evil. That was the reason he couldn't go. He'd already seen it first hand, and had been lucky enough to get out alive once. Going back would be suicide.

"Sorry, man. I can't help you. If you're smart, you'll get out while you can. They ought to do everyone a favor and burn that hellhole to the ground." With that, he hung up and headed for the shower.

* * *

Amanda watched the unit manager trying to comfort the grieving family as she led them from the ICU cubicle where their son lay dead. The eighteen-year-old had lost his battle to overcome car accident injuries that had left him in a coma and the family without hope. Amanda fought back tears as the mother crumpled onto a visitor couch and buried her face in her hands.

Experience had taught Amanda that death came with the job, but she never got used to it, especially when it called someone so young. It reminded her of Grant and forced her to think about her own reaction if he would be taken from her. His past behavior had landed him close on several occasions making her more protective and paranoid than most parents. She knew she tended to smother him, but her job had trained her to expect the worst at times. Danger had become one of life's harsh realities. *Like an unexpected warning?*

She bit her lip and recalled the teacher's phone call. Why had Mr. Cooper angered her so? The truth hit before her mind could rationalize it away. She had guilt. She'd ignored her own son's pleas and concerns because she didn't know what else to do with him. Her fear of losing him had caused her to blow it as a parent.

Sending Grant to Knollwood had proven more punishment for her than anything. She'd already lost her husband, first to another woman, and then to death. She couldn't lose Grant, too. Perhaps she deserved to suffer after her show of lousy parenting skills. She seemed unable to care for any male in her life. Knollwood had provided the hope that someone else might do a better job.

"Damnit," she cursed her pride. Why hadn't she seen it before? She'd sent Grant to the academy for *her* sake, not his. The gnawing in her solar plexus told her she'd been wrong.

As the night shift began taking report, Amanda couldn't wait to get to Knollwood and make things right. Tonight her son would sleep in his own bed.

* * *

Grant had finally fallen asleep and turned over feeling the pleasant drowsy sensation completely relax his body. Still wearing his clothes, he couldn't make himself get up to undress. Through bleary eyes, he saw Joe hadn't returned yet and wondered where he might be at this late hour. Sinking deep into slumber, his mind drifted back in time and he smelled the unmistakable aroma of fast food fries. He saw himself at eight, sitting beside his dad in the family car. Whenever Mick would come home from the road for a few days, he made it a point to take Grant to their favorite burger place for a celebratory grease-feast. Boys' day out.

Grant savored the salty taste against the ketchup as he reached for another handful. Sweating rivers in the penetrating heat of the old car, he found it didn't matter. He had his dad all to himself.

He heard his little boy voice ask, "Dad? How come I can hear Mrs. Bo and no one else?"

Mick coughed down the last sip of his drink. "What do you mean?"

"You know. You and I can hear people thinking."

"Yeah. I told you it's not something you should go around telling people."

"I don't. I just want to know why I can hear the crossing guard thinking about her dog and her daughter, but I can't hear anyone else unless it's an emergency."

Mick frowned. "You know, buddy. I think you've got yourself an angel."

"A what?"

"An angel. See, angels are God's messengers. It says so in the Bible. Anyway, if He wants to tell you something, He sends a servant."

"So why can we hear angels?" Grant stared at his father.

"Because they want us to. If you're hearing everything Mrs. Bo thinks, I'll bet it's a message from God. He wants you to hear her."

"But why?"

"Don't know. You'll figure it out someday."

Grant welcomed his father's callused fingers on his chin, but the dream began to fade and he fought to hold the moment. Too late. Mick was gone.

Grant moaned on the edge of waking and pulled the covers up to shut out the damp air. He knew he'd closed the window. His pulse bounded when the same gray mist he'd witnessed in the basement hovered over his bed.

The cloud covered him before he could get up, weighing down on his chest, making it difficult to breathe. He struggled to free himself, but his limbs were paralyzed. When he opened his mouth to call for help, it filled with the pungent fog, choking any sound he might make.

He grew strangely calm and wondered if he was still dreaming. A moment ago, he'd been fighting for his life, and now he only wanted to sleep. He sighed deeply as the mist filled his lungs. Grant lost all conscious thought and slipped away.

* * *

Grant yelped when his legs buckled nearly jerking his tethered arms from their sockets. He managed to get his footing against the damp floor and tried to focus his eyes. Dressed only in his briefs, he didn't feel cold. The damp air smelled like worms, but he sensed no temperature at all. Where could he be?

His last memory surfaced bringing with it the overwhelming fear he'd felt. Suddenly he knew it hadn't been a nightmare. Burning shards ran up his arms. His wrists had been fettered to the wall behind him. He stared at his translucent limbs in awe, but saw no bones or veins, not even muscle. His body looked spirit-like.

He grimaced at the death chamber around him. Human shells were pinned to the walls and ceiling. The boys looked as though they'd been sucked dry and left to petrify; their skin yellowed and taut, like dried leather. Hollow eye sockets stared at him from all sides. Tufts of brittle hair clung to the corpses' scalps, and most of the victims' teeth had fallen to the floor. Thick dust covered the bodies, and Grant wondered how long they'd hung there.

He could almost hear their tortured screams escaping the gaping mouths. Their faces held twisted expressions as though they'd witnessed something shocking before they'd succumbed. Each body had been posed and nailed to the wall like Christ on the cross. Grant knew there was something unnatural about the way the boys had died and the fact that their bodies remained intact. They looked like trophies.

His eyes stopped on a pile of clothing in the corner and he strained to see it clearly. It looked out of place in the death cave—like somebody's laundry. He recognized the shirt and scanned it carefully. A clump of dark brown hair hung past the mangy shirt collar, revealing Mr. Peterson's shriveled face. His tight lips wore an unnaturally large grin, causing his teeth to stand out like chalk. The empty eye sockets stared back at Grant in shock.

He turned away to see a corpse nailed beside him and jumped when it shook. A small mouse crawled from the murdered boy's mouth.

"Get me out of here!" Grant squirmed against his shackles.

But the manacles held fast against his efforts, and he knew no one could hear him.

Grant wondered what had happened to all of the victims. How could this be happening without anyone knowing? He scanned the rest of the cavernous room. Bright with candlelight, a large altar draped in red velvet across the room supported an empty bookstand centered between two goblets. The dusky walls shined like wet skin and had an unusual texture. To his right an engorged puckered area in the wall repeatedly constricted and relaxed. Its surface resembled the same muscle-like material he'd seen inside the manhole. He knew he'd found the end of the tunnel.

Not far away, six-foot cocoons stood upright, against supportive stands. Shadows moved inside and he feared there might be some sort of giant insects or hungry creatures trying to eat their way through. Something told him it wouldn't be butterflies. Then he heard faint cries, like the ones he'd heard in the basement. He squinted to see through the gray web-like material and made out human silhouettes writhing inside.

He must be next. This would be his fate too, if he didn't come up with a way out. But how? He had no other option but to wait and see what would happen next.

His attention moved to an incubator in the far corner where a plump red object quivered. He watched in fascination as the shiny vessel beat out a perfect rhythm. Its engorged veins pulsed with each contraction and Grant knew by its size it must be a human heart.

Across the room to his left, Mumsford suddenly entered through a crudely cut section of tissue-like wall. The headmaster paraded through the room dressed in a black cassock held by a golden braid about his waist. His flushed face shone with sweat as he hurried toward Grant.

"Ah, Mr. Taylor. Welcome to Malik's lair. I see you've arrived on time. We are running a bit behind schedule and I feared you would be late."

Grant eyed him carefully. "Late for what?"

"Why, you're induction of course. You've been chosen." The man beamed with delight and turned to the altar. "You do know we wanted you to find the book, don't you? All of the chosen ones have found it. That's what makes all of you special. Only a pure heart can see true evil. Congratulations, Grant. You will be one of the seven leaders of Satan's grand army!"

"Who the hell is Malik?" Grant stalled trying to figure out what to do next.

"Malik is my master, young Grant. He is a servant to the great one. It is the proper chain of command. I serve Malik, he serves our great father, Satan, and the others here will serve in the army of Armageddon."

"What have you done to them?" Grant's gaze fell over the cocoons.

Mumsford followed his gaze and smiled. "Your friends' souls are safely tucked away until it is time. I assure you I take good care of them. I am their keeper."

"Seven? That's not a big army. My money's on God."

"Don't be ridiculous. The harvest of souls has been going on for centuries." He motioned toward the bodies on the walls. "Their souls can't all be housed here. These are but a few souvenirs. But do not worry, Satan's army is nearly complete. We need only the seven commanders. That is where you and your friends come in."

"So, what was the point of all the accidents? I mean, why not just steal our souls?"

"I always liked you Grant. You have a fresh spirit about you, which simply won't rest until it knows all the answers. I don't suppose it matters now if I tell you. Very soon, you'll understand everything.

"The accidents served two purposes. First, soldiers need to have a certain respect for their commander and the threat of physical pain and suffering tends to seal that bond. Call it boot camp in Satan's army.

"Secondly, the time away from the academy brought a sense of reality to the other students and faculty. If boys simply woke up *changed*, it would hardly go unnoticed. Most of the boys here have already experienced trauma and after a final horrific incident, it seems acceptable that the student might appear odd."

"Why weren't the last few of us sucked dry and walled up like trophies?" Grant asked.

"The last seven are special, for you will lead the great army of Armageddon to defeat God and finally place Satan on His rightful throne."

"So what's going to happen to our bodies?"

"You will have no use for them in the battle, for it will be a spiritual war. Your birth from the cocoon signifies new life and therefore your bodies will be burned as a sacrifice. The ceremony will seal you to the master forever." Mumsford smiled.

"What's in it for you?" Grant wanted to know.

The man looked puzzled. "Me? Why, nothing, except the honor of obeying his majesty. I have served him for so long."

"What about Thomas? He's still in the hospital. You need one more."

Mumsford frowned at this. "Yes. His recuperation is taking longer than we planned. Nevertheless, there is a replacement. His brother Terrence has had a great change of heart since his brother's accident. Don't worry yourself about that. He will serve us well."

Grant struggled to gain his freedom, but discovered it useless. The shackles held tight and he couldn't gain any leverage. He watched as Mumsford moved toward a tall metal stand.

"This is for the seventh and final soul."

Grant's heart raced as the man headed his way.

CHAPTER 27

Coop looked out the window of the staff lounge to see the last car pulling out. It looked like he was finally alone. The lights of the school and administration building had long been turned off as he sat in the dark sipping coffee. As far as he knew, no one had a clue he'd stayed. It had been a brisk walk from the gymnasium parking lot across the campus, but he'd had to hide his Jeep behind the gym in order to remain after hours. He had to get inside the main house without being seen. Fortunately, there was no security guard on duty at night, only the overnight chaperones that patrolled the house once every two hours. Once inside, it would be easy to get to Grant's room.

He checked his watch and noted it was time. The first rounds should be finished by now, leaving him a two-hour window to work with. His plan seemed simple—get Grant out of Knollwood and back to his farmhouse without anyone knowing. He'd deal with the repercussions in the morning, and realized his teaching days were once again about to come to an abrupt end.

As he made his way past the first floor windows of the main house, he glanced back to make sure no one had noticed him. He kept a stealth stride through the dried grass as he tried to make sense of the whole situation. It angered him that he had to go to these extremes because Amanda Taylor wouldn't listen to him. Things would have been so easy if she'd removed Grant herself. Realistically, Coop knew he'd probably sounded like some kook on the phone trying to convince her Grant's life was in danger. After all, what real proof did he offer her?

When he couldn't give her any solid reasons, she'd practically hung up on him.

He opened the front door of the main house and slipped inside the dark foyer. At the top of the stairway leading to the bedrooms, he heard a muted thud and ducked behind the famed armored knight. The metal mascot had become a familiar emblem proudly displayed on banners everywhere, but right now it better served as a shield. Coop waited and watched, letting out a breath when Mumsford's cat strolled by like a stealth little spy.

A fleeting thought threatened his plan. *What about Joe?* He'd been in such a rush to save Grant, he'd forgotten about the boy's roommate. He'd have to find a way to get by the cocky bulldog.

He hesitated at Grant's door before turning the knob, cursing under his breath when it opened easily. Hadn't he told Grant to keep it locked?

It took a moment for his eyes to adjust to the room's darkness. A wave of anxiety poured over him at Joe's empty bed. *Where could the boy be at this hour?* He knew he had to hurry before Joe returned.

Fear gripped him when a sharp, tangy smell met him half way across the room. Even in the room's dim light, he could see Grant's skin had grown pale. The boy stared at the ceiling without blinking, and Coop shook him hard.

"Grant! Wake up."

The boy didn't move.

"Oh God!" Coop flipped on the bedside lamp. "Grant!" He grabbed the boy's blood splattered wrist.

Coop's fingers slid along the cold skin as he checked for a pulse. Both wrists had been cut deep, soaking the bed. The faint throb in Grant's throat told Coop he had to get help.

As he reached into his coat pocket for his cell phone, a familiar voice startled him from behind.

"That won't be necessary, Coop. It's too late."

"You!" Coop's anger surged. He wanted to grab the punk by his throat and tear him apart. Instead, he kept his head as he dialed. "You knew about this, Joe?"

"I said, you're too late. Put your little toy away."

Coop pressed send and waited. To his horror, the phone had no service. He redialed.

Sharp laughter cut the silence and Coop suddenly understood, pitching the phone aside.

"*You're* the one."

The boy's eyes glowed white in their sockets. His facial skin twisted and writhed like an amoeba. "I am *not* the one. Not yet."

"Then who?" Coop tried to stall. He had to get help.

"The master. You'll see, as Grant and the others have."

Coop backed away as the teen moved closer. His face had contorted back to that of Joe Blockman, basketball star.

"Come. Let me take you to the chosen ones. As an art teacher I think you'll find my lair quite beautiful."

Coop raised his hands to defend. "I'm not going anywhere until I get help for Grant."

"You're right about one thing, Mr. Cooper. You *do* need help."

Coop felt his chest implode and he dropped to his knees.

"That's right. On your knees before your master!" The voice no longer belonged to Joe.

Joe's lower half had changed shape and a snake-like tale grabbed him by the throat and Coop fought for release. His body grew weaker as the creature dragged him behind. Coop heard his heart slowing to a stop.

* * *

Amanda floored her car's accelerator. "C'mon you piece of shit," she coaxed.

The engine chortled and coughed after a brief hesitation, then gunned forward.

The night hung pasty gray and bitter cold. She couldn't recall a worse November and thanked God it wasn't raining. She drove faster, replaying her last conversation with Grant. How could she just shut him out and dismiss his concerns? A niggling voice in her head repeated a point quickly wearing thin. *You did the same thing to Mick. That's why he found someone who would listen.*

"That's bullshit!" Tears brimmed in her eyes as she sped on. "Mick didn't know how good he had it till he gave it all away."

Her years as Mick Taylor's wife had been the happiest of her life, until he'd gone astray. She'd forgiven him for Grant's sake, but eventually there wasn't enough emotional glue to hold their fractured relationship together. Then he'd died and she planned a funeral instead of a divorce.

Amanda cursed when the car's engine light blinked on. "Damnit!" Once again, she'd neglected her vehicle and now she might pay with her son's life. The car sputtered and groaned, forcing her to pull over before the engine blew.

The tires skidded as they cut the roadside gravel. She managed to stop safely, but moaned when the motor died completely. She pounded the steering wheel as tears spilled down her cheeks.

"No! No! No!" Her fists became numb.

Amanda got out of the car wondering what she would do. Her hair cut her eyes in the vicious wind, and she cursed when the first heavy drops of rain splattered onto her thin windbreaker.

The car's hood opened with a loud moan, and Amanda stared inside the dark mouth. Rain pounded her face forcing her to lean as far under as she could. Her hope died when she realized she couldn't see a thing against the night sky and she didn't have a flashlight. Mick's repeated warnings to carry roadside emergency supplies cut through her mind and she wished she had listened. She closed her eyes in defeat. Her only chance seemed far and remote—she needed a guardian angel.

She jumped when a penetrating horn blared into the night, followed by a wet gusting wind that nearly knocked her over. A semi rolled past, then hit the brakes, pulling to the roadside. She watched the great silver giant slow to a stop, like a knight in shining armor.

The driver jumped down from the rig and ambled toward her in the blinding rain. She squinted to see him in the light from the blinking taillights as he came past the rear of the truck. His strides reminded her of Mick. *Must be a trucker thing.*

"Hey there," he called out with a wave. "You all right?"

Shivers raked up her spine at the sound of his voice. She shook them off.

"Just a stubborn engine," she called watching him close the distance. His dark shoulder-length hair dripped with rain, yet she could see enough of his face to appreciate the surreal likeness she'd tried to ignore. Even his faded jeans and rolled up flannel shirtsleeves matched Mick's dress style.

A stroke of lightening cut the sky and she gasped in disbelief. The trucker was Mick.

He moved past her and stuck his head under the car hood.

Amanda moved to the side and watched in shock. Her mind told her it was impossible. If it really *were* Mick, he would have recognized her. She watched his nimble fingers move over the engine like a professional musician with an instrument.

"Get in and try it," he told her.

Amanda backed up toward the door and slid in. She couldn't take her eyes from the man. Inside, she turned the ignition and listened as it whined twice and stopped.

The open hood hid the trucker from her sight and she caught a brief flash of reality.

"It's not Mick, you moron. You're letting fear take over." She tried the engine again and this time it turned over with a roar. "Thank God!"

She jumped when the car hood suddenly slammed. Amanda fumbled in her purse for a few bucks and then noticed the man eagerly heading toward the passenger door. Before she could act, he jumped inside and turned to face her.

"Man, it's a bitch out there."

The money slipped from her fingers when she stared into her dead husband's eyes.

"What's wrong, honey? Everything's fine now. You should be able to get home. But you really need to get this baby tuned." He pushed back a lock of black hair and grinned.

Amanda was speechless. She eyed his clothes, the familiar point of his chin, and even his skull and crossbones belt buckle. "Mi...Mick?" she heard her voice squeak.

"Yeah?" he looked puzzled.

"What are you doing here?" she asked.

"I think I just helped you with your car. Can't really think of any other reason I'd stand in the pouring rain."

"I...you're...dead," she managed.

"That's right, Amanda. I am. But I'm still around. As you can see." He grinned and pocketed the bills from the floor.

"I know I'm dreaming. No, I'm having one helluva nightmare." She rubbed her eyes with her palms.

"No, you're not. I'm here."

As crazy as the situation had become, Amanda couldn't help her reaction. Even if this were a dream or a hallucination, she couldn't stop her anger.

She glared hard at him. "Yeah, I see that. You weren't here for me the last few years we we were married, but *now* you are. That's great, Mick. Thanks."

"That's just like you, Amanda. Ungrateful."

"First you have an affair, then you die. How am I ungrateful?" She couldn't believe she was having this conversation.

"I just fixed your car so you can go off and save Grant."

She stopped. "How do you know about that?"

"The same way I knew you were stalled out here in B. F. Knollwood."

"So now what? Are you going with me?"

"No."

"Our son is in danger and you're not coming? What the hell is going on?"

"He's not in danger. He's safe."

"Safe? Mick I have reason to believe he could die tonight. So if you're not coming along, then get out." With that, she reached across his lap and shoved open the passenger door. Leaning against his firm thigh muscles, she realized he was no ghost. This couldn't possibly be Mick.

His vice grip held her as rain pelted her face. The man's glowing eyes were stone-white orbs. She cringed as a gravel voice filled the car. "You will do what I say! I am master of this realm!"

Her body grew weak although she desperately tried to fight. His fetid breath filled her nose as he drew close to her face. His gnarled leathered skin brushed her cheek and she screamed.

* * *

Rock music blared from the living room stereo speakers as Mitch combed his hair in the bedroom. He nodded and sang along, taking a final look in the mirror. He grabbed his keys off the dresser and headed toward the door.

The roads were slick from the earlier rain, but the skies were clear. He could still make good time on Route 41. Running late as usual, he knew Sandy would kill him if she had to wait more than fifteen minutes for her ride. He really couldn't see the big deal. She'd sit and smoke herself into a nicotine coma until he arrived, shooting the shit with all the drunks at the bar.

He opened up the Harley on the stretch of road that would take him past the freshly cleared fields and into town. The cycle's speedometer read eighty-five when he passed the car and semi on the roadside. It didn't look like an accident to Mitch. If a rig that size had clipped a car, there'd be Chevy pretzels all over the road. Then he caught the wild thrashings of someone inside the car. He grinned. *Looks like someone's getting some.* He slowed briefly trying to see clearly. The car looked familiar.

He remembered working on the same car not too long ago. The

woman had come in complaining about her oil light.

As he drove, he argued with his conscience. If the babe wanted to do a trucker on the roadside, it was her business. But the woman he'd met hadn't struck him as the slutty type. Something wasn't right.

"Shit," he growled and turned the bike around.

When he pulled up behind the rocking car, he regretted his heroics. It looked like a backseat tryst, after all. Still, he couldn't shake the feeling that something was wrong. He cut the bike's engine and listened for cries of ecstasy. Instead, he heard muffled screams and the sound of kicking against the door panel.

Mitch yanked open the driver door and grabbed for the woman. He couldn't see the attacker, but knew he had a strong hold on her. She clutched Mitch's jacket tight and cried into his chest as he tried to pull her free.

"Help me! He's not human! He's going to kill me!"

Mitch's temper flared. He wasn't much of a hero, but the idea of some coward mistreating a woman never failed to send him over the edge.

"Let go of her. Now!" he commanded

The man let out a low pitch growl releasing a foul stench into the car. Mitch gagged as he grabbed the woman around the waist and pulled hard.

They both fell onto the pavement as the attacker let out a raucous laugh. Mitch froze when he heard the familiar voice from his past. He knew it was impossible.

Fear reflected in the woman's eyes against the truck's flashing taillights. He and the woman backed away together as the man climbed out of the driver's side.

"Mitch! How's it goin' buddy?" the man said as if they'd met casually on the street. "You want a crack at 'er?"

Mitch stared, his mind fighting to make sense of things as his old roommate, Cliff Travis leered, waiting for a response.

Cliff's chuckle broke the awkward silence. "You're still a jerk. Can't even speak like a man, can you?"

The man turned to the woman. "Hey, Amanda. Is this what you like now? You know, the loser, grease-monkey type?"

Mitch stepped in front of Amanda. He saw Cliff's night-crawler scar gleaming against the truck's flashing emergency lights. His old roommate stood before him, except he hadn't aged. He still looked seventeen and even wore the same clothes he'd had on the last time they'd been together.

"What the hell?" Mitch mumbled as he backed up toward his bike.

"Now you've got it, pal. That's exactly where I'm at—Hell. Go figure. But you got lucky when you're parents died, and you left before I could show you the grand prize. That's the story of your life, Mitch—lucky. You came to the academy when you should have gone to jail, and then you left Knollwood before I could make you part of the plan. No brains, just luck."

"Keep moving toward the bike," Mitch muttered to Amanda.

Cliff moved forward. "Where you goin'? I'm not done with you yet. You've got lots of potential my friend. That's why you were chosen so long ago."

Mitch ducked as his old roommate swung at him with a knife.

"Get on the bike!" he yelled to Amanda, and rushed Cliff. He caught him around the waist and they both went down.

Cliff's guttural growl reminded Mitch of an animal. He dodged another hit and kicked the guy in the groin. Cliff never flinched and grabbed Mitch by his hair, forcing his head to the ground with a quick shove.

Gravel cut Mitch's cheek as the man's boot pressed against his head.

"You always looked for the easy way out because you're a coward. Too bad you picked tonight to finally show some balls. You should have kept goin' when you had the chance, hero. Now you're gonna die."

Before Mitch could act, the knife's blade sliced into his back. His sudden anger dulled the pain of the cut. Years of harbored guilt rose to the surface, and he realized what he'd known all along—he had nothing to lose by confronting his fears and the evil truth of the past.

The dim glow of his attacker's eyes told him Amanda was right; he wasn't human. He sneered at the would-be Cliff saying, "You can't kill me. I died years ago."

Mitch reached up and grabbed the knife by the blade. Fire sliced his palm. He fought the pressure of the knife as Cliff pressed it toward his throat. Blood raced down his arm as he pushed with all of his strength. He knew he would probably die, but found comfort knowing he'd at least confronted the horror that had imprisoned him most of his life. He would finally be free. He would die a hero.

"One more thing," he said glaring at Cliff. "Remember poor Jake Connally? Before he died that day in the pool, he told me about you.

You were exposed years ago. I wasn't lucky, I *outsmarted* you."

The glowing eyes blazed and Cliff let out a deafening screech. The knife jerked from Mitch's hand and he awaited the blade's final plunge. His eyes closed tight and thought of Sandy for the last time. He heard Amanda scream.

Then silence jarred him out of his fear and he opened his eyes to find he and Amanda alone on the roadside.

CHAPTER 28

The putty colored altar candles had burned into pools of melted wax around their golden holders. In the dying light of the foul smelling lair, Mumsford bustled about, humming to himself. Grant tried to buy time.

"Hey, Mumsford?"

The headmaster wore an annoyed expression. "What is it? I'm busy."

"Why haven't I been put into one of those cocoons, yet?"

"Only the master has the power to do that. Soon enough." Mumsford turned back to his work.

"When is all this going to happen?"

"The ceremony?"

"The war."

"When all of the commanders of Satan's armies are in place. That is why tonight's ceremony is so important."

"What kind of ceremony?" Grant watched the man placing the boys' personal items on the altar.

"The one that will bind the souls to Satan forever."

Grant's anger surged when the man picked up his father's key chain. He glanced across the room at the pumping heart inside the incubator. Everyone in the room had fallen victim, all held hostage by Satan's demon, Malik.

"You're a slave, aren't you?"

The man paled and looked over at the incubator.

"That's *your* heart, isn't it? That's how he keeps you working for him. What did he do, promise to give it back to you?"

Mumsford turned back to his work.

"You silly bastard. Do you really think he'll live up to his end of the bargain? He's a demon for Christ's sake! Think about it!"

"Stop!" the man commanded. "I will not have you speaking with disrespect for my master."

"What are you going to do, Mumsford? Kill me? I think it's a little late for that. I'm not even human any more. But you *are*. Why don't you save yourself? If you leave right now, he won't know it until it's time for the ceremony. Then it will be too late."

Grant knew he had his attention when the man's pudgy lips worked against each other in an inaudible dialogue.

"What's the worst that can happen if you leave? You'd end up the hero for a change."

Before Mumsford could answer, Joe Blockman stepped into the lair.

Joe ran a hand through his short-cropped hair and grinned. "Taylor. Glad you could make it." He turned back and motioned for someone behind him to come forward. Grant's hopes disintegrated when Coop stepped inside.

"Coop! Get out of here before it's too late!" He tried to tear free.

Mumsford led the entranced teacher to the last stand.

Joe shrugged at Grant. "We'll have to secure your friend for now."

Grant couldn't believe it. Coop followed orders like a brainless zombie.

He struggled against the chains holding his spirit form. He yelled as Joe moved toward his friend.

"No! Coop wake up!"

Joe offered a patronizing glance. "Sorry, man. That won't help you. Your efforts are all in vain."

"What do you want from me? I'll do it. Just leave Coop out of it!" Grant kicked once more to try to gain his freedom.

"Your soul, Grant. It is needed for the final battle. You see, Armageddon will be a spiritual war that will be won by my master, Satan. All of you have been especially chosen for this job." Joe waved his arm toward the other cocoons.

"Your army won't be very big. There are only so many students at Knollwood."

"As you can see, worthy souls have been taken for centuries. Knollwood isn't the only place to find an army. The soldiers come from all over the world."

"Why us?" Grant asked glancing at the cocoons.

"The evil ones of this planet have made their choice. There is no hope for them. But you all have the potential to do good. Your light is as His, and for God to destroy you would be to destroy a part of Himself.

"Therefore, you will all be the perfect army to battle against Jehovah. He would smite an army of evil, but not his pure creations. His Bible teaches that He is perfect, without fault or limitations, but that is a lie. He has a weakness, His biggest limitation. God is unable to destroy something He loves, something with good in it. The victory is mine."

"I thought the victory belonged to Satan?" Grant countered.

"Of course. If you choose to give your soul freely to the fight, you will be rewarded. If not…let's just say it is in your best interest."

Grant eyed him carefully. "Why are you doing this?"

"A quick history lesson, Taylor. And then we have business." Joe paced before him. "There is an ancient truth that tells of a great warrior angel called, Malik, who followed Lucifer when he fell.

"For centuries, Michael the Archangel defeated Satan and his legions in countless battles. But one glorious day, Malik found a way to kill Michael, making him superior among the demons in Satan's eyes.

"Malik fled God's angelic army to the Zion foothills in human form to escape punishment and ultimate destruction. Satan came to him with promises of greatness as a reward for killing the Archangel and placed Malik on the throne in the stone city of Petra to hide him. He sent a legion of demons, also in human form, to serve him and guard his black bible.

"As king, Malik enjoyed the adoration and power he received from his subjects and housed Satan's bible safely in the burial tombs encased in the city's mighty stone walls. His time as king served Satan's purposes well, and he learned to embrace the idea of his future greatness. Safely hidden in the Jordanian desert, he had only to bide his time before he would rise from his temporary human form to pursue his goals.

"After Petra fell, Malik returned to a high ranking demon in Satan's army. But the army suffered one defeat after another against the children of earth—that selfish lot created for so much more than they are aware of."

Joe stopped, fixing his eyes on Grant. "And Malik knew what he must do. This time he would not fail."

Grant met his burning gaze. "Nice bedtime story. So, this is all about some sick war against God? And who the hell is this Malik character?" He regretted his tone immediately.

A thunderous voice pierced his ears as his roommate's chest ripped open like a weak seam. "You will show respect when speaking to me!"

Grant watched as Joe's body sloughed to the ground and pooled around the towering serpent inside. Its head fanned like an angry cobra as his tail whipped around and caught Coop by the ankles.

"You're Malik?" Grant couldn't believe it. "What are you doing?" he cried as Coop's body slid along the lair floor.

The serpent turned briefly, his face unlike any snake Grant had ever seen. It was human. As Malik spoke, his features formed a familiar face.

"You do what you got to do, Grant. Remember I used to tell you that all the time?" Mick Taylor said.

"Dad?"

Mick's laughter echoed throughout the lair as Malik turned to Coop.

A thick foamy substance spewed out of the serpent's tail, covering Coop's feet and ankles in seconds.

"Wait! Leave him out of this. He didn't do anything." Grant knew he couldn't stop it.

Soon the last of Coop's face disappeared behind heavy gray mesh.

Grant squirmed against his shackles. "What do you want?"

"I am chosen to form Satan's army for the battle of Armageddon. I am serving my master as you will serve yours!"

Grant had a thought. His father's image a moment ago triggered a memory he might use against Malik the demon. He hoped for the right opportunity. Grant baited the beast.

"So you're just a servant boy, huh? Jeez, *Joe*, you had more glory as the star basketball player. Don't you think?"

"Silence!" Malik's great body moved quickly for its size. He slithered to Grant's side in an instant.

Grant pressed against the fleshy wall to avoid the creature's breath. Its skin glistened with an oily substance and black smoke curled inside the beast's transparent belly. Malik's forked tongue flicked between hideous jaws, clipping the edge of Grant's chin.

Thick folds of decaying slough replaced snakeskin. The serpent's almond shaped eyes glowed in their sockets and Grant fought to turn away from their penetrating gaze.

Malik's acidic voice grated Grant's ears as the serpent's face contorted into the old crossing guard's. Suddenly Grant heard Mrs. Bo's voice whisper inside his head.

I will defeat Beelzebub and take his place over all principalities to rule my kingdom, as it should have been long ago. Satan will be destroyed!

Grant understood why Malik's thoughts finally came through. When the demon shape shifted out of his true form, his guard was down as a human. Now Grant knew the plan.

Mick Taylor had been right. Mrs. Bo had been an angel. There were bigger forces at work and for some reason he didn't understand, he'd been targeted to play a major part. Grant's hopes soared. Although his purpose remained unclear, he knew his whole life had somehow led to this day.

He swallowed hard when Mumsford leaned Coop's cocoon against the tall metal stand announcing. "Everything is in place, master."

"Let the sacrifices begin," Malik commanded.

* * *

Amanda buried her face into the back of Mitch's leather jacket. Images she couldn't believe or comprehend burned in her brain. She kept seeing her dead husband turning into a creature with stony, white eyes and then into some pimple-faced adolescent. The frigid air blasted her cheeks when she raised her head.

She kept her arms tight around the mechanic's waist. She'd become too cold to think, but too frightened not to. What if she was too late? *Grant can't be dead*, she told herself. *I won't allow it.* She knew for sure, she'd never let Grant out of her sight again.

Stricken with conflicting feelings of fear and relief as they made the turn onto the long stretch of road leading to the school, Amanda held tight. Soon she'd rescue Grant from whatever evil lived here. She'd already seen the impossible for herself. Now she knew her son had told the truth.

The trees looked menacing and she found herself wanting to duck as they went by. Suddenly, an arm-like branch reached across the road like a barricade. She heard Mitch's warning too late.

"Hold on!"

She nearly fell off the bike when he swerved. The sudden motion caused an imbalance and Mitch fought hard to right the Harley. Amanda's heart pounded in her ears as the pavement drew dangerously close. Then he regained control, but her heart sank when she heard the engine wind down. They had about two blocks to go. Mitch pulled over to the side of the road and cut the motor.

"What are you doing?" Amanda sputtered.

Mitch got off. "We'll have to walk from here."

"What do you mean?"

"Do you want them to hear us coming?"

She hadn't thought about that. She couldn't feel her fingers and had to force her numb lips to speak. If they didn't get going soon, she feared she'd be frozen in place.

"Let's go," she said.

* * *

The academy grounds were dark. The only visible light came from the lamps illuminating the brick and mortar marker bearing the school's name. It provided just enough light for Mitch and Amanda to make their way to the main house. Mitch motioned for her to follow him and keep close to the building.

"How are we going to get in?" she whispered.

"Don't worry about that. Just keep down."

By the time they reached the front doors, a familiar sense of foreboding surged through her system. If caught, Grant's life could end tonight.

The white doors loomed ahead, and she waited for Mitch to quickly open them while she stayed low behind the nearby bushes. He had no trouble with the lock, which told her he was either crafty, or the doors hadn't been locked. She didn't bother to ask when he nodded for her to follow him inside.

The winding staircase went on forever in Amanda's estimation. She wanted to get Grant and leave, and fought to keep from racing upstairs to get her son. Mitch carefully tested each stair for squeaking boards and she parroted his steps. Finally, they reached the upper hallway and headed toward Grant's room. She found herself running at the sight of the open door. Something was wrong.

Mitch grabbed her back before she entered, raising an index finger to his lips. He placed his palms up as a sign for her to wait, his eyes asking for her silent promise not to go in. She nodded and let him go ahead of her.

Seconds later, he came out and grabbed her hand, pulling her back toward the stairs. She yanked back breaking his grip.

"No!" came his coarse whisper.

Too late. Amanda had already rounded the corner into Grant's bedroom.

The empty, blood-splattered sheets revealed that her son was gone.

CHAPTER 29

Grant watched in sick fascination as Billy Parker, Artie Sikes, Terrence Treybelle, and several other boys entered the lair single file. When they moved past him to the altar where Mumsford waited, the physical signs of their accidents became clear. Billy's arms and face wore deep scars where he'd nearly scratched himself to death, and Artie's mangy bandage hung in tatters. Terrence had no apparent injury, but walked past Grant trance-like. Grant kicked his foot in front of the boy to get his attention, but Terrence never flinched. Mumsford had stayed true to his word when he'd said Terrence would be Thomas's substitute.

Grant gasped when his own body brought up the end of the line.

He saw his face wore the same blank expression as the others, and his arms and wrists were coated with dried blood. The physical Grant never looked his way as he took his place with his back to him, facing the altar. Grant squirmed violently against the chains and called out angrily to Malik.

"What did you do to me? What gives you the right to take us?"

Malik slithered closer to the zombie-like boys. He moved slowly past each one, letting his serpent tail rub their ankles. "I did not take you. You came willingly, remember?"

"No! I don't!"

"Of course you did. The minute you came looking for your personal items, you invited me into your head. Each of you wanted your pathetic junk returned in order to link yourself to the world. Without these trinkets, you all felt void of a vital piece of your life. How easy you made it for me.

"But now you must all make a choice. You may have your items back, but you must give yourselves over to me. Once you offer yourself freely, you will no longer have need for your bodies and they will be destroyed. They served their purpose in avoiding suspicions."

Grant caught sight of a moving shadow inside Coop's cocoon. Coop was alive! He had to keep Malik busy.

"And if we refuse to come freely?" Grant challenged.

"Your body will be destroyed, anyway. While I cannot take your soul, I *can* take your life."

Coop's container shook once more. Grant realized Coop's soul must still be intact.

"Let us go, Malik. What the hell are you going to do with a bunch of delinquents in a war? You'll lose."

"I've already explained that. Victory is ours. After all, it is written." With that, he nodded for Mumsford to start the ceremony.

The headmaster turned with a smile and began to read from the black bible. Grant didn't recognize the language, yet he found he could understand the words perfectly. The other boys understood as well and moved to stand beside the cocoons with their soul inside.

"It is written." Mumsford bowed and kissed the black bible. "In the last days, Satan gathered his elected army for the battle of Armageddon. Behold the thief comes! Blessed is he who prepares to meet the army of God."

Grant's physical body stood beside his spirit now and he longed to slide back inside where he could feel again. He wanted his life back no matter how screwed up it was. Joe Blockman's words replayed in his head about making amends and the ultimate sacrifice when the time came. He'd said Grant would do it for his mom. He hoped he would get the chance.

Mumsford's commanding voice cut through the lair and the boys moved to the altar. He handed them each their personal item. Billy held his football, and Artie clutched his hamster wheel. Terrence Treybelle stepped up to receive a small trophy and then Grant's body accepted his father's key chain. The procedure resembled some sick award ceremony to Grant; only he knew their reward would be death. Mumsford finished handing out the items to the remaining boys.

Malik tore open the cocoons with his razor sharp tail. Their souls emerged looking lost and frightened. They went to their bodies and tried to touch them finding the skin merely slid through their phantom presence.

Mumsford motioned the boys to step up to the altar. "The time has come. If you make the decision to follow your chosen path, you will no longer have need for your bodies," he waved a hand toward the huge fire pit blazing in the center of the room, "but you will have eternal life. If not, you will reunite with your body to receive your eternal punishment. Your master awaits you."

He stepped aside, awaiting their decisions.

Grant willed his body not to move. He refused to make the choice. All eyes fixed on him at the foot of the altar.

* * *

Mitch wondered when he'd crossed from reality to the weird zone, and realized it had been years ago. His whole life had been one, strange, out of tune nightmare since he'd left the academy. He always figured things would straighten themselves out after he left. But things had grown progressively worse, until he'd given up and simply existed day to day.

Tonight was the most bizarre of all of his Knollwood experiences, yet a dark excitement filled him at the prospect of returning to academy turf. In some twisted way, he knew this could be his one chance to make things right. He might even be able to finally live without guilt— that is, if he lived at all. The brilliant plan he'd come up with would most likely get him killed.

He tugged Amanda's hand hard to lead her down the steep staircase and into the foyer. He stopped to listen. Nothing.

"What the hell are you doing?" Her eyes reflected tears against the lighted wall sconces.

"There's nothing we can do up there. C'mon." He didn't wait for her answer and pulled her to the small hallway behind the stairs. "Stay here for now. I don't care what happens, don't come out."

"I'm *not* staying here. Forget it."

"Yes, you are. You can't come with me, it's too dangerous. Besides, you need to stick around in case Grant shows up."

"You saw his bed. Do you really think he's just going to *show up*?"

He knew time grew short. "Just stay put. If I'm not back in twenty minutes, get yourself to my bike and ride for help." He tossed her the keys and backed away slowly.

"I don't understand, Mitch. Where are you going?"

"Trust me."

"Right. My husband used to say that. Now tell me where you're going."

"Hell." He heard her bitter retort as he opened the door to leave.

"Say hi to Mick for me."

* * *

Outside, Mitch recognized the overhead flutter of bats. He scurried close to the building like a fearful mouse and tried to take his mind off the task at hand. If he'd stuck to his original plan, he'd be sinking deep into pleasure with Sandy right now instead of plunging headfirst into the academy's asshole.

He reached the backyard and found the manhole cover with no trouble. It took all of his might to edge the heavy disk far enough over for him to fit inside. His eyes met the blackened void as he peered over the edge. After all these years, he didn't really know what he expected to find down the hole, but he never would have guessed a black void of pure nothing. No sound, no stench of death or decay and most of all, no light. God, he hated the dark. He took a deep breath and slipped inside headfirst.

If he'd ever been grateful for the workout time he spent at Haley's Gym in town, it was now. He grabbed onto muscle-like tufts of the slippery wall to ease himself along. His biceps bulged beneath his sleeves as he paced himself against gravity. It was like descending a mountain upside down.

He'd never been claustrophobic, but the tunnel narrowed as he went. He wondered what he would do when he reached the bottom—if there was one. His hand brushed against a gristle-like mound and he jerked back. He squinted, seeing something white in the darkness. It moved and he knew he wasn't alone.

Suddenly it jumped.

Mitch pushed back and the pulsating muscle missed his chin. He forced himself back up the tunnel against the cramping in his arms.

The mound reached up again and this time slapped his cheek hard.

His face burned where the creature hit him. Rubbing his skin against his shoulder, the fire eased. The thing had a mean punch and a chemical weapon to boot. He wedged his knees tight against the walls and arched slightly, giving himself enough room to maneuver his hand into his jeans for his knife. He switched open the blade. With the knife between his teeth, he continued on, hoping to meet his attacker.

He didn't have to wait long. The bulbous form shot upward and hit his nose. Mitch saw bright lights flash at the pain. He felt blood pouring up his cheeks toward his eyes.

He slashed at the beast, but wasn't quick enough and the creature sunk back down out of range. Mitch vowed he wouldn't be defeated by a giant, writhing gristle.

He probed deep with quick slashing motions in search of his foe. Finally, the knife connected and sunk deep into the rubbery mound. A deafening screech filled the tunnel and he knew he'd hit his mark. He continued to strike, tearing into the mass until it lay in shreds.

Mitch worked his way down until he could go no further. If the tunnel came out where he suspected, he would be out in seconds. If not, they wouldn't have to bury him.

He took a deep breath, and plunged headfirst into the pile of gristle fragments.

* * *

Amanda crouched in the darkened corner of the small foyer. She'd sworn she'd heard footsteps several minutes ago, but never actually heard them leave the stairs. Could someone be standing there waiting? Her legs ached and she knew she'd have to change her position soon.

She couldn't believe she'd let Mitch leave her like this. Abandoned again, she mused. He'd left her vulnerable and without protection. The guy reminded her of Mick. His self-assured, almost cocky attitude made her feel like she'd stepped back in time as Mick's wife. Could she count on someone like that to help her save Grant?

Although she hardly knew him, she *did* know they'd shared some scary moments back at the roadside. He didn't know her. Didn't owe her. Yet he'd risked his life. She had no choice but to trust him.

Amanda wasn't sure about anything, except time was running out for Grant. How could she find him alone? The answer stood out clearly in her mind. She couldn't. Like it or not, she had to rely on Mitch.

She took a deep breath thinking, maybe the time had come to shirk her hurtful past and trust, not only another person, but herself as well. She owed it to Grant to try.

Amanda checked her watch and noted the twenty-minute mark drew close.

She winced, stretching her legs out to rest her bottom on the foyer tiles. If anyone came around the corner, she'd be an easy target. As she waited, she heard a low humming close by. It sounded like chanting.

She crawled to the wall on her right and pressed an ear against it. A human voice!

If only Mitch would return, he might know who could be on the other side. Her watch told her the twenty minutes had come and gone, and she needed to get to the Harley. Instead, she listened closer. Drawn to the singsong drone behind the wall, Amanda made her way to the door that Grant had tried to show her that day. As before it remained locked.

The singing grew louder. Her heart pounded a counter rhythm. What if Grant was trapped in there?

She tried to think of who would be chanting behind a locked door. Grant had been right—something strange lurked inside the academy.

The sharpness of Mitch's keys inside her coat pocket reminded her there wasn't much else she could do now, except go for help. Pulling the keys out, she looked them over and spotted a miniature speed pass card for fast food payments hooked onto the key chain. She thought about all of the times she'd locked herself out of her house and how her credit card had become a second key. It was all in the wrist. To her surprise, the knob turned easily. Amanda slid inside the darkened room.

Black silhouettes lay in silence across the room's floor. Their shadowed shapes became clear against the dusky light penetrating the far wall opening. Amanda squinted as she made her way down the basement steps. Careful to avoid bumping into boxes and old desks, she navigated her way to the slim shaft of light. The sound of muffled voices caught her attention and she strained to hear if one of them belonged to Grant.

She saw the wall partition led to another room. At any other time in her life, the idea of a secret passage would have been exciting, but tonight it scared the hell out of her. She pressed her cheek to the cool cement and tried to peer into the room, but the bright light blinded her. When the chants rose to a heightened crescendo, she pushed the partition open enough to slip inside. Suddenly, her vision blurred, her mind a total blank.

CHAPTER 30

Coop fought to awaken from his nightmare. He couldn't move his arms or legs against the tight surrounding tomb. He thrashed for freedom, turning his face from side to side, but his mouth filled with a cottony substance tasting like sour milk. Unable to see past a gray haze, he feared he'd gone blind. Then Grant's voice cut the murmurings outside his crypt. Suddenly everything came back to him, the bloody sheets, Joe Blockman, and finally his blackout. This was no nightmare.

Coop determined he'd been locked in some sort of plastic wrap prison. He struggled to move his arms inside the murky shell, without success. *What in the world is this stuff made of?* The smell of candles burning told him the material must be porous enough to breathe. That meant it had to have a weakness. His cheek brushed the cotton candy-like substance, and suddenly he had an idea.

Coop grimaced and pressed his tongue against the fuzzy barrier. The rancid flavor made him gag and he forced out a soggy mouthful over his lips. He repeated this motion until a small gap opened between his cheek and the mesh. Slowly, he worked, disintegrating small portions with saliva like a moth eating its way out of a chrysalis.

Eventually, the wetness gave and his surroundings became clear through the remaining layer. Like looking through a dirty window screen, he found he could see clearly enough to make out the scene. The large room glowed orange against a large fiery pit near the center. The walls were shiny and covered with petrified corpses of boys.

Several students, including Grant, stood with their backs to him before a large altar not far from the pit. Mumsford towered over them from the top step in dark robes. Beside the boys were shaded silhouettes, exact replicas of each student.

Across the room, six empty cocoons obscured a shadowy figure chained to the far wall. Coop recognized Grant, or his spirit-like facsimile. Everyone in the room stared at the boy as if waiting for him to act.

Suddenly Grant's wrist shackles fell open with a clank. A large, serpent-like creature slithered toward the boy and escorted him to his physical likeness before the altar. Coop shuddered to see the same creature that had attacked him in his home.

He forced himself to take the final mouthful that would allow him to expose his face. His saliva seeped through the wall in front of him as it dribbled down his shirt. He hoped the barrier had weakened enough for him to break through.

Mumsford's voice had changed to a commanding throng, echoing throughout the room.

Coop cringed at the sight of the headmaster holding the black bible high above his head. How had he gotten it? He'd purposely left the book with Dr. Batten to keep Grant safe, not thinking that it might put his good friend in danger.

Coop worked his arms up through the soggy mush around him. *That's it you sick little bastard. Keep chanting.*

He didn't have a clue what he'd do after he gained his freedom. The hideous serpent gave him pause about any heroics. After all, he hadn't done any good trying to protect himself at home. He was lucky the attack had only been a strong warning, or he would be dead. The serpent had probably been looking for the black bible.

When Coop's face broke free, he gulped a deep breath, and smoky incense filled his lungs. No one noticed him. His attention shot to the far side of the room where Grant's shadow had been chained. An area of glistening tissue protruding from the wall pulsated. Its puckered, middle section stretched wide, creating a two-foot opening. He watched in amazement as the area grew in size.

The wall suddenly burst open and a man's hand jutted through.

Everyone turned to see a second hand, followed by a human head.

Mumsford pointed as Mitch's full body slithered out of the hole and dropped to the floor.

The serpent hissed and rose up to its full height screeching, "You have defiled Satan's mouth! For that you will suffer!"

*   *   *

Grant surveyed the standoff. Man against demon. Not good odds, he decided.

"Mitch!" Coop shouted across the room.

With Malik's attention temporarily diverted, Grant stared at his physical form before the altar trying to think of a way to fight back. He willed his body to move its left hand, and to his astonishment, it did. Now the right foot. It moved at his mental command. If he had control over the body, he might be able to do some serious damage, at least enough to create a chance for Coop to act.

He set his sights on the altar candles, intending to overturn them and set the red velvet altar cloth ablaze. He willed the physical Grant to move forward, but stopped when his mother suddenly entered the lair.

She levitated into the room, with arms outstretched.

"Mom!" Grant yelled. "Wake up!"

Her vacant gaze told Grant she was unreachable. He watched in horror as she hovered upside down over the great fire pit intended for the boys.

"No! Leave her alone, Malik. It's me you want. Let her go!" Grant watched her sink lower.

Just then, Coop broke through the cocoon. "Grant! Remember, a soul must be freely given. He can't take it!"

He watched his mother's body dip dangerously close to the roaring flames. Suddenly his decision became clear.

Grant's physical body stepped up to the altar and clutched his father's key chain. He allowed his body to hand it over to Mumsford, while keeping his own gaze on his mother. He hoped his sacrifice would be enough to save her.

"A wise decision, Mr. Taylor." Mumsford accepted the trinket.

Mitch made a sudden move for Amanda, but Malik struck him hard with his tail, slamming him into the wall.

Grant heard Mitch's thoughts before he slipped into unconsciousness. *Darkness dies in the light. Expose the demon to the truth.*

He saw Coop's eyes burn in fear as the physical Grant followed Mumsford toward the fire pit.

Malik inched closer to witness the sacrifice and accept his new recruit. He nodded for Mumsford to continue.

The headmaster turned to Grant. "Do you freely give your soul to Satan?"

"When my mother is free." He held Malik's gaze.

Mumsford looked back and forth between them unsure of what to say.

Finally, Amanda's body returned upright and to the ground. She broke from her trance and slumped to the floor.

Coop helped her up, his eyes fixed on Grant. "Don't do it!" he shouted.

Mumsford continued, "As an act of submission and final acceptance of your new life, you must destroy the last physical link to this world. Your body must enter the pit."

Grant forced his body to the edge.

His mother screamed and reached for him, but Coop held her back.

"Do the right thing, man," Malik said in Joe's voice.

Grant's physical body teetered on the fiery ledge, while his spirit form turned to Malik. The demon's almond eyes gleamed in anticipation of the final plunge that would send Grant into hell.

Grant recalled the creature's earlier thoughts and he spoke so all could hear.

"Before I enlist in your little army, I think everyone should know the real plan of attack. *You* plan to take over for your master! Just as Satan planned to take the place of God, you want to remove Satan from his evil throne! I heard your thoughts, Malik. You can't deny the truth!"

The words triggered a violent reaction inside the lair. A towering flame spewed up from the fire pit, falling dangerously close to Grant's physical body. The blazing geyser took on a life of its own as it changed in color and form.

Malik rushed to push Grant's body into the pit, but faltered against the floor's quaking. His granite eyes darted back and forth as the walls swayed, threatening to topple at any moment.

Mitch tackled Grant's physical body from the ledge as it started to tumble over.

Coop herded the other boys' bodies away from the rising fire, with Amanda clinging to his arm.

Grant's soul stood mesmerized by the flames as the pit grew in size. He heard his mother's calls to get away, but he didn't move. A sound like the ocean's roar filled the air, and Grant's soul broke from its daze. The room shook with electricity.

The spiked corpses on the walls collectively gasped. Their mummified faces turned upward, with empty sockets wide in wonder.

Grant looked up to see. The fire pit flames spiraled into an illuminated form of great size. An angel hovered above the flames, powered by broad, pearl colored wings beating with astonishing grace. The angel's hair framed angular features of a glowing face, and draped over brawny shoulders in ebony ringlets. A thick, purple sash held secure about his waist beneath a shimmering, golden breastplate. His left hand rested on the gilded hilt of a double-edged sword, ablaze against the bright flames below.

Grant pictured angels as beautiful, gentle, creatures, but this heavenly messenger looked more like an angry Herculean god. For a moment, Grant wondered if he could be another demon in Malik's army.

The terror subsided when the angel's crystalline eyes scanned the lair, and briefly met Grant's. Filled with déjà vu, Grant knew he'd seen those eyes before. Then he heard Mrs. Bo's voice in his head.

"Do not fear me. I am guardian of man."

His angel had returned.

The angel's penetrating gaze fell upon Malik as the demon slithered to the furthest corner with no place to hide. The angel drew his sword.

Mumsford ran to the incubator, screeching at Malik, "My heart! Do something! I served you well. Give it back before it's too late!"

The organ exploded within the incubator like a potato in a microwave, and Mumsford fell to his knees clutching his chest. He fought for breath, his face ashen and sweaty. Grant turned away as the man fell over in a heap.

Cornered, Malik raised to fight. He taunted his foe in defiance. "I defeated you long ago. It is easily accomplished twice."

Michael's reply thundered across the lair. "Today the spoken truth of a child has exposed your darkness, giving me life. Twice your plan has failed."

Before Malik could reply, an ear-splitting screech erupted over the flaming pit. Thick, ebony smoke encircled Malik completely, quickly forming about his head. Malik struggled to pull away but an invisible force drew his jerking form toward the edge of the blazing hole.

"Master, have mercy!" the demon cried.

The vibrating walls toppled the altar with a crash as the lair's floor split open.

Grant covered his ears as Satan's deafening roar exploded from the pit.

"You cannot deceive me! The servant is never greater than his master. You have proven yourself unworthy. It is *you* who has been deceived!"

Swarms of demons emerged from the muscle-like walls, Rajan and Tau among them. Their voices chanted an ancient dirge, steadily rising to a crescendo.

"Spare me, master!" Malik pleaded.

"I give you your army!" Satan's putrid vapor tightened its grip around the serpent's body holding him in place.

The demon's screech rose as he struggled for freedom.

Above the din, Grant noticed high-pitched grating as the metal spikes pinning the petrified bodies to the walls slowly slid out. The dead boys' remains dropped to the floor, coming to life to slink on all fours toward Malik. They growled like a hungry pack of dogs, bits of their hair and teeth falling to the floor. The hollow leathery bodies creaked as the hardened skin bent to move.

Grant jumped aside as more bodies dropped to crawl toward the demon that had murdered them.

Malik thrashed within Satan's invisible clutches as the bodies formed behind him. He teetered on the pit's edge, the throng pressing against him. The dead boys stood soldier-like as if awaiting orders.

Malik raised his eyes to Michael amidst the throng and pleaded, "Help me, comrade. We were once brothers in battle."

Michael sheathed his sword, his wings still beating the burning air behind him. "The battle is won."

With that, the corpses seized the serpent and lifted him high overhead, pitching him into the flames. Malik's form exploded, but his caw-like screams continued as he fell deeper into the pit.

For a moment, everything stopped. No chanting. No sound. The dead boys stood frozen, their tortured expressions remaining. Then a tremendous flaming spiral shot out of the fire pit and Grant heard his mother scream.

He backed away from the molten fire splattering the air. The intense heat burned his arms and face. He could feel his arm hairs singeing. He was back in his body!

The other boys had returned to their bodies, too, and hovered near the wall opening with Coop. Grant jumped when a heavy hand clamped his shoulder. Mitch grinned down at him.

"Let's go. Class dismissed."

THE ACADEMY

CHAPTER 31

"Move it!" Coop's voice shouted over the rumbling air.

Grant shook himself from the scene and followed the group. He pushed his mother ahead as he brought up the rear. The narrow opening rocked as the walls started to disintegrate.

The group clawed frantically at the debris blocking the way out. It looked like a job for a backhoe. Another deafening tremor shook the lair and they covered their heads. More rubble plundered down, mixing heavy, white dust with the smoke pit fumes. Grant choked from the burning in his throat and fought to see through tearing eyes. He heard Coop's orders to *keep digging*, even though it looked hopeless.

A rush of wind brushed Grant's cheek and he looked up to see Michael racing overhead, wielding his gleaming unsheathed sword. The angel easily gutted the wreckage to create an opening large enough to accommodate their exit. Then he disappeared. Grant lingered a moment saying a silent thank you to *his* angel.

He headed toward the others, glancing back in time to see the cocoons ignite into torch-like plumes. The dead boys' bodies began to melt in the intense heat, taking on life as their faces twisted into misshapen grimaces. The human shells smoked and charred in the intense heat.

A leathery head dropped and rolled from a nearby corpse before shriveling into a pasty lump at Grant's feet. He quickly turned away.

Mumsford's smoldering torso lay near the incubator, jerking and twitching. Peals of gray smoke rolled over his blackened tongue when he choked out one final plea for help. He stared in terror, and died.

Grant knew there was nothing left to salvage except their lives.

A sudden quake knocked everyone to the ground, except Terrence. His stubborn expression fueled his words. "C'mon y'all. Let's do this. Do it for Thomas!" He dropped to his knees and plowed through crumbling passageway.

"Keep going!" Coop followed.

Grant forced himself past the yellowed corpses nailed against the walls inside the narrow passage. He could see the basement door only a few feet ahead. They had to move faster to make it in time. The air had become hot enough to make him light-headed.

In front of him, his mother stopped to fight a bout of coughing. He nudged her to keep going. Just a few more feet.

Suddenly Artie came to a halt ahead of Amanda. A thick trail of blood oozed from his infected stump.

Amanda tried to coax the boy forward, but he wouldn't move.

"We've got to get out of here. You can do it. C'mon," she pleaded.

Grant knew they had to get Artie moving before the passageway collapsed on top of them, but he couldn't get to him. He couldn't believe his eyes when Billy turned back and grabbed the former bully by his collar.

"Snap out of it, man. We're all gonna die!" He slapped the boy hard.

Artie's dazed look lingered a moment and then his eyebrows knitted together. "You got a death wish, Parker?"

Grant smiled at Billy. "Let's go."

The basement provided relief from the heavy smoke and the group hurried up the steps and out. They burst into the foyer to pure chaos. Chaperones and students raced from the main house as it quaked on its foundation. Large cracks split the walls around them as the ceiling crumbled above, filling the air with dust and falling debris. Suddenly the enormous chandelier crashed to the floor, pinning one of the chaperones. Coop and Mitch motioned the others to go ahead as they stopped to help her.

Grant knew it was too late by the woman's blank expression. He hurried outside to find his mother.

"Grant!" Amanda called, running in his direction.

People scurried for their lives away from the burning buildings. The school and the main house had become huge bonfires. Students and chaperones stumbled as they tried to run on shaking ground.

Grant pulled his mother close. They had to get away from Knollwood Academy.

"Where's Coop and Mitch?" he asked her.

"I think they're still inside."

"Get the others together and I'll find them." He tore away from her grasp.

"Wait! You can't go back in there!" she called.

Grant plowed inside without looking back.

Coop's voice came through the thick dust. "Get back! The building is going!" Coop raced out behind Mitch just in time, sending Grant sprawling into the grass. A firm grip dragged him backwards as the air filled with a deafening explosion.

The main house gave one final shudder then imploded onto itself and sunk into the ground. The foundation became a larger version of the lair's fire pit as it spewed out flames into the smoke-filled sky.

"We've got to get to my Jeep behind the gym!" Coop shouted over the noise.

The group followed him across the school grounds as it trembled beneath their feet. The soil moved in a waving motion, like a giant, pulsating muscle.

Amanda screamed when a large mound of earth rose up and wrapped around her ankle like a fist.

"Get it off!" she screamed.

Mitch grabbed his pocketknife and began slashing the earthen fingers. A viscous liquid poured over the dried grass and seeped into the surrounding ground.

Amanda back-crawled away from the area panting, "What the hell was that?"

"Let's go," Coop ordered, and started jogging toward the gym.

The entire field house had been reduced to a fiery mound and the group surveyed the ruins in shock. Charred bodies lay strewn across the yard and the stench of burned flesh filled their nostrils. Billy Parker dropped to his knees and vomited along with several of the other boys.

Grant caught up with Coop.

Coop grabbed a pipe from the rubble and plunged it into the ground. The earth split open like a sore, spurting more of the oily black substance.

"The ground is alive, isn't it?" Grant jumped out of the way.

Coop nodded. "This place is Satan personified. We have to get out of here."

He turned to Grant. "The Jeep won't hold everyone. I'm going to have to take the team van. Can you get the others together and meet me in the west parking lot?"

"Give me five minutes." Grant took off toward the others.

* * *

Coop jogged ahead, hoping to locate the vehicle before it was too late. He breathed a sigh of relief when he saw the van remained intact a few yards away. His hoodlum days as a youth had taught him certain tricks of the trade, such as hot-wiring. He wasn't especially proud of it, but he didn't regret it now.

The van turned over easily, but as he got up from the floorboard, his eye caught something shiny on the passenger floor. He grabbed it and climbed into the driver's seat. Coop examined the identification bracelet, with the initials J.B. etched onto the faceplate. A surge of fear spread through him when he realized it belonged to the star basketball player, Joe Blockman.

He pocketed the bracelet as the group approached the van.

Mitch helped Amanda and the boys inside and slammed the side door closed.

"Let's hit it," he told Coop.

Grant landed in the front passenger seat and glanced back to do a quick head count. "Everyone's here."

Coop floored the gas pedal and headed toward the frontage road that would take them to the main road and away from academy property. The gyrating road continued to rock the van as it traveled at top speed past the school's crumbling buildings.

He slammed on the brakes when a security guard ran in front of the van. He'd been badly burned, his face bloody and raw. Shouting out the window, Coop tried to call the man back, but it was too late. He didn't seem to hear him and continued running without a backward glance.

As he sped on, Coop tossed Grant the bracelet.

"What do you make of it?"

"It's Joe's. I've seen him wearing it." Grant stared at it.

"It's probably the only thing left of him."

"Yeah. Now we have *his* personal item. Do you think it's safe to keep it?" Grant asked.

"Hold on to it for now. We're almost out of here."

As the van turned onto the darkened road leaving the school, Coop reveled in the quiet. The past few hours had been chaos and he welcomed the break. Glancing in the rearview mirror, he saw the boys leaned back with their eyes closed. Amanda stared out the window, apparently deep in thought.

Mitch had taken the opportunity to light up a cigarette. "What the fuck!" he shouted.

Coop followed the mechanic's gaze out the window when he jumped up.

A crumpled mass of twisted metal lay on the roadside. A pair of handlebars reached up like praying hands from the Harley's corpse.

"You see that?" Mitch met Coop's look in the rearview mirror as they passed the wreckage.

Coop nodded.

"How did that happen? It wasn't close enough to the buildings."

"Look out!" Amanda screamed.

Coop hit the brakes. The trees that lined the road swayed wildly as if pushed by hurricane winds.

Grant pointed. "The trees are alive!"

A loud scrape filled the air and a tree branch tore through the top of the van creating a ragged opening. The trees clawed at the vehicle nearly knocking it onto its side.

Coop hit the accelerator.

The windshield splintered, forcing Coop to swerve into a ditch. Several thick branches punctured the van's sides, skewering it like a piece of meat. Coop tried to reverse, but the wheels spun in place.

With a sound of crunching metal, the rest of the van's roof tore off, and thousands of black beetles poured in over the top.

The backseat passengers screamed as the large, sharp-clawed bugs covered them. Their needle-like legs made a hideous clicking sound as they ran along the van's metal.

Terrence yelped in pain when he pulled one from his face, its claws clinging deep into his skin.

Coop grabbed Grant's shoulder and yanked him out of the driver's door. They both fell out onto the beetle-covered pavement. The van filled so quickly the passengers were trapped, unable to move. He and Grant ran around to the side of the van.

"Mom!" Grant called, tugging at the door.

Coop yanked hard, but the latch wouldn't give. Panic gripped him as the swarm of beetles filled to the top of the van.

The trees overhead returned to normal, standing watch over the morbid scene.

A hand pounded against an inside window, smashing one of the black devils against the glass. They were suffocating.

Grant grabbed a rock and threw it at the window, but it bounced off without making a crack. "Do something! They're all going to die!"

As cries rose from the van, helplessness washed over Coop. How can you fight a demon? Then he had an idea.

"Give me the bracelet," he told Grant.

"Why?"

"Just do it!"

Grant tossed it over and Coop quickly threw it inside the van.

"What good is that?" Grant yelled at him.

"Remember when the demon attacked me at home? I think it was looking for the physical evidence of Satan's plan. In that case, the black bible. When it didn't find it, it left. Just like the Academy is sinking into the ground. It's the last physical manifestation of Satan. It has to be destroyed."

"So?"

"Don't you see? We had the only physical proof that Joe Blockman ever existed. His bracelet. It was one loose end Satan didn't want unraveled."

Coop stopped abruptly as the beetles poured out of the van.

Grant ran to the side door, stepping and smashing the bugs as they ran past his feet. This time the door opened.

Coop started pushing the insects out in armfuls to clear a path. He grinned when Mitch fell out onto the ground, cursing.

After him came Artie, Billy, and the rest of the boys, frightened, but unharmed. Finally, Amanda crawled on the floor toward the opening, her face scratched and bleeding. He lifted her out and carried her to a safe spot away from the trees.

"Is it over?" she asked with fear in her eyes.

Before Coop could respond, he heard a deafening explosion and everyone watched the academy grounds open with a roaring rumble. The area sunk into the earth with a violent shudder and then the sky went black.

"What happened?" Grant asked against the sudden quiet.

"I'm not sure. But I think your mom's right. It's over." Coop glanced at Amanda.

Mitch rested his hands in his jean pockets and looked out over the empty land. "Look at that."

The moon shown bright in the night sky revealing that each building on the property had vanished. The smoke and fires had ceased to burn. There was no trace of Knollwood Academy.

CHAPTER 32

Coop stoked the fireplace logs, bringing the flames to full heat. The overnight snow had floated in on frigid temperatures, blanketing Knollwood under a numbing deep freeze. He stared into the flames wondering how the recent events could have been possible. They'd fought and defeated one of Satan's demons. But had it all been real? Would he wake up and find it all a nightmare?

Safe now, the boys slept upstairs on make shift beds. He knew none of them would ever be the same and wondered what effect their experiences might have on them in the future. Fortunately, the academy had no future at all.

Amanda awoke and stretched on the love seat, grabbing a nearby afghan. Her blue eyes reflected the flames. She caught his stare and offered a small smile.

"Can I get you anything?" Coop asked.

She shook her head and covered her sleeping son beside her.

Grant's mouth hung open slightly in a silent snore. The long trek from the school grounds to the farmhouse had taken its toll on all of them. Fortunately, the subzero temperatures hadn't arrived until late in the night. No one had spoken in the cold darkness of his home. No one had the strength.

Amanda, Grant, and Mitch finished hot chocolate and Coop's attempt at nourishment. Coop figured they didn't mind peanut butter and jelly sandwiches for breakfast. After all, the fact they'd even survived the night had probably been foremost in their minds. They'd all found a place to "crash and burn," as Grant called it, sleeping for several hours now.

Mitch lay sprawled on the recliner with one shoe off. He'd managed to polish off the last of the sandwiches before collapsing into a near coma. Coop doubted the mechanic had ever had an all-nighter quite like this one. He predicted its lasting effects would be far more memorable than a bad hangover.

The phone rang, jarring Coop from his daze. He grabbed the portable device before it woke anyone.

"Hello?"

"Coop?" An elderly man sounded unsure.

"Yes." Coop said.

"Are you all right?"

He finally recognized the voice. Thank God his friend was alive. "George? Yes, everything's fine." He made his way to the kitchen.

"You sound a little distant. I didn't wake you, did I?"

"No, no. I've been up for hours." Coop rolled his eyes.

"Good. Listen, I have some bad news. It's about the black bible."

Coop's stomach churned. He wanted this nightmare to end. "What's that, George?"

"It's gone. Missing."

"Really?" Coop tried to hide his relief.

"I don't know what happened, Coop. I promise you I'll launch a full investigation, although I'll have to be careful not to expose its suspected identity. In all my years, I've *never* lost a piece like this. I'm extremely embarrassed…"

Coop cut him off. "You didn't lose it, George. I can't talk now. But I *will* tell you that you were right about the army. Have you ever heard of a demon named, Malik?"

"No. I can't say that I have."

"I'll have to fill you in when I see you. Just know that the book is gone, probably forever."

"Did something happen at the school?"

"There is no school. It's gone, too."

George hesitated. "There's something else. I heard from Dr. Pearlman yesterday. The carbon dating results proved quite encouraging. It looks like the mysterious book can be scientifically dated back to about 2500 B.C. It would need further study, but now that's impossible."

Coop decided that wasn't a bad thing.

"One more thing. Pearlman tested the ink and found it was blood—human. Can't say whose, and I suppose that's for the best. Still, the professor in me can't help but wonder about the book's true identity. I guess we'll never really know, will we?" He sounded disappointed.

"Maybe that's best."

"Is everyone all right?"

"Yes. It's all over." Coop tried to sound convincing.

"I know you don't want to hear this, but you still need to be watchful."

"I was afraid you'd say something like that." He tried to smile. Goose flesh speckled his arms at Dr. Batten's reply.

"I'm afraid it will never be over. This Malik you spoke of might be gone, but Satan has many other demons in his legions. I'm certain his plan to build an army is still underway."

* * *

Grant jerked awake. He smelled smoke and jumped up before he had his bearings nearly losing his balance.

"Grant, its okay. Where are you going?" his mother asked.

He stopped and looked around. Now he remembered. It had all been real, but now he hoped it was over.

He sat beside his mom watching the fireplace flames die down to the sound of Mitch's snoring. They shared a grin and she ran her hand through his curls.

"Hungry?"

"Nah. Just tired. Where's Coop?"

"He took a phone call in the kitchen."

"When can we go home?" He pinned her with a stare. What if she sent him to another school?

"As soon as we can find a way. My car is shot, and it looks like Mitch and Coop have the same problem. We'll get there, don't worry."

"I *am* going home, right?"

"Absolutely. Whatever our problems are, we'll have to work through them. You'll probably have to go to summer school and you'll be a year behind. Can you handle it?"

"After last night, I can take anything."

"Grant," her voice became a whisper. "I'm so proud of you. The way you took responsibility for all our lives and put yourself last. That was brave." She reached out and touched his cheek.

He didn't shy away as he usually did. He'd almost died for the sake of her love. Grant knew he'd changed and would never forget the events they'd shared.

Coop came into the room with a tray of cookies and several more mugs of hot chocolate.

"Brunch." He grinned grabbing a mug for himself as he sat on the couch.

Grant took a handful of cookies and leaned back.

"Someone going to wake Mitch?" Amanda asked.

"I'm up," a groggy voice came from across the room. Mitch sat up and tried to find his shoe.

"Welcome back," Coop teased. "We thought you'd died."

"Not the way *he* was snoring." Grant laughed.

They sipped their drinks for a moment, letting the silence wash over them like a summer breeze. Finally, Amanda broke the stillness.

"What do we do now?"

Coop shrugged. "I think we should lay low for a while."

"Can't go anywhere without a ride anyway," Mitch chimed in.

Coop pressed the remote device turning on the television. He surfed the channels waiting for news about the school's disappearance.

A helicopter camera showed an aerial view of the academy grounds. Grant expected to see nothing but charred grass and huge smoking craters where the buildings had once stood. He frowned at the scene. The snow covered area looked like a Christmas card with a glistening white blanket lying serenely across the acreage once known as Knollwood Academy.

The newscaster's voice announced what everyone in the room already knew.

"Officials are baffled by the unusual circumstances of the facility's disappearance. The mayor has declined comment until further investigation. The only sure fact at this point is that the town of Knollwood has seemingly lost one of its greatest assets."

They watched several more minutes, enough to learn that police chief Lucas Koch, had perished in an attempt to save a young boy. Coop frowned at the line of bull. If Koch was missing, it was because he'd known too much. He caught Mitch's knowing glance.

Coop shut off the television. "Listen, everyone. I think the best way to handle this is to move on. Don't say anything to anyone."

"No one would believe us anyway," Grant stated.

"The kid is right. We all know what happened and why. It's over." Mitch set his mug down hard on the coffee table.

"I don't think so, Mitch. I spoke with Dr. Batten this morning."

"He's okay?" Grant asked.

"Yes. But he said he feels this is far from over, and I tend to agree. By the way, the radio carbon results on the book came back. The date indicates that it's most likely the black bible. But I guess we already knew that. Of course, further testing isn't possible now. It's gone."

Grant shook his head. "If I hadn't been able to hear Malik's thoughts, it would have turned out a lot different. I wonder why I couldn't read Joe, but Malik's words came out loud and clear."

Amanda broke in. "When Malik transformed into Mrs. Bobis, he lost his defense because she was an angel. Your dad had that much right."

"Turns out he was right about a lot of things I never gave him credit for." Grant turned back to Coop.

"I still don't understand what happened. How come Satan didn't just kill us all?"

"You spoke the truth and Satan knew it. When you exposed Malik's plan to deceive him, the light of truth destroyed Malik's deception. The demon didn't realize until it was too late, that the whole thing had been a sham to expose his plan to overthrow Satan. Don't forget, Satan has experience in thwarted takeover plans." Coop relaxed into an overstuffed chair.

"So what makes you think it isn't over?" Amanda grasped Grant's hand.

Coop shrugged. "Until the final battle is fought and won, I expect Satan will continue to build his army."

Grant had moved to the window that overlooked the front yard and Route 41. In the distance to the west, he watched the sky above what should have been Knollwood Academy. He jumped when a whisper spoke loudly inside his head. This time, it wasn't Malik's voice he heard.

* * *

The teen bent down and brushed the snow from the metal plate. The other boy looked on, keeping his nose buried inside his coat collar.

"What are you doin', man? My balls are frozen."

The teen looked up with penetrating eyes. "Yeah, and they'll get a whole lot bigger when you see what we're going to do next. I haven't told anyone about this place. It's between you and me. Got it?"

The younger boy leaned over for a closer look as the teen shoved open the manhole cover. "What is that?"

Buell smiled. "The beginning..."

SCARLETT DEAN

Horror fiction author, Scarlett Dean, has been a true horror fan since childhood, and has always enjoyed creating her own dark worlds and characters. "I remember racing home every day after school to catch the last fifteen minutes of my favorite daytime soap, *Dark Shadows*. It was also a Friday ritual to curl up with a big bowl of popcorn and watch scary movies late into the night. The horror world intrigued me so much that I started writing my own stories."

She is an avid reader who is always looking for a really good scare. As a full-time author, she has published her own quarterly magazine of other author's works in fiction, non-fiction and poetry. She enjoys motivational speaking at area schools to promote the gift of writing and encourage reading.

In addition to her love of books, Ms. Dean finds music, especially Rock, to be her second greatest passion. "Since I can't dance, sing or play any instrument well, I'll stick to writing."

She has three children, and a Siberian Husky who is more like a fourth child than a pet. Her husband is the computer genius who bales her out of her e-messes with the patience of God, and supports and encourages her in all of her writing endeavors. Of course, her characters are practically family when she's writing a book, often keeping her awake at night. "Being a writer allows you to get away with hearing voices, without being committed!"

You can visit her website at: www.scarlettdean.com

AMBER QUILL PRESS, LLC
THE GOLD STANDARD IN PUBLISHING

QUALITY BOOKS
IN BOTH PRINT AND ELECTRONIC FORMATS

ACTION/ADVENTURE	SUSPENSE/THRILLER
SCIENCE FICTION	PARANORMAL
MAINSTREAM	MYSTERY
FANTASY	EROTICA
ROMANCE	HORROR
HISTORICAL	WESTERN
YOUNG ADULT	NON-FICTION

AMBER QUILL PRESS, LLC
http://www.amberquill.com